TEN OF SWORDS

Midlife Zombie Hunter

THE FORTY PROOF SERIES

SHANNON MAYER

Midlife Ghost Hunter
Copyright © **Shannon Mayer** 2020
All rights reserved
HiJinks Ink Publishing
www.shannonmayer.com

All rights reserved. Without limiting the rights under copyright reserved above, no part of this publication may be reproduced, stored in or introduced into a database and retrieval system or transmitted in any form or any means (electronic, mechanical, photocopying or otherwise) without the prior written permission of both the owner of the copyright and the above publishers.

Please do not participate in or encourage the piracy of copyrighted materials in violation of the author's rights. Purchase only authorized editions.

This is a work of fiction. Names, characters, places and incidents are either the product of the author's imagination or are used fictitiously, and any resemblance to actual persons living or dead, business establishments, events or locales is entirely coincidental.

Mayer, Shannon

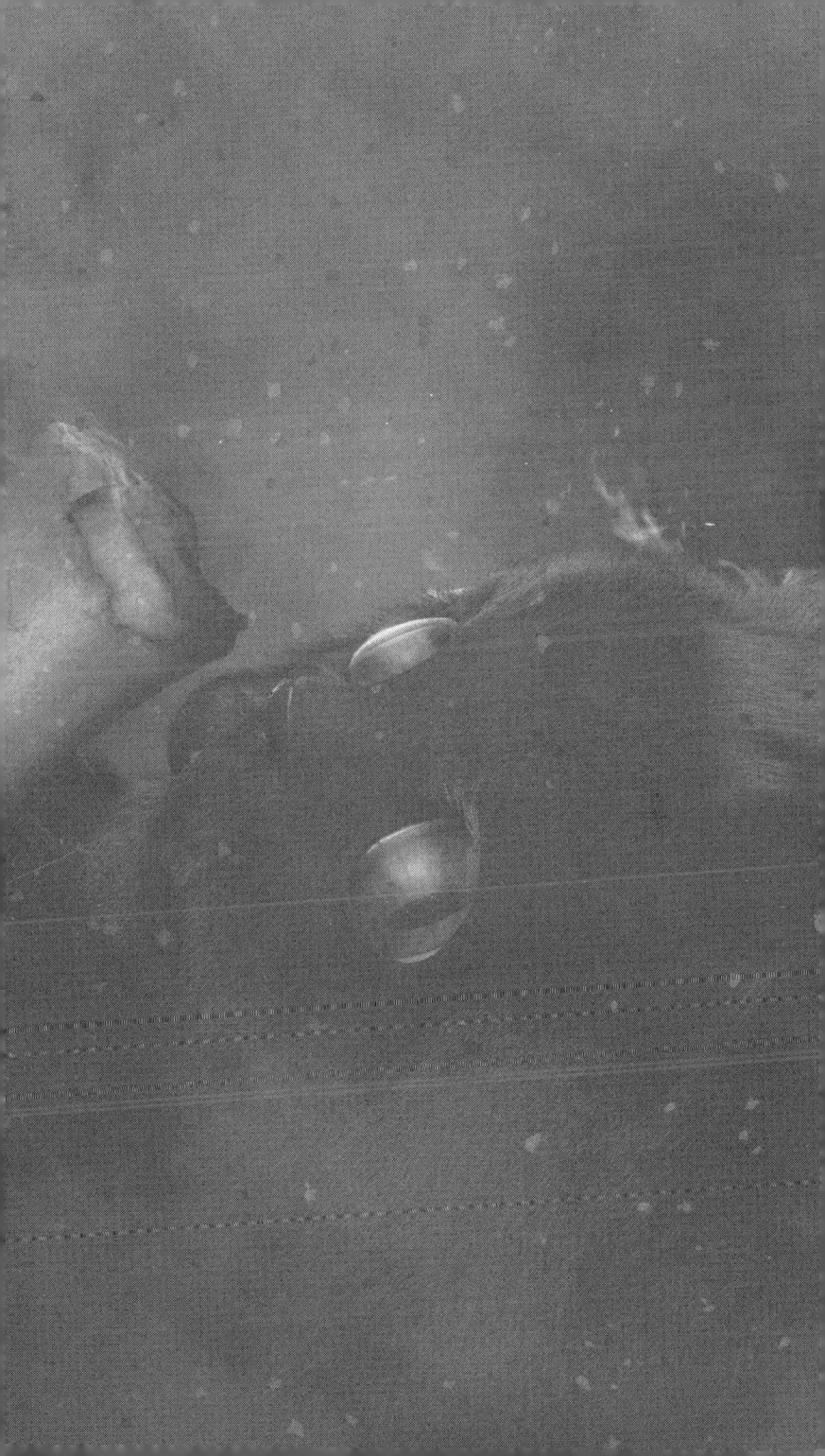

Acknowledgements

Huge, monstrous thanks to my friends across the board who've seen me through the last couple of months. Your patience, love and support as I've burned both ends of the candle has been immeasurable in my life.

Buckets of thanks to my editors who pulled out all the stops to help me make this deadline. I could not do this without you Angela Polidoro, and Shannon Page, and am so grateful you haven't told me to duck off when I tell you what the deadlines look like.

Quiet, grateful thanks to Bree, Crash, and all the characters in this series, for giving me a place to run to when the world gets dark.

I hope my characters are that place for you too.

1

Maybe the forge is exactly the place to heat things up.

Most people wouldn't think that standing in your gran's basement that had been converted to a forge would be a place where you'd want your first time with a guy to be.

Most people would be dead damn wrong.

Crash's words zinged straight through my head and down to that spot between my legs that pretty much hadn't seen action in so long I was afraid there would be cobwebs. Dust bunnies.

God forbid, mold.

Sure, sure, there had been that moment—minutes at best—in the shower with Crash, but that felt like it had been a dream, and let's be honest, the job hadn't been what I'd call completed. Nope, coitus-interruptus was a real thing in my world and something I greatly feared would happen again now that we had another moment together.

I took a deep breath. "You sure? I would hate to think I was coercing you into—"

Crash slid his hand up my neck and cupped my jaw so he could run a callused thumb over my lips, rubbing them lightly, making them tingle. "Coercion isn't even possible with you, Bree. You could never force me."

That was an interesting turn of phrase. What did he mean by that? Was it going to be a problem? We'd been home from New Orleans for just over a day, and I was still more than a little jacked up on leftover nerves and suspicions.

"Stop overthinking," he growled as he stepped closer, placing himself up against that now-throbbing juncture between my thighs, his hard body a delicious feeling against my own less than hard body. Okay, okay, slightly squishy body. Crash tipped his head to the side. "Your eyes tell me that you aren't really with me, Bree. Stay with me, right here, in this moment. So I can breathe you in. I need you here with me."

I let a slow breath slide out of me. "I'm here. I've just got, like, a hundred tabs open at once."

Many of those tabs were related to the shadow creatures that I'd faced in the last very short while. Witches. Demons. Ghosts. And at least two dozen were reserved for my fears about what was coming next. Would it be Clovis, the necromancer, or some other awful being? Would we be able to overcome whatever 'it' was? Also what if my breath was bad? Which pair of panties was I wearing, the cute red ones or the beige pantaloons that came up to the bottom of my boobs?

His smile was soft as his eyes dipped to my lips, his hands circling my waist. "Tabs?"

I waved my hands in the air. "You know, like on a web browser. I always leave all these tabs open, and it can be kind of overwhelming. Like I don't know where to start."

His smile widened even as a definite twinkle danced in his eyes. "It's so sexy when you talk about computers. And tabs." One eyebrow quirked up even as he tugged me flush against his front. "Dare I even say, hot? But let me help you. Tell me what you are worried about and get it out of your system. Then we can focus on other things."

My hands rested on his biceps, fingers curling around his muscles as I pushed him away a little so I could see his face. He was offering to slow things down when I could tell all he wanted was to get his freak on.

His finger brushed across my face. "Talk to me, Bree. I can take whatever it is you have to say. Let me help you carry things for a little while."

Damn it, why had he gone and said something so perfect? Not that I wanted him to make another mistake, but this was unreal. And that worried me. Of course, that wasn't what I said.

"I'm worried about the spell that we only have bits and pieces to." I tightened my hold on him and closed my eyes. The spell was wicked enough that Gran had been killed for her efforts to find and hide the elements. "I'm worried about Clovis just disappearing like he did—you and I both know there is no way he's done. Sure, we got the feathers before he did, but he's not going to give up until he can do that spell. I'm worried about Missy taking my gran's book, and . . . " I had to swallow hard on this next part before I said it. "I'm worried this is too good to be true. That I'm dreaming and you won't be here when I open my eyes. That this is just a fairy tale and we both know how the real fairy tales end."

I forced my eyes open and looked up at him.

"Let's start with the hard stuff." His smile was devastating in its softness, and I realized just how deep he'd gotten under my skin. Just how much I'd let him in, in such a short time.

"You say that like any of it is easy." I squinted an eye at him.

His chuckle rumbled against my skin. "The spell, and whatever it was supposed to do, is disrupted—the pieces needed for it, the fairy cross and the feathers, they're gone. We burned the feathers"—he motioned to the forge across from us—"and you hid the fairy cross."

I nodded. "I just feel like Clovis will keep trying."

Crash shrugged and smiled at me. "And when he does? What are you going to do about it?"

Damn it. My lips wobbled. "I'll stop him."

"Exactly. It would take one mighty fine distraction to knock you off kilter. No point in borrowing trouble, lass." His accent curled around me. "And that spell book of Celia's, Missy won't misuse it."

"But it was helping me get through all this shit, it was helping me deal with the shadow world," I said. "And what if I can't survive this world without it?"

"You have something better than the spell book. You have your gran's ghost." He pulled me closer, so our chests were pressed together. "You aren't alone, Bree."

My bottom lip and chin wobbled suspiciously. "But I was for so many years and now . . ." And now I had friends I loved and trusted. I had a chosen family that meant the world to me, but I was so scared to lose them.

His lips brushed over mine, sending a delicious tingle through me. "And that last bit, that is the piece you need to worry about least." He sunk his fingers deep into my hair and held me gently. "I will always be here, Bree. You can't get rid of me now. No matter," his eyelids flickered and his voice hitched, "no matter what comes."

My damn lip wobbled some more as my insecurities tried to flow out my eyes. "You'll tell me if you change your mind? I mean, just in case someone better comes along. For me, I mean." I grinned up at him as my wavering confidence flared hot.

"Love all, trust few, and do wrong to none," he said. "Will Shakespeare got it close, but maybe it should be love deeply the one you love, trust few, and do wrong only to those who need an ass kicking."

I couldn't help the laugh. "That *is* good advice."

A buzzing in my pocket twisted me around. My brand-new phone vibrated and blinked lights at me with a name that surprised me.

Eammon.

"Take it," Crash whispered as he began to nibble on my ear. "Or he'll just keep calling until you answer. Ask me how I know?"

Smiling, I hit the green button and put the phone to my other ear as Crash's hands slid up and under my shirt, fingers skimming my spine giving me a rather lovely distraction. "Hello?" Yup, a little breathless.

"You been running, girl?" Eammon barked. "Out of breath still. You gotta work on that!"

I bit back a groan as Crash nipped gently along my neck. "Sure. What's up?"

Crash chuckled and pressed his hips to mine—yes, he was definitely *up* for this game.

"Louis crawled back into town today. All beaten and bruised, and he said he wanted to talk to you."

That was a buzz kill. Louis had been working with Clovis. If you asked me, he'd earned those bruises. "How come you don't just kick his ass out of the Hollows?"

Eammon gave a heavy sigh. "It's complicated. Will you come talk to him when you get a chance?"

My turn to sigh, and I leaned back so Crash had better access to my body. "Sure. Tomorrow, okay?"

"Tomorrow. That be good." Eammon hung up, and I flicked my phone shut and set it on the counter across from me.

"Anything else? Any other tabs need closing?" Crash's mouth was wet against my skin, my body so hot I was surprised there wasn't the sound of sizzling.

"Nothing but you," I said. My worries hadn't disappeared, but Crash's confidence in me, in us, soothed them. He gave me the ability to believe in myself and in him. As impossible as we should have been as a couple.

I slid my fingers up to his chest and then ran them lightly down the front of his body to his belt buckle. I left them there, a light tremor running through me. I could be bold. I could show him how this was done. I tapped the buckle with the tip of my finger.

Right.

He sucked in a sharp breath. "Bree."

"Crash." I stared up at him, taking in his blue, gold-flecked eyes. The tousle of dark hair kissed here and there with silver streaks. The jaw line that begged to be touched. The body that begged to be fuc—

Okay so here's the thing. I've warned you before when stuff was about to get hot, for those who would rather not see what's . . . er . . . *coming*. Like the shower scene. (Seriously, y'all missed out on that one.) I can respect that some of you want to keep it clean.

Back to the good stuff. Educational if you will. Rest of you, skip on over to Chapter 2!

I let myself reach up to trace the edges of his face, my fingers dancing across his skin and reveling in the bit of stubble on his cheeks until they reached his mouth the way I'd been thinking about off and on pretty much since we'd met. He kissed the pads of my fingers, his tongue darting out to lick along the tips, followed by a skim of his teeth.

"Gods, I have wanted you for so long," he breathed out across my hands.

The urge to cross my legs tightly together had me breathing hard. And we hadn't even lost a single article of clothing. Yet. Please let there be more to this.

His hands skimmed up the sides of my body, brushing up the curve of my waist to the sides of my breasts while his eyes stayed locked on mine. His thumbs slid over my nipples, and even through my bra and shirt they hardened, begging for more.

Hussies.

I loved it. Loved the feeling of him touching me and knowing that he really wanted me for me, not for any nefarious purpose like breeding rights. I'm looking at you, Corb, with that one. My magic and his intertwined in such a way that it had triggered his siren's need to procreate.

No, no I would not think about Corb. He'd abandoned me when I needed him most, because he hadn't gotten his way. He wasn't really my friend. It was good that he was gone. That I wouldn't have to look at him again. That I wouldn't have to send him away—

"Stay with me," Crash urged and I swallowed hard even as the heat in my belly notched upward, curling through my body and sending bright signals of desire to every part of my being. The heat of the forge next to us had nothing on the temperature rising between us, the tension that had been building from the first moment I'd seen him standing in his forge in nothing but a white sheet loosely wrapped around his waist, eyes still full of sleep, body aglow with a bit of sweat. I could get used to seeing that every day, I could get used to waking up to this man, this fae, every morning.

For however long it lasted, I would take the moments as they came and believe in the dream.

I didn't look away from him as I unbuckled his belt and loosened the waist of his jeans. I didn't look down as my hand brushed the top of his cock.

Yes, I said it. Cock.

It felt like soft velvet wrapped around steel, and that single touch sent a groan rumbling out of him. It took everything I had not to peek. But I wanted to see his face. To see him react to my touch. Because, let's be honest, once you've seen one, you've seen them all, am I right?

"Bree, goddess I need you," he whispered my name and his body shuddered as I kept up the careful exploration of that one part. Sliding my fingers around and over, reveling in the fact that every time I adjusted my hold his eyes fluttered shut and his breathing grew erratic. Me, I was doing that to him, Crash of all the hotness. The king of the fae was struggling to breathe as I touched him.

His hands went over mine, and he pulled me away. "I won't last if you keep that up."

"I doubt we have time for a five-hour epic session," I whispered. "We've got maybe ten minutes at best before Feish comes looking for us. So *not* lasting is going to work solidly in your favor."

His chuckle was low and dark, and he nodded even while his eyes lowered to my mouth. "Good point. Quick and dirty it is, though I'd hoped for more for our first time."

There was no time for me to respond. His kiss was sudden and crushing as he pulled me tightly up against his body, our lips and tongues tangling in a rush of heat and taste. Smoke, he tasted a little like smoke and vanilla with a hint of what I could only peg as the smell of a summer night. Luscious and addictive, and I couldn't get enough of him.

He ground his hips up between my legs, and the tip of his cock pushed hard against my core even through my pants. I groaned and wiggled, my ass still firmly on the edge of the big anvil. He'd been right about the height.

It was the perfect setup for getting freaky in the forge.

I wrapped my legs around him and pulled him closer still, but all our clothes were in the way.

His hands caught at the edge of my shirt, and he slid his palms under it, ghosting them over my ribs to my bra and the swell of my breasts.

"The devil's device," he muttered as he fumbled with the front buckle of my bra. A growl followed, and for a second I thought he'd given up.

Nope, he had better plans.

He grabbed either side of the top of the bra and gave a sharp tug, snapping the thing off me.

My breasts fell from the contraption, and he caught them, palming and rolling them in his hands, my body responding to his every touch. I tipped my head back, and his mouth landed on my neck, nipping and kissing along the edge of my clavicle and then back up to my ear. Each love bite sent a shiver racing down my spine, coursing heat straight to my wanting center until I was panting, my body moving on its own as it fought to get closer to him.

He hadn't even touched my nipples yet, just held my breasts, massaging them lightly, and I was squirming with need, moisture pooling between my legs and soaking my panties. I don't think I'd ever been so wet in my life, certainly not without my clothing already off and lube manually applied.

"Crash, please, I can't take much more," I moaned. Not caring that someone upstairs might hear, or that someone—namely Feish—would very likely come looking for us soon. We wouldn't be denied this time. I could feel it in my bones and in the urgency with which he touched and kissed me.

His growl against my neck had me arching my body, pressing my breasts into his hands even as I kept my legs wrapped tightly around his waist, hips grinding upward. He dipped his head and took a nipple in his mouth through my thin cotton shirt, using the material as well as his mouth against it.

Sweet Jaysus, I was going to die, but I would die a happy woman as my nipple hardened and sensation shot liquid heat straight to my core. Much more heat, and I would damn well explode on the spot.

The sounds escaping me were nothing I'd ever heard before from my vocal cords. Whimpers, moaning, begging. I was begging him to strip me naked and take me right there on the anvil.

Magic, this had to be magic that he was working on me.

His mouth slid to the other nipple and one of his hand slid down between us, into the front of my pants.

His fingers slipped between my very, very wet panties and flesh, and his whole body stiffed as he let out a low groan. "Sweet goddess, you are wet, so damn wet."

I wanted to tell him to hurry up, but my ability to speak was lost somewhere between his first stroke across my swollen and throbbing clit and the next. His fingers dipped deeply into me, drawing the moisture out across my flesh as my hips tried on their own to buck against him, begging for more.

He stepped back suddenly, letting me go, leaving a gasp on my lips.

I was balanced precariously on the flat of the anvil, bra torn, front of my pants undone, panting as my chest heaved and my body ached.

"I just want to look at you, there, on my anvil." His eyes swept over me, the hunger in them so unflinching I didn't doubt it. He stepped back to me, lifted me up with one arm and grabbed the waistband of my pants with the other hand so he could push them down, taking my sopping wet panties with them.

He lifted me back up onto the anvil, the heat in the steel seeping into my now very bare and sensitive skin. I didn't question why the anvil was hot rather than cold. More magic probably.

Crash stepped closer and slid his own jeans down, and I finally let myself look at what he had going on down there.

I couldn't help myself. "Holy Dinah, is that even going to fit?"

My eyes shot to his, and my mouth may have dropped open. Big boy didn't quite cut it. I mean . . . I was fairly innocent, seeing as I'd only ever slept with Alan before, but holy crap on a toasted sesame bun, Crash was . . . big. Both in length and umm . . . girth. I swallowed hard, imagining far too many things. Like the way he would taste. Like how his cock would stretch me as he slid in, inch by delicious inch, and I started to squirm once more. I couldn't help it.

"I'm quite sure it will be a perfect fit." His voice deepened again, his accent a little heavier than usual, drawn out by the lust curling through him, no doubt.

He put his hands to my thighs. I thought he was just going to slide on in, and I braced myself a little for the magnitude that was Crash.

Nope, not Crash, he was in no rush despite having already admitting we were on a time crunch.

"I want you to come in my mouth. I want to taste your desire on my tongue before I make you come around my cock," he whispered against my belly as he bent to kiss the soft flesh there. Then another kiss as his mouth drifted lower.

Yeah, I had no words, but I surely wasn't going to say no to an offer like that. He sucked the skin hard just below my belly button, then went to my inner thigh and did the same, letting go just at the edge of pain and pleasure. I groaned and writhed as his mouth went to my aching center, his tongue swirling across my clit first, just the softest of touches, the flutter of wings against my sensitive places.

My back arched as I lifted my hips involuntarily to give him better access. He let a single finger drift across my opening, back and forth, as he lapped at my clit, gently at first, then sucking it into his mouth, pulsing those sucks in time with his finger as he slid it into me.

I gripped the edge of the anvil—the only solid thing in my world in that moment—as slow pressure began to build in my belly.

Leisurely yet intense, the swirling pleasure ebbed and flowed with the rather passionate and dedicated attentions of the man crouched between my legs. He groaned even as he lapped at me, whispering words I couldn't hear but could feel rumbling against my sensitive flesh.

He pulled his mouth back and slid a second finger in with the first, pressing against my g-spot.

"That's never happened," I whispered. "So don't fuss yourself."

He looked up at me from between my legs, eyes bright with the question. "Never?"

I shook my head, taking note of the way he smiled. "It's not a challenge, Crash."

His smile was wicked as his tongue darted out across his lips. "Oh, I do believe it is. To be your first."

My first.

Jaysus, he was going to—

His two fingers slid in and out, pressing on that elusive spot even as his mouth went back to my clit, suckling and dancing across it in time with the pulse of his fingers.

I whimpered as I clutched hard at the anvil, the only steady thing around me.

Once more that pressure began to build, growing, deepening as my muscles contracted and tensed, lifting me closer to a high I'd never experienced. Heard about, yes. Wondered about, of course. But experienced?

Nope, not even close.

The pressure kept building, coming from all directions. My body was unsure of how to react, and so I just shook, as if I were being electrocuted. But damn, what a way to go. I leaned backward, eyes closed, as the sensation crawled up my body, tingling everywhere.

I gasped as it notched up further and then . . . frowned.

My body convulsed in a way that I didn't remember from a building orgasm. I mean, I was definitely rusty, but then again maybe this was super-duper special because it was Crash and a g-spot orgasm? Somehow, I didn't think so.

"Wait," I whispered, trying to sit up even as Crash sucked my clit into his mouth again. "Crash, wait."

He blinked up at me and blew out a slow breath that I felt all across my overstimulated parts. "What is it?"

Something deep within me convulsed that had nothing to do with pleasure. An arrow of shooting pain lanced through my belly and back. I groaned, and he took it the wrong way, sliding his fingers back into me.

"No." I shoved him off with a foot and hopped off the anvil and promptly collapsed as pain rocketed through my body in a wave that displaced every bit of pleasure Crash had been wringing from me.

I couldn't breathe, and my vision darkened, fading even as Crash put his hands on me. The pain was too much, and I could feel myself blacking out.

Jaysus. It would be just my luck to die right before I had the best sex of my life.

2

On the floor of Crash's forge, I writhed for all the wrong reasons. I was situated on my knees and bent so that my forehead was pressed to the dirt floor and my bare ass was in the air. Normally this position would have mortified me, especially as a squeaker snuck out, but right then, I didn't give a flying duck who saw my butt or heard me fart because another wave of pain came rolling through me that stole my breath away in all the wrong ways.

Groaning, I rocked in place, barely breathing, sucking air between my teeth.

Crash dropped beside me, one big hand on my back as he tried to get me to sit up. "Bree, did I hurt you? Talk to me."

"No." Or at least I didn't think so, but I couldn't think past the rapidly spiraling pain that had wiped away every last ounce of the desire he'd drawn up through me. Tears leaked from my eyes as I stayed there, sucking in coal dust from the floor. "Not how I imagined this ending. I'm sorry." I gasped as another roll of agony cut through my innards, sliced up my back, and had my muscles spasming.

Crash's hands never left my back. "I know, lass, but there be no apology required. What can I do? What do you need?"

Like the pleasure he'd given me, the pain grew in leaps and bounds, tightening my body in all the wrong ways. Could I ride it out? Or was I really in trouble?

Trouble, it felt like trouble.

An especially sharp, muscle-contracting wave rolled through me, and my stomach decided to make its own protest. I turned to the side and threw up on the floor, the pressure of puking only intensifying the discomfort as I heaved.

A cool cloth wiped across my face. "Hospital it is," Crash said as he carefully picked me up and rolled me in his arms.

"Half naked. Need clothes," I mumbled but kept my eyes closed as I focused on breathing through each roll of pain—like a tsunami of hurt, all wrapped up inside of me.

"Well, yes, but such a lovely bum to let the world see." He kissed me on the forehead. I managed a weak smile but truly couldn't think past the next mind-numbing wave of pain that cut through me. It circled around my sides and dug into my back, arching my body in his arms. Sweat slid down me in rivulets as my stomach heaved again. He held me so I could gag to the side. At least nothing came out this time, though it didn't relieve any pressure either.

"Feish, Suzy!" Crash hollered as he carried me out of the basement and around the side of the house. Even the bright sunlight hurt me, and it was all I could do to crack an eye open. At least I had a longish T-shirt on. Because I wasn't stopping to get dressed.

"What now?" Feish yelped, rushing toward us, her pale blue shirt with the sparkling mermaid on it all I could see. Her fish mouth bobbled open. "What you do to her? You said you wouldn't hurt her!" For good measure, she slapped him on the arm with a webbed hand.

Crash shot her a look. "We need to get her to the hospital. Now."

I barely registered what he was doing as he stuffed me into a vehicle.

Crash did not get in. "I'll meet you there. There isn't enough room for me."

He wasn't wrong, Suzy's car was small on a good day, and he was a big man. I lifted a hand and managed to give him a thumbs up.

"I don't really want to die alone," I mumbled. "So don't dawdle."

"You aren't dying, Bree." He leaned in and kissed me on the forehead. "I don't think."

My lips twitched as he gave me one last hand squeeze, and I closed my eyes. "Comforting as ever."

Feish climbed *over* me, only jabbing me in the guts once, and then cradled my head on her lap. She stroked my face with her webbed hands. "Nothing good comes of sexy times as far as I can see. Despite those romance books I been reading. They are lying, I think. All those roses and amazing mountains climbed."

I stared up at her, which gave me a good view up her strange nose slits. "Mountains?"

"All those heights people be climbing, all sweaty and panting. Seems like that isn't as fun as they want you to believe." She patted my face, her skin sticking to my sweaty cheeks.

Suzy leapt into the driver's seat.

"Hang tight, I'll get you there!"

She sounded confident, but I remembered her driving all too well. We might get there in body bags. "Hang on," I said. Feish grabbed the holy-shit handle above the door, and I braced one foot on the back of the passenger seat.

The screech of the tires and the hard corners Suzy took were enough to send me over the edge of pain. The blare of other drivers as they honked and slammed on brakes left me less than confident. I closed my eyes and prayed that the accident would at least be swift because if whatever was going on with my body didn't kill me, Suzy's driving surely would.

I focused on my breathing, trying to work past the pain that was coming in waves. Almost like . . .

like cramps when you had your period, only a thousand times worse.

Could I be . . . no, there was no chance it was a miscarriage. I hadn't had sex in over a year, long before Alan and I split, unless there was something else at play. Except . . . a terrible thought worked its way through me. One I did not want to think but it hovered there in my head whispering a horrible 'what if'.

What if Corb had done something? What if Mr. Siren who wants a baby had somehow knocked me up without my knowledge? Although we'd never had sex, we had shared a bed before, and I didn't actually understand much about a siren's magic. A groan slid out of me, along with a couple wayward tears.

More and more the rolling pains came in perfect rhythm to a miscarriage. I'd know.

"You gonna be okay," Feish burbled softly, "I promise. Pain is just weakness leaving the body. Sometimes also a bad angry worm, but I don't think you have worms."

Hand it to Feish to make me smile when I felt like I was dying.

"Worms would be bad," I whispered.

"Oh, terrible, and they make your butthole itch like fire ants been biting down there."

I shouldn't have laughed, really I shouldn't have. But I did. The contractions of the laughter on my belly only intensified the pain, but I didn't care. Maybe dying laughing was the way to go?

As suddenly as the driving had started, it stopped, and then Suzy was at the door with a wheelchair.

"How did she move so fast?" I whispered.

"You pass out for a few minutes." Feish pulled me out by my arms and Suzy grabbed my legs and they sat me on the wheelchair. All gentle and womanly like, my bare ass sticking to the fake leather bottom.

"Nice hickey," Suzy laughed. "Was he any good?"

I glanced down at my bare legs, the tops of them only just covered by the bottom of my shirt, to see a set of twin hickeys high up on the inner sides of my thighs. Another time I might have blushed. As it was, I leaned to the side and dry heaved as they pushed me in through the emergency room doors.

"Never got there," I mumbled. "No mountains climbed."

"What?"

"I knew it!" Feish said.

Once we were through the swoosh of the automatic doors, Suzy and Feish handed me over to a pair of nurses. They hustled me onto a bed in a small room and wrapped a heated blanket around my body.

My eyes were closed as I shook, cold sweat rolling down my face as my arms bumped up all over with gooseflesh.

"You're in a bit of shock, honey." A woman's thick Southern drawl drew my eyes open. The nurse bent over me had a whack of white hair, though her face didn't look as old her hair color suggested. Her eyes were a deep amber brown full of compassion. She patted my arm.

"Shock?" I mumbled.

"Real bad pain will do that, especially if it's your own body causing the issue." She tapped my arm again. "We have to wait for the doctor, but we will give you some pain meds as soon as we can."

"Sounds wonderful," I whispered even as I began to shake and my vision darkened, blinking in and out.

My mind, however, was not turning off. What if this *was* a miscarriage? Sure as shit felt like the last one. Only about ten times as painful. Gawd damn Corb if he'd done this to me. And damn me for trusting him.

A second nurse, a man in his early twenties, tapped my arm to draw my eyes to him on the other side of the bed. "Slow your breathing or you're going to pass out. I'm going to check you over for any injuries."

"Right," I whispered even as I struggled to do what he asked. His face was a blur as he lifted the blankets and took a quick look for . . . oh shit. He was going to see the hickeys. The lack of underwear. The evidence of what I'd been up to. Did I care? Not really, but I knew how judgey people got, and it was the last thing I needed.

"Nothing here," he said and flipped the blanket over. "You're not hurt?"

"No."

"What were you doing when the pain came on?" asked the woman—Helen by her name tag—all innocent like, those amber brown eyes glowing.

Now, I could have said it happened when I was in the shower. Or asleep. Two very plausible reasons for why I would have no underwear and be in a T-shirt with a torn bra.

But I had Feish and Suzy with me, being ever so helpful.

"She was banging the boss," Feish called through the door. "Those marks on her legs are hickeys, that's what Suzy said."

I closed my eyes. Die. I wanted to just die right there and let it all be over.

Helen laughed, but there wasn't an ounce of meanness to it. "Oh, Lordy, this is not the way to end a moment like that. I hope you got what you needed first."

The male nurse grunted and left.

Helen patted my arm. "I'll be back in a jiff." Then she left too, and Suzy poked her head in through the door. "Sorry about that. I'll try to keep her under wraps."

I managed to nod. I mean, it wasn't like I could leave. All I could do was just ride out the waves of pain that were not getting any better.

"Did Corb do this to me?" I whispered. Suzy stepped fully through the door, glancing over her shoulder once before letting it close.

"You think Corb would hurt you?" She came to my side and took my hand. Her fingers were warm as she took hold of me. "Crap, you are green and clammy looking. This is bad, Bree."

"Shock. This is what shock looks like," I said as my body went through another round of shaking.

"Did he do this? I mean, we both know what he wanted from me."

Suzy shook her head. "I don't think so. He's gone. No one knows where he went. If I were to guess, I'd say he swam out to the ocean to get away from you."

A low moan rolled out of me that I couldn't catch. "Could he have . . . knocked me up without my knowing? I slept beside him a few times," I managed to spit out the question. Because this really did feel like a ramped-up version of the miscarriages I'd had. Sure, it was way worse, but it was close enough.

Before Suzy could answer me, Helen the nurse came back in, two needles and an IV hookup with her.

"Bless you," I whispered as she expertly slid the needle into my arm. The pin prick had nothing on what I was living with.

"It will take about five minutes for the morphine and the anti-nausea to kick in. This third one is an anti-spasmodic. The doctors will get a couple of scans going on you soon to make sure it's nothing serious." She depressed the plungers into the IV and I watched the fluid slide down the little clear tube. The lovely, beautiful tube.

I sighed as a rush of warmth flushed through me, chasing away the pain.

"Well," Helen laughed softly, "that was quick. You are what we call narcotic naïve. It normally doesn't work that way."

I closed my eyes, and someone put another warm blanket over me.

I may have dozed off. I may have dreamed about Crash holding me tight and whispering something in my ear.

Don't believe me. Please.

What the hell did that mean? I reached for him, and my vision blurred. A man stood in front of me, and it took me a moment to orient myself because it wasn't Crash.

The doctor had come in, and his face was all fuzzed up, as if he were wearing a mask. I reached for it to pull the mask off, and my fingers slid through the fuzziness. I tried again and could feel something hard and scaly, definitely not human flesh.

"You aren't human, are you?" I spat out the words.

He cringed, his human mask slipping more as his features tightened. What was left was a strange mix of human features and something more . . . monster-y, for lack of a better word in my stoned brain.

I needed this mixture for the next time I was sore after a run—my muscles were limp like overcooked noodles.

"I'm Dr. Mori," he said in a clipped foreign accent. "And you are . . ." He flipped my chart open, and his eyes widened for just a brief flash. "Breena O'Rylee. Is that correct?"

"Bet your ass it is." I gave him two thumbs up and tried to smile, but it turned into a jaw-cracking yawn.

Dr. Mori smoothed a hand over his thick dark hair, but his smile was off as his eyes took me in again. "I think the meds are getting to you. We're going to do a CT scan to see what you have going on. It could be kidney stones. That is our best guess based on where the pain is radiating from."

I did not mention to him that I could be pregnant. Kidney stones sounded gravy right then.

I was given a hospital gown, and Dr. Mori himself rolled me through the halls to the CT machine. I looked up at him, knowing that the filter inside my head was even more broken than usual. Did that knowledge stop me? Not for a second.

"You aren't human."

His eyes shot to me. "You need to learn not to speak when you see something unusual."

"What are you then? Tell me, and I'll be quiet," I whispered. Or thought I whispered. Judging from the side-eye I was getting from another patient; I wasn't being as quiet as I'd thought. I knew a *you're crazy* look when I saw one. I'd been in a mental institute once, a long time ago, although not out of need. It had been Alan's version of being helpful.

Dr. Mori wheeled me into a side room, spun me around and crouched in front of me. "I have remained hidden here for a long time, Breena O'Rylee. I know who you are, and what you are." He leaned in closer, and his voice hardened as the human mask completely slipped away. Scales adorned his face, and he had a mouthful of sharp teeth. "So, unless you want us both to be found out, I suggest you stop talking. Do you . . . who is your trainer?"

I blinked up at him. "Okay. I'll be quiet." I blinked up at him and grinned. "Mostly self-taught."

He rolled his eyes.

Yup, I was a real winner when I was stoned. A great conversationalist. I should have asked him just who he thought should be training me, why he recognized my name, and what the hell kind of supernatural he was. But did I ask any of that? Nope.

He rose from the crouch and smoothed his hair before wheeling me the rest of the way to the imaging room. From there I was handed off to another pair of nurses. So much of it was a blur that I started questioning whether the whole scaled face piece had been a dream.

I wondered if what had come before—the time with Crash—had been a dream. Because he wasn't here. He'd been gone a long time when he'd said he'd be right behind us.

I giggled at the nurses as they helped me lie on my belly, hands above my head. "Stop tickling!"

"We are not tickling!" one of them laughed at me.

I may have proposed to one of them when she said I was too skinny, which made it hard for them to distinguish my organs from one another.

I may have started singing "You are my sunshine," and to be clear, I am not what you'd call even a mediocre singer.

The next thing I knew I was in a semi-private room on the fifth floor of the hospital with the drugs slowly wearing off, which left me immensely tired and confused. Suzy and Feish were sitting with me, talking about the best way to spice deep-fried catfish.

Still no Crash either but I was too tired to even speak the question.

My mind kept wandering back to other things. Had I seen a monster in Dr. Mori?

With my eyes closed I smoothed a hand over the less than lovely sheets pulled up to my armpits. Someone cleared their throat, and I opened one eye. Then frowned at Dr. Mori as he leaned over me. No monster face now.

"You did not have kidney stones, Ms. O'Rylee. You had two large ovarian cysts that burst at the same time, one right after the other. There is a great deal of loose fluid in your belly from that, which was the cause of all the pain—"

"You sure that isn't just loose fluid from being flabby?" Feish said from the corner of the room, ever helpful. Dr. Mori glanced at her. "She been working hard, but ways to go you know."

Leave it to Feish.

He seemed a bit taken aback. "Quite sure. But because we aren't a hundred percent certain what caused the pain and you've been in here recently with other injuries—" he flipped the chart in his hand open, his eyes skimming the page, "—I think it's best if you stay the night. We will likely release you first thing in the morning, barring any other issues arising."

I stared up at him, trying to break through the glamor or whatever he had going on. Or had I actually imagined the scales on his face? For all I knew, the drugs really had been that good. I narrowed my eyes and concentrated until my back began to warm and bead up with sweat.

But no, it wasn't the drugs. His human mask slipped, and there was the monster face again—long snout, skin covered in gold and black scales, glowing eyes of deep green. Maybe not as scary as I'd first thought. Kinda awesome actually, the more I stared. Almost dragon-like.

Green eyes narrowing, he snapped his fingers, and it felt as though I'd been slapped across the face. "Stop," he spoke with a great deal of authority and took a step closer. Human features did not disguise the irritation etched into his face. "You need to understand that you cannot unmask me, Ms. O'Rylee. I have no quarrel with you, but I have no desire to lose my home here. Which would happen should you continue this game." His eyebrows arched upward. "Is that understood?"

I put a hand to my cheek, feeling the heat of embarrassment roll over me. "Sorry about that. And I am crystal clear." But that didn't stop me from turning over his words. What the hell did he mean by losing his home? Why would unmasking him do that? I mean, I wouldn't do it in front of humans. "Will you at least tell me what you are?"

His dark eyebrows rose further upward. "You don't have a clue, do you? Were you trained so badly for your job that you don't know the simplest of etiquette for our world?"

I shrugged and the sheet slid down. His eyes went to my collar bone and I flushed, already knowing there was a giant hickey there. "Don't be dissing my gran. It's not her fault I left the shadow world for twenty years."

"Don't be so sure," Feish mumbled, and I twisted around to see her staring out the window as if she hadn't spoken. What the hell was that comment about?

Dr. Mori put down the chart. "One friend can stay, the other has to go. Visiting hours are up in thirty minutes. Please do not . . . ." He shook his head. "Good day, Ms. O'Rylee."

Dr. Mori left before I could formulate any more questions—of which I had a few.

I looked over at Suzy and Feish. Suzy flipped her long blond hair over her shoulder. "How are you feeling? I went back to the house and brought you some clothes." She put her hand on the pile of clothing folded on the side table.

"I am feeling better. Just, really tired," I said.

"Maybe you get a good sleep, feel better in the morning," Feish said. "Especially with no one pawing at you and forcing you up a mountain."

Suzy sighed and stood up. "I'm not even going to argue about who is staying. Feish can't drive." She patted Feish on the shoulder, came to me and kissed me on the cheek, and whispered in my ear, "See, it wasn't Corb after all. Not a miscarriage, you weren't pregnant."

She stood and backed up into the form of Crash, who was right behind her.

He waited for her to leave, watching her go. His shoulders were tight and there was coal dust on his forearms in smears like he'd been working. Maybe that's what he'd had to do before he came to see me?

My eyes traced his arms down to his hands where they rested against his thighs and clenched so tight the knuckles were turning color.

"What has Corb got to do with you and . . . this?" he asked, his blue-gold eyes raking me head to toe.

I blinked up at him, not understanding for a good thirty seconds why he was looking all pissed off and dangerous, eyes sparking. "What?"

He laid a bouquet of wildflowers on the table beside my bed and stepped back as I reached for him. "You made your choice then. I wish you all the happiness in the world."

"Wait, what?" Stick a donkey in a dentist's office, and you could not have had more confusion than I did in that moment. "What choice? What are you talking about?"

But Crash turned and left, the door shutting behind him. "What choice?" I repeated, a hand to my head. "We were making out, I was about to have what I'm sure was the best orgasm of my life, maybe of my entire existence, and then I started writhing in pain. Now I've made a choice?"

Feish clucked her tongue. "He thinks you bang-bang with Corb because you thought you might be pregnant."

Oh. My. Gawd.

Crash had overheard what Suzy had said? And now he thought I'd been sleeping with Corb all this time and that I was pregnant with his child.

Suddenly I felt like I was in the center of my own damn soap opera, one I had to find a way out of.

Secret baby with the siren I'd never slept with, here I come.

3

Horror rushed through me, and I sat up with a groan in my less than comfy hospital bed. Suzy was already gone, and my legs were numb, so there was no way I'd be able to rush down the halls of the hospital, my gown flashing my bare ass. At least not in a normal situation. But this was no normal situation.

I couldn't let Crash think I'd been sleeping with Corb behind his back.

"Feish, did you bring the new phone Sarge bought me?"

She bobbled her head, gills flapping. "Yup, here you go."

I took the phone from her and hit Crash's contact number. It rang on his end, once, twice, three times. "Pick up!" I growled at the phone. The phone clicked.

"I have nothing to say to you," Crash's voice rumbled through the speaker. Hard, and not like himself. He sounded like he was walking, hurrying. His voice echoed. Maybe he was in a stairwell of the hospital?

"I did not sleep with—"

"We're done, Breena. I don't suffer faithless women. I will never allow myself to be in that position again. Not even with you."

Jaysus, what in the hell had just happened to the guy who'd said he'd always be there for me? "Crash, would you listen to me?"

The phone clicked off, and I stared in disbelief at in my hand. "Damn you, Crash."

I handed the phone off to Feish—not like I had any pockets. I leaned back in the bed, tired beyond belief, the shock of his accusation doubling down on my heart.

"Nope, I am not going out like this. Even if we're done, you're going to listen to me."

"Who are you talking to, me?" Feish stood at the end of my bed. "You losing your marbles already? I knew you were old, but—"

I cut her off with a wave as I forced myself out of bed, grabbed the IV, and started walking. One hand on the pole, one hand clutching the back of my gown, I shuffled gracelessly to the door. Feish beat me to it.

"You need to get back into bed. Doctor says you have to stay." Her bulbous eyes said it all. She wasn't moving. I sighed.

"Then you need to find Crash, wherever he went, and tell him that I didn't sleep with Corb. I thought he'd used some of his magic on me since that was all he wanted. Or, better yet, tell him to get his ass back here so I can tell him myself."

I would not let my heart hurt over this. I wouldn't. The squeezing inside my chest and the way my eyes prickled at the edges told me I was a liar, but that lie was all I had right then.

Feish gave a slow blink and then burbled a sigh. "Fine. You stay here. No leaving hospital. Okay?"

She slipped through the door.

I made my way to the big window that looked out over the entrance to the hospital. A second later Crash strode out and was in view and my heart clenched. His head was bowed and shaking.

A short man approached him from a long black limousine. What the hell was a limo doing here?

They talked, Crash pointed hard at the little guy. Damn, I wished I could hear what was going on.

A moment later Feish joined them and there were more hand gestures. Little guy shook his head several times and then turned and went to the limo. Crash followed him but not before he gave Feish a look. She bobbled her head and clasped her webbed hands.

The limo pulled away and Crash was gone.

I slumped away from the window and onto my bed. What the hell just happened?

I'd not felt this alone in a good long while. Alone. Or so I thought.

A low cough turned me around to the bed directly across from me. The room had beds for four individuals, and only two of the beds were taken. Me and whoever was behind curtain number one.

The curtains that went around the bed were mostly closed, and through the gap I could see the shape of a body under a sheet.

"Hello? I'm your roommate for the night," I said.

No answer. A low gurgle that didn't sound particularly healthy.

I found myself stepping carefully toward whoever it was behind those curtains. To open them fully, I'd have to either let go of the back of my gown or the IV pole that was holding me up.

Ah well, my ass had been seeing a lot of people anyway lately. I let go of my gown and pulled the curtain back a little.

A woman lay in the bed, her face sallow and her gray-flecked hair pulled into a messy braid. I would guess she was in her early sixties, but it was honestly hard to tell. With her eyes closed and her mouth hanging a little open, she was clearly not doing well, but the question came out anyway.

"Are you okay?" I asked. Then suddenly realized what she might have overheard if she'd been awake long enough. Sirens. Magic. Daytime soap opera drama. I mean, assuming she was with it enough to process all of that?

Another low cough and then she drew a breath that sounded less than dry. In fact, it reminded me of Feish's burbling.

That could not be good unless she was secretly a river nymph like Feish, which I highly doubted.

I made my way to her bedside and grabbed her call button, pushing it several times. Up close she looked even worse, her cheeks sunken and her shoulder and collar bones prominent under thin skin.

I put a hand on her shoulder, sorrow swelling in me. It felt like she was in her last hours at best. Someone who loved her should have been there, but she was all alone.

The tapping of shoes and then the curtain flung open. Nurse Helen stood there next to me, her eyes wide as she lifted the woman's hand and took her pulse. "How did she hit the call button?"

I shook my head. "She didn't. I did. Her breathing is really bad." I didn't take my arm from the dying woman's shoulder.

Helen bustled around, her blue smock a bit too tight around the middle, as if she weren't ready to give in to sizing up. Girl, I knew that feeling all too well. "She is . . . not going to come out of this. And she has signed a DNR. We are keeping her heavily medicated for the pain, but that's all we can do at this point. That's why she's on the IV and nothing else."

No heart monitor or oxygen mask. Nothing but pain meds and a lonely death.

I blinked and took a step back. "No one is here with her."

"She doesn't have any family left," Helen said. "She was very sweet when she was still awake. Kind to all of us despite the pain she was in—not everyone is, you know."

She brushed a hand over the woman's face, then used a wet cloth to wipe her lips, dipping it into her mouth to take away the dryness. I found myself sinking into the chair closest to the bed and picking up the woman's hand. It was frail, like bird bones, and cooler than it should have been.

"I'll stay with her for a little while." I found myself staring at the woman, wondering how she'd ended up here all alone.

Helen patted my shoulder. "You're a good one. I'm glad it wasn't anything serious for you today. But don't stay in that chair too long, you need your rest too."

She left me there. Feish didn't come back, and I clutched the woman's hand as the minutes ticked by and the feeling of approaching death curled around me.

I just wished I could give her some . . . release. I bowed my head over her cool hand, not understanding this sudden need to be with her.

My back warmed, and a trickle of sweat slid down my spine even as cold pulsed through my hand. I gasped as the sensations collided inside of me—heat and cold forming a kind of steam that flowed through me and pooled around me.

Like standing in a fog. Was this my magic? Was this—

"Hello, who are you?"

My head snapped up, and I stared at the woman on the bed, who was now staring right back at me. Gray eyes, face flush with health, and skin pink and almost glowing. She smiled, her expression gentle and curious. "Who are you?"

"Um. Breena. Breena O'Rylee. Who are you?"

Her smile widened. "Eleanor Meredith Jackson, pleasure to meet you." She squeezed my hand, and I shook my head in disbelief.

"How do you look so good right now? You . . ."

Eleanor looked down at herself. "Cancer has been eating me away a long time. Palliative care is what they said the last time I remember talking to the doctor. I'm dying, I know that."

I frowned. "Okay, but how are we having this conversation?" Really, did I expect her to know? Didn't I have enough issues without finding myself suddenly talking to people who were unconscious and dying?

But I didn't let go of her fingers. I couldn't. Somehow I knew that as long as I held onto her we could talk. That fog I'd called up floated around us, wrapping us up in its embrace.

"You're special, I think. I can feel it." Eleanor smiled. "And I'm glad you're here. I didn't want to die alone."

My heart clutched in my chest because the person I loved most in the world had died alone. Gran had died without anyone to comfort her as she passed.

And in the quiet moments of the night that truth still ate at me.

Eleanor's hand tensed around mine. "You know, when I look at you, I see a beautiful woman, but I also see so much confusion. You don't know who you are yet, do you? Or where you're going?"

I stared down at her. "No. Not really. I'm a bit late to the game."

She closed her eyes a minute. "Can I give you a piece of advice before I go?"

I cupped my other hand around hers, so I was holding her fingers between my palms. "Of course."

"This life . . . we only get one shot at it. There are no do-overs. No second chances. We don't always know when we are saying goodbye for the last time." Her eyes opened, glittering with unshed tears. "I learned that the hard way. Follow your heart, my young friend. Follow it and don't be afraid of change. Don't be afraid to chase after what makes you happy." She did a long, slow blink. "You need this. Someone on the other side says you need this."

She lifted her other arm, outside of the fog surrounding us. Untouched by magic, her flesh was nearly skeletal, her fingers as bony as my skeleton friend Robert's, but my focus was on the card in her hand.

A tarot card, to be exact.

Shaking a little, I took it from her and turned it over.

The ten of swords stared up at me, blood on the edges.

Pretty much the worst card you could turn over in the deck because it meant whatever was going on in your life really was as bad as it looked.

Awesome.

"How did you—"

Her eyes fluttered. "You should go now. Someone is calling my name. I think it's my boy. Oh, how I've missed him! I've waited my whole life to hold him again." Tears trickled down her cheeks to a smile so tender and gentle it broke a piece of my heart.

The fog to the right of me thickened, and a figure emerged. Small, maybe four feet tall, and no distinct features. Still, I could tell he was a little boy. He held out a hand to his mother.

A reunion with a child lost was no small thing. I sure as anything didn't want to come between her and her son. She reached for him, and her soul peeled away from her body.

"Goodbye," she whispered to me and bent to scoop up her boy.

"Be at peace," I whispered, and the magic humming around me slid away. The fog dissipated, and the woman's glow of health gave way to a gray pallor. She took a deep breath, her chest rattling with the effort, and the exhale puffed out of her. No inhale followed.

I untangled my hand from hers, and I felt it in my left hand. The tarot card.

I'd seen something that was definitely a sort of hallucination, yet I'd taken something very physical from it. Like a crossing between worlds.

Bringing the tarot card up, I studied the ten of swords, the blades glimmering silver and covered in blood. Shaking, I took in the familiar details. The longer I looked, the more certain I was that it was from the same deck as the one that Annie, the tarot card reader above Death Row, had given me the death card from all those weeks ago.

From the same deck of cards I'd taken from Sean O'Sean at the river's edge.

I shook my head. It shouldn't have been possible, yet there was no denying the card in my hand. I tucked it . . . nope, I had nowhere to tuck it in my lovely hospital gown. Sighing, I clutched it in one hand.

"Be at peace, Eleanor," I said again as I pressed the call button and stood with a wobble in my legs that was part medication, part fatigue, and part whatever I'd just experienced. My magic? It was interesting, though I wasn't sure how it would help me when I was facing down a werewolf or some other monster.

"Fear the fog," I whispered to myself.

Leaning against the railing of the bed, I breathed through the bit of vertigo and took one step. One step was all I got before a hand clamped down on my forearm with supernatural strength.

I did a slow turn—you know, the one from the horror movies—that brought me face to face with the flat, empty eyes of the woman who'd been Eleanor just a few minutes before.

She bared her teeth at me, blood dripping past her lips, and her hand tightened even more on my arm, sharp and broken nails digging into me.

"Eleanor, let me go!" I pried at her fingers, already knowing it would not be enough. Something was very, very wrong. I'd detected no spell other than my fog. No one else was here, so what in the world . . . had *I* done this?

Jaysus Gawd in heaven. *Was this what my magic was for?*

She ground her teeth, and the sound of the molars cracking and splitting was enough to send me flying backward. Her hand was still attached to my arm, so the motion jerked her more upright. I didn't have my knives anymore. I didn't have my friends—I wasn't even sure I could call on Robert here in the hospital. Heat radiated from her hand like it was a red-hot iron, and my attempts to twist free did nothing but give me a serious burn on the skin.

Panic clawed at my still-aching belly. How the hell was I going to get out of this one?

"Feish!" I shouted her name, hoping she wasn't far. I reached for the call button again, pressing it rapidly.

No one came.

But . . . I did have a connection to the dead. Maybe that fog wasn't all I could do.

I calmed myself and pulled on the power that was in me, if a bit elusive at times. My back warmed, even as my hand cooled. I held onto that power and said in my most confident tone, "Eleanor, release me now!"

Her hand sprung open so abruptly her fingers cracked, and I stumbled back, my arm seared by her touch. My magic raced around where she'd scratched me and the heat dissipated.

"Lie down!" I pointed a finger at her, and she slammed back onto the bed, flopping about as though she were a child having a tantrum. Her arms shook at her sides, hands clenched in tight fists, and a low growling began to emanate from her.

Staring at her, I could only think of one thing. Those Tonton Macoutes I'd run into in New Orleans that had been run by the necromancer Clovis and his employees.

Was she somehow connected to them? Was my last job catching up with me?

Footsteps, and then Helen was in the room, cutting off my train of thought. "What happened?"

"Don't go near her!" I grabbed Helen as Eleanor lurched up into a sitting position, teeth snapping and clawed fingers reaching for the nurse.

"Sweet baby Jesus in the manger, have mercy!" Helen put a hand to her bosom. "What in the world . . . ?"

"Yeah, this has very little to do with Jesus unless he was the first undead," I muttered as I pulled Helen back a step.

I had given up any pretense of keeping a hand on my gown and one on the IV pole. I pointed a finger at Eleanor again. "Stay!"

She turned her head toward me, bared her teeth, and let out a long, low snarl. But at least she didn't get out of the bed.

"Maybe you should get Dr. Mori?" I suggested. Though what he was going to do about this I wasn't sure. But he had a good monster face, and obviously he knew how to heal people. Though I wasn't sure how he would heal Eleanor.

Eleanor stiffened, her head tipped sharply to the left, and let out a low sound. At first, I thought it was a moan. Then I realized it was a single word drawn out past dead lips.

"Nooooooo."

"Yup." I pushed Helen out of the room as the curtain around Eleanor's bed fluttered. "Go get the good doctor."

Eleanor stepped out from behind the fluttering curtain, and I could feel her pushing against the strength of my magic.

"Stay!" I snapped, but my power decided to short circuit right at that minute for no apparent reason. Damn it all to hell . . . well, maybe not that far.

I clenched my hands. "Eleanor! Don't make me kick your ass! I really don't want to do that. I thought you were a nice old lady!"

Her lips pulled back, and she clacked her teeth at me as she took another step, and then another and another, and shook her head sharply. Apparently, she was done listening to me.

I mimicked her, circling backward to keep her in the room but also because I was still attached to the damn IV. The thought of it ripping out of my arm made my stomach roll in a horrible, awful way that had me swaying on my feet.

Dragging the IV, both our gowns flapping in the whirlwind breeze we were creating, I could only imagine what Dr. Mori saw when he stepped into the room.

I mean, I know exactly what he saw because my back was to him.

"What is going on?" he said, his voice a careful clipped neutral as I stepped out of his way so he could see Eleanor. I waved a hand at Eleanor.

"Well, she's dead, but kind of not, and seeing as you are who you are"—see, I didn't say anything about him not being human. I could learn—"a doctor, I figured you could help." I lurched as she lunged for me, but I wasn't quick enough.

Her hand caught hold of the flesh on my hip, her fingers dug in, and then she tackled me straight to the ground in a tangle of limbs, IV line, flapping green gowns, and bare older-lady bodies. My back hit the floor with a thwack of bare flesh on cold tile. But that was a distant concern compared to my more pressing need to keep my limbs from being chewed on. Although human stories about the shadow world were usually incomplete if not flat-out wrong, I didn't want to test the bit about zombie bites.

I managed to drive my forearm up under Eleanor's snapping jaws. The tile was cold on my backside, and I could only hope I didn't leave a sweaty bum print.

"Little help here!" I yelped as I rolled Eleanor to the side, flipping her onto her back.

A bony arm shot out from the shadows and pinned Eleanor to the ground as my help whispered a single word.

"Friend."

4

"Robert!" I yelled his name as Eleanor fought against him, but he was stronger than her and managed to hold her down.

I carefully got to my feet, and Dr. Mori helped steady me. His touch sent a strange shiver of recognition through me that had me staring hard at him. I realized that he'd not touched me before, even in my examination. He'd been very careful to avoid it. Now, he released me as soon as he could, wiping his fingers off as if I were filthy.

"Call your pet off," Dr. Mori said as he closed and locked the door behind him. "I will deal with the ghoul."

"Ghoul? She's not a Tonton Macoute?" I asked.

His already dark eyes seemed to grow even darker. "No. A Tonton Macoute still has a soul trapped in them. She is . . ."

"A zombie?" I offered.

"That is one name—" Crouching beside her, he drew symbols in the air over her face. They glowed for a moment, glittering gold and black like the scales on his face. "—though it is not the name I would use."

Robert jerked back from Eleanor as the symbols landed on her forehead. As if he were afraid of them. As if those symbols could do to him what they were doing to the zombie.

Eleanor's body crumpled and a heavy sigh slid out of her, flapping her lips like a last hurrah, and then she was face down on the floor in a lumpy ball.

Dead. She was *dead*-dead now. I hoped.

Pulling my IV with me, I put a toe to Eleanor's body. There was no zing, no magic left in her. "What would you call her?"

Before he could answer, a scream erupted out in the hall, followed by several more.

"More?"

"Impossible, there are not that many dying people here." His voice was sharp. Irritated.

"Imports? Could someone have brought more bodies in to be . . . reanimated?" I offered, and he gave me a shrewd look as if perhaps reconsidering me.

"Perhaps."

Dr. Mori glanced at me and my IV. Before I could ask what he was doing, he reached over and expertly removed it. I hissed out a breath but otherwise was okay. Taking me with him, he walked over to a small supply cabinet and quickly wrapped the IV site. "Get out of here, Ms. O'Rylee. It seems as though this . . . zombie . . . is not alone. Which means I have work to do. And you are far from being up to this."

He gave me a quick nod, then spun on his heel as he left the room in a rush of floral-smelling air. Was that the smell of his magic, or did he have questionable taste in cologne?

I was exhausted, but my adrenaline was pumping once more and I was going to use it to get me out of here.

"Robert, we have to go." I clutched my tarot card and the back of my gown with one hand, reaching for Robert with the other. I glanced at my clothes but the sensation in the air was that there was no time.

Bare ass it was.

He slipped under my arm and helped hold me up as I left the room and entered what could only be called complete and utter chaos.

There were . . . shit, I could only call them zombies . . . zombies shuffling, running, biting all around me. How had this even happened? Had a whole slew of people died at once, or had someone snuck the bodies inside? Dr. Mori thought there weren't enough bodies in here, which meant someone had set this up.

And my money was on a necromancer.

Hanging tightly onto Robert, I headed for the EXIT sign at the end of the hall. Sure, we'd have to go down a few sets of stairs, but I had no desire to get stuck in an elevator. And, knowing my luck, that was exactly what would have happened.

"Where the hell is Feish?" I yelped as a zombie came straight for me and Robert. He let me go and grabbed the freshly dead undead with his skeletal hands, all but throwing it behind us. "Thanks, Robert."

"Friend," he growled.

He slipped back under my arm, and we made it to the end of the hall as sirens erupted outside the hospital.

"We have to hurry," I said even as I fought another wave of vertigo. I could do this. I stared down the long flight of stairs. Shit, I wasn't sure I could do this.

Robert tugged on me, but I shook my head. "I have to go slow."

Letting go of my gown once more, I put a hand on the railing, keeping Robert close with the other arm.

Halfway down the flight of stairs, I heard a familiar voice yelling at the top of her gills.

"Stupid dead thing, get away! Gross! This is not romance! No biting!"

I forced my feet to move faster. "We're coming, Feish!" I yelped as we hit the next landing down. Feish was tangled up with a large male zombie wearing a gown just like mine. Only it was on backward. Which meant it wasn't his ass we were looking at swinging around like a wrinkled-up elephant trunk. I mean . . . it was even gray.

And suddenly I understood the "it's not romance" comment. I shouldn't have laughed, but it spilled out of me as I stepped up next to them, grabbed the zombie's arm and yanked him sideways, toward the stairs going down.

The one thing I'd say for these zombies was that they weren't particularly graceful. The Tonton Macoutes I'd dealt with in NOLA had been much better on their feet.

The zombie and his little friend teetered for a moment before crashing down the stairs, two and three at a time. There was a crunch of bone and then silence.

Not that I thought he was *dead*-dead. Just sidetracked.

Robert grumbled, "Dumb friend," under his breath, and then the three of us were rushing down the stairs. The two of them pretty much carried me the rest of the way down and out the bottom door into the lobby of the hospital.

"Hurry," Feish said. "A spell is going to trap us."

I blinked up at her. "Wait, what spell? What are you talking about?"

"Council is going to shut down hospital. Hide it from rest of humans while they deal with the outbreak." Feish was running now, fully dragging me along with her, and Robert shuffled along on the other side, never losing sight of me.

She'd been gone a long time, but I didn't think she'd been gone long enough to get to the council and back.

"The council knows about the zombies? And how do you know what they're up to?" I shouted as we dodged around another zombie crawling across the floor and reaching for us.

She misunderstood my question and answered it slightly to the left. "Yes, of course they know about this! Big problem in the shadow world right now! And I overhear talking when I was trying to explain to Crash about you not sleeping with Corb, just worried about baby from him." She hit the front doors with the flat of her webbed hands, shoving the doors open wide as the three of us stumbled out and into the sharp night air. Okay, it was only sharp because I was naked under the thin gown. I was regretting leaving my clothes behind.

There was a tingle on the skin of my back as we took one more step, and I turned around in time to see a shimmer of magic flow down and over the entrance to the hospital. The shimmer was opalescent with brilliant red streaks that moved and slid like a nest of snakes. Less than a second later and I'd have been caught. If I'd gone for my clothes, I'd have my butt covered but . . .

I recoiled from the magic, not liking the feel of it. "What will it do?"

"Keep all supernaturals locked inside hospital for questioning." Feish lowered her voice as she dragged me backward. "That was close. Almost didn't get you out! Phew!"

I stared up at the hospital, thinking about Dr. Mori. He'd be trapped. But at least no one knew what he was. I mean . . . I didn't even know what he was, to be fair.

We kept moving backward, our eyes on the hospital and the glimmering spell covering the whole thing.

A few people came running out.

"Humans?" I asked quietly, and Feish nodded.

"Yes, humans can come and go from under spell, but no one else. They will clear out the hospital so they can find the person responsible for this mess. Then deal with it."

I looked over at her, a strange feeling in my gut. "There is no way you could have heard all of that in the last hour." I was surprised she'd even found him, given I'd heard the sounds of a vehicle through the phone.

She pursed her lips and looked around as if to see who was watching us before she bent close. "Boss has been talking with council a lot lately. I listen in." She tapped the side of her head where her ear slits were. "They been planning this. Boss knew it was happening soon. He sent me back to get you out. Council can't know he helped you one last time."

Crash had known this was going to go down? I didn't think that the council had that kind of sway over him. I would have thought he'd warn me or, better yet, stayed and gotten me out himself. And why in the spitting fires of hell did the council want me to go down *now*?

I didn't understand how this could all be because he thought I'd been unfaithful, which made zero sense since he hadn't asked for a commitment from me. And. I. Hadn't. Slept. With. Corb. My sadness and hurt over being poorly labeled was rapidly transforming into anger.

Anger was better. Anger gave me motivation to move.

I frowned as more people came flooding out of the front doors of the hospital. The sirens behind us grew louder as the emergency vehicles came shooting in around us.

Robert growled as a few of the cops got too close.

"Hello, Ms. O'Rylee." The familiar female voice turned me around.

I blinked once at the cop, her bright red hair pulled back and tucked under her cop hat. Yes, cop hat. Give me a break. I have no idea what they are actually called. "Officer Burke," I said. "You got reinstated?"

She snorted and then gave a nod. "Yes."

I raised both eyebrows. "We good?"

Her face was tight as she looked me over, not one ounce of friendly in her expression. It didn't take a rocket scientist to figure out I'd lost an ally. She'd tried to help me learn about my parents' murders, only to be kicked off the force for being seen with me.

Then again, it was all bunk. My name had been cleared, and she'd obviously gotten her job back. So, it was all good, right? Except she clearly didn't see things that way.

"What are you doing here?" Officer Burke asked. "This is a crime scene."

I looked down at my gown and then back up at her, not sure at first whether she was serious. But if she wanted to play that game, I'd play. "Oh, you know. Just out for an afternoon stroll. Thought I'd try my hand at a new fashion." I whipped around and flashed her my ass. "What do you think?"

Feish burbled a laugh. "Oh, it's a fashion some people love."

"Yes." I waved a hand at the other patients in gowns just like mine. "I've started a trend. Look at all the people copycatting me."

Officer Burke's eyes tightened. "Stay out of the way, O'Rylee. You've caused me enough grief to last a lifetime. You and your . . . friends."

I smiled at her. "You're about to walk into a hospital full of zombies. I suggest you take whatever help you can get. Especially if it comes from me and my friends."

Her face paled, and her eyes slid to the doors of the hospital right before a body slapped into it. Heavy fists hammered on the door, and her face lost more color until she was nearly as gray as the zombie.

"This isn't real," she whispered as her hand went to her side holster.

I shrugged. "Sure, you keep telling yourself that. You going to let me help you? If you can fill me in on your side of things—"

"I'm not at liberty to discuss this case." Her eyes shot to me again. "You're a civilian."

Case. Did that mean she actually had an idea of what was going on? Could this mean this wasn't the first round of zombies? Undead. Ghouls. Whatever.

Her car was right behind her. Light flickered inside of it from a glowing screen of some sort.

I wasn't much of an actress, but I was going to try. I buckled my knees and closed my eyes. "I don't feel so good. I need to sit down."

"Then sit down!" she said, her voice sharp, an edge of fear to it. Yeah, I suppose the first time I'd seen an undead thing coming around I hadn't responded too well either.

"Can I sit in your car, so I don't have to sit my bare butt on the sidewalk?" I swayed again for good measure, and Feish gave me a look like she wondered what the hell I was doing.

Officer Burke waved a hand at me, and I fake stumbled away as she continued to watch the zombies slam into the front door of the hospital.

I reached the driver's door and let myself in. The seat squeaked against my bare skin, but I barely noticed as I looked across at the tablet screen that was lit up in its own holder that hung from the ceiling.

Case #6666
Supernatural at large
Undead popping up like daisies.
Narrowed down to hospital. Local shadow council prepped to help us lock things down.

Suspect a doctor at the hospital according to the shadow council.

I stared at the screen. That had to mean . . . they thought Dr. Mori had done this? They could be talking about another doctor—that was possible—but color me suspicious. It seemed like a hell of a coincidence.

I might as well have been in the Scooby Doo gang given the way trouble always seemed to find me.

I frowned and looked up as a slew of police slid through the doors, guns up, and then came the steady pop, pop, pop of rapid fire.

I tensed. What the hell did I do now? Go in and try to help Dr. Mori?

What if he wasn't a good guy?

I thought about his touch and the strange tingle it had given me, but he hadn't hurt me. No, he'd laid poor Eleanor to rest.

We'd just dealt with Clovis and his Tonton Macoutes in New Orleans, only to come home to zombies in Savannah. I didn't like the timing one bit.

Unless . . . unless Dr. Mori really was responsible. Or maybe even . . .

A terrible, gut-twisting thought rolled back up from where I'd stuffed it in my subconscious.

The zombies had shown up right after that fog had rolled out of me.

What if these undead had something to do with my changing abilities? Dr. Mori had said I didn't know who I was yet. What if I was the one who'd somehow risen all of those dead people? I knew that I had talent there—I mean, you just had to look at Robert to know that.

I looked out at Feish, seeing the worried creases in her fishy face as she glanced from me to the hospital and then back. She'd never be a good poker player.

She'd been listening in on council meetings.

Crash had abandoned me, but she'd hurried back inside to get me out.

Had they know it would come down to this?

That I'd be the cause of some undead plague as my weird mishmash of abilities showed up?

I closed my eyes and settled my head on the steering wheel, feeling wobbly for real this time as the questions and fears piled on top of one another.

A bang on the window jerked my head up and Officer Burke glowered at me. "Not the driver's seat."

I nodded and stumbled out of the car, clinging to Feish and Robert.

Jaysus, I was in trouble this time, and I didn't even know what I'd done.

5

Feish and Robert managed to get me home on the bus, though it was neither easy nor pretty, and I had to give my epic resting bitch face more than once to get people to stand down.

One of them was part fae, and he made a reach for me and Robert that was not friendly at all.

"You can tell Karissa to duck right off!" I snapped at him and he recoiled to the back of the bus as if I'd hit him. And, sure, I didn't know that he worked for the fairy queen, a.k.a. Crash's ex-wife, but it was a pretty good assumption considering our history. Frenemies had nothing on the two of us.

Another man took one look at the flapping backside of my green gown and took my lack of cover to mean that I was a buffet for groping. Two broken fingers and a black eye later, he knew he was incorrect about that.

"I am nobody's tidbit," I grumbled as I limped up the steps to my gran's house.

Feish snickered. "He was surprised that you were so mean! And that either of us could fight!"

I snorted and checked over my shoulder to see Robert position himself in his usual spot under the oak tree. Then I put my hand on the door, staring at it. Remembering the eviction notice I'd found there before our New Orleans trip. Who'd placed it there? Because Crash had said it wasn't from him, and Karissa hadn't done it either.

I sighed. Another mystery. I was so full up on ducking mysteries I could puke.

Pushing the door open, the smell of fresh baking hit me first. I stood in the foyer and tried to identify it. Pastry, but there was a richer smell under it, savory and mouth-watering even in my less than perky state.

Meat pies maybe?

I looked down at my bare feet, the coating of dirt that curled up around the edges and through my toes. Sighing, I headed straight upstairs. "Feish, can you tell them—"

She waved her hand at me. "Yeah, yeah, I tell them you filthy."

Hanging onto the banister, I pulled myself up a step at a time, really feeling the fatigue now that I was home. It was closing in on dinner time, and I'd been at the hospital for most of the day.

At the top of the stairs, I paused and looked across to what had been Gran's room. She was there, her ghostly back to me as she stood in the middle of the room.

"Gran?"

She turned and frowned. "Aren't you supposed to be at the hospital? What in the world are you doing back here already?"

I crooked a finger for her to follow me and went into my room, dropping the hospital gown on my way to the connected bathroom.

"Gran, you would not believe what happened." I flicked on the water and stepped in before it was fully warm. I need the quick burst of adrenaline from the cold water if I was going to stay awake for any period of time.

Her voice echoed through the bathroom. "Let me guess, someone died and came back to life? Maybe a few someones?"

I poked my head out of the shower to stare at her, not caring that my hair dripped water onto the floor. "How did you know?"

She sighed and clasped her hands in front of her body. "The dead can communicate with one another, Bree. And those who can speak to the dead sometimes warn us if trouble is coming." She paused and then went on. "Also, I overheard Crash and Feish talking when they didn't realize I was close. Something about the council having problems with the undead, and moving them elsewhere."

I blinked and ducked back into the shower, scrubbing between my toes. The world went wobbly, and I sat down in the bottom of the tub. *Those who speak to the dead.* Like me? Or Dr. Mori? Worse, had Clovis been talking to her?

"You've never mentioned that before, communicating with people outside this house. Dead or otherwise." I didn't want to think too hard on just what Crash and Feish had known.

I didn't want to *not* trust my friends. Bad enough that Crash thought I'd been sleeping with Corb all this time and wouldn't listen to reason and didn't trust me. I sighed and lathered up a bit more, wishing life was not quite so damn complicated.

"It was not pertinent information prior to now," Gran said, her voice sharp. Which meant she felt foolish about not mentioning it earlier. Such was the way of my gran.

I wasn't sure she was right about that, but I wasn't in the mood to argue. It was more important to find out whether she understood my abilities . . . and whether it was possible I'd been the one to make the mess in the hospital.

Back in New Orleans, Jacob, the necromancer from the council, had called me a sentinel. From my understanding, that meant I was some kind of guardian of Savannah, but the title raised as many questions as it answered. I knew my mom was part witch, part fae, seeing as my gramps was apparently fae. But my dad's side . . . of him, I knew very little.

There were no grandparents, aunts, uncles, or cousins there that I knew about.

"Gran, what was my dad?" There was no answer. "Gran?"

"He was human," she said. "He was no shifter or fae."

I yawned. Well, so much for that train of thought. She clearly didn't intend to talk and if she thought I believed he was a straight up human she was not on her game. "These undead zombies, they aren't very quick. Any thoughts on them? I mean, obviously they aren't good, but they aren't like the Tonton Macoutes."

Gran poked her head into the shower, the water running straight through her face, reminding me that she was very much dead. "If you had my book, you'd be able to look them up."

I grimaced. "I know."

Damn Missy again for stealing Gran's spell book.

Gran sighed. "I hate to suggest speaking to Louis, but he is likely your best place to start if you want to understand what these undead are capable of and how to stop them."

My frown deepened. "He's a dick, and he worked with Clovis."

"I know, but who else has knowledge about this sort of thing?"

"Jacob," I said. Assuming he'd talk to me. Yes, I'd saved his butt back in NOLA, but from what I'd learned over the last months, saving someone in the shadow world didn't mean as much as you might think.

"He wouldn't break the council's confidence for you," Gran said. "They would crucify him."

I cringed, wondering if she meant that literally.

There was a flash of Dr. Mori in my head, but I shook that away. He seemed to want nothing to do with me and thought me an untrained fool. Besides, he might be a council prisoner by now.

"How did the council know that the zombies were going to show up? That's the real question," I said as I absently scrubbed at my legs. "Or was it a setup?"

I stuck my head out of the shower again to see that Gran had left. I sighed and stayed sitting in the bottom of the shower for a few more minutes, letting the water hit my shoulders until it began to lose heat.

I flicked the water off, towel dried, and pulled on some clothes. Winding my hair up into the towel, I stared at the bed. Yup, exhaustion won over food.

I lay down—just for a few minutes is the lie I told myself—and closed my eyes. Sleep rolled over me.

Sleep that had me twitching and jumping as I dodged undead and fought Tonton Macoutes.

My dream softened, and I found myself standing with Crash, holding his hand.

"Don't believe me," he whispered, and I looked up at him.

"Is it a spell?"

He shook his head. *"Don't believe me."*

I jerked awake, tears tracking down my cheeks. What the hell did that dream mean? That I shouldn't fight for him? I rolled over, and while the room was dark with night, I could still see that I was alone. I sat up, winced at the twinges in my lower back, and headed downstairs. I thought that everyone else would be asleep, but they were not.

I found my friends in the kitchen—our usual hangout, as it was the room that we all seemed drawn to the most. Eric and Suzy sat next to each other. While they weren't all over one another by any means, it was obvious from their subtle touches and looks that they were totally 'shipped' as the young ones say.

That is what they say, isn't it?

Feish sat at the end of the table with a cup of tea in front of her, bulbous eyes blinking rapidly as I came into the room. "Feeling better?" she asked.

"Yes." I thought about my dream of Crash. "Maybe."

I smiled and lowered myself into a chair across from Eric and Suzy. At least someone was finding relationship bliss.

"Tell us what happened," Eric said softly, his voice as calming as ever when he slipped into psychologist mode. "Let's see if we can figure this out."

A fluttering of wings, and Kinkly flew down from the light fixture to land in the middle of the table.

"Before we get to that, I want the good stuff. Did you actually have sex with Crash this time before you got interrupted?" She scooped up a grape from the fruit bowl next to her and grinned at me over it.

Feish snorted but didn't answer for me.

I stared at the ceiling to avoid looking at any of my friends as the heat rose in my face. "No. And now he thinks I've been sleeping with Corb, and that I could be pregnant with Corb's baby. You know, just to make things interesting."

There was stunned silence for three, two, one . . .

"WHAT?" Kinkly's voice was a shriek. "Wait, you weren't sleeping with Corb! Were you?"

"I was not," I sighed and then smiled as Eric pushed a personal-sized meat pie in front of me. "Thanks, I'd probably die of starvation without you."

Kinkly snorted. "Please. Starvation isn't what's going to kill you. Maybe a werewolf. Or a necromancer. But you will never die of starvation."

I ignored her and dug into the pie. The pastry flaked perfectly on my tongue, and the filling was as luscious as the smell—beef, garlic, ginger, and a spice I couldn't identify, all wrapped in a thick sauce that was the perfect consistency. I had to fight back a groan as the warmth soaked through me.

"You need to start a bakery," I mumbled around a mouthful.

Suzy smiled up at Eric and fluttered her eyelashes. "I said the same thing. As good of a counselor as he is, he's an even better baker."

Kinkly made a gagging noise. I tapped my shoulder, and she flew to me, perching there so she could whisper in my ear. "They've been ridiculously sweet," she grumbled.

Of course, Eric had been in love with Kinkly not too long ago. She'd turned him down, understanding what he didn't—a bigfoot and a tiny fairy could never really have a relationship. Of course, that didn't mean Kinkly didn't know he was one of the good guys.

Hence the gagging.

"Honeymoon stage," I said as I shoveled in another spoonful. "Give it time. She'll be hitting him with a frying pan soon."

I winked at Suzy to soften the words, and she winked back. Despite looking like a total Barbie doll, she was sharp as a tack and understood as well as I did that Kinkly's feelings were bruised.

Kinkly sat on my shoulder with a huff, leaning against the towel. Feish sipped at her tea.

Feish, who Gran had overheard talking about or to the council.

The others waited while I finished my meat pie. The sound of the back door turned us in time to see Sarge saunter in, his nose in the air. "What is that amazing aroma?"

"Meat pies, my mom's recipe," Eric said. "You want one?"

"Imma steal you from Suzy if that tastes as good as it smells." Sarge waggled his eyebrows at Eric, who flushed bright red.

The werewolf chuckled and sat down to my left. "Heard you had some excitement. The grapevine is all but vibrating with news."

I scooted back in my seat. "What have you heard?"

Sarge moaned as he took the first bite of meat pie. "Damn. This is good. You need to start a bakery, man!"

It was hard to wait, but finally Sarge leaned back and patted his belly. "I've heard a new kind of supernatural is in town, raising the dead to cause havoc. Trying to situate themselves to gain influence with the council. The council is having none of it, though, and they're throwing everything they have into shutting the whole thing down. Problem is, the person or persons are hiding." He pursed his lips. "Far as I can tell from the news, what I'm hearing isn't that far off. The smell of the undead is all over the place. I haven't seen any zombies or Tonton Macoutes, but their stench is everywhere."

I stared at him. Kinkly flew up and unwound the towel from around my head and started to play with my hair, weaving it here and there.

"Like where?" I asked. "Because let's be honest, there are dead under every damn square foot of Savannah."

Sarge and Eric both nodded. "Agreed," Eric said. "There is not truly a place here that hasn't seen death over the years."

"But there are places that have been cleaned of the dead," Sarge said. "Places they've been dug up, displaced, and moved. Old death and new death smell different. And the undead smell different yet. They're the ones I'm smelling everywhere."

Kinkly tugged on my hair, turning my head away from Sarge so that I was looking across the table at Feish, who was being uncharacteristically quiet through the whole conversation. Kinkly was being more subtle than usual, but the second tug when I tried to turn my head away was enough for me.

Gran had said there had been a conversation that Feish had at least been there for, even if she hadn't taken part.

"What about you, Feish? You knew something would go down at the hospital, didn't you? That's why you were there with me. Why you came back for me."

Feish grimaced, her lips squashing together as if someone had squeezed her face. "I am not supposed to say."

"Little late," Sarge rumbled. "You might as well spit it out now."

She stuck her tongue out at him, but before she could answer, there was a knock on the front door. It had to be past midnight. I checked the clock above the fridge. Strike that, it was just past one in the morning.

With a raised eyebrow, I put a finger to my mouth and headed to the door.

Who was I kidding? My friends got up and fanned out behind me, my own little parade to meet whoever was on the other side of the door. At one in the morning.

The one thing I knew was this . . . it wouldn't be anyone looking to borrow a cup of sugar.

6

A visitor after one in the morning was a sure sign of trouble. I half expected it to be Officer Abigail, following up after seeing me at the hospital. Maybe to accuse me of making some zombies.

I also half expected it to be a brand-new monster looking for trouble and ready to pick a fight.

The last half of me thought it was for sure going to be a solicitor—maybe Girl Scouts looking for a new midnight munchie market for their cookies?

Sure, three halves are a lot, but math never was my strong suit.

Before I could reach the door, Sarge got in front of me, blocking me from view as he whipped it open. "What the hell do you . . . oh. Hey."

I couldn't see past him. "Who is it? Girl Scouts selling cookies?" Hey, one could hope for the best, right?

Sarge grunted and stepped to the side.

I stared up into Roderick's chiseled face, his cravat perfectly in place. He tipped his head toward me. As a member of the council, I'd run into him on a few occasions and he'd worked with Sarge and Corb when they'd been undercover for the council. I couldn't quite decide if I liked him or not. "Ms. O'Rylee. I would like to speak to you on a matter of business." His gaze shifted over my group of friends. "Alone."

Behind him, from under the oak tree, Robert let out a low growl that was less than welcoming. "Not friend."

Yeah, although Roderick always referred to Robert in friendly terms, the feeling was not mutual. One day I would find out the history between them, but it hadn't happened yet. I took just one step and stopped as Kinkly buried herself in my hair, hiding under the strands.

"Rod, listen, I'm not sure that would be smart of me," I said. "The council hasn't really made any bones about not liking me. Or about throwing me to the wolves." I shot a look at Sarge. "No offense."

Sarge draped an arm across my shoulders. "None taken. And you're right, it probably isn't smart to talk to him. Especially at this time of night. Especially with all the zombies around."

Roderick's eyes didn't slide away from my face. "Outside, perhaps? Your friends can keep an eye on us then."

Ole Rod was playing a game. He knew there was no way I could trust him, but he was making the point that he was in the council, so he was in charge. Or at least that's what I took from it.

Sarge gave me a squeeze and then let me go. I sighed and looked past him to where Robert stood swaying. "Sarge, you stand in the door here. Robert will be right with me."

I thought about the tarot card Eleanor had given me. Ten of swords.

Maybe that had been about Roderick's visit? What could be worse than undead zombies, and Crash freaking out?

I followed him down the steps and then joined Robert under the oak tree. He swayed lightly side to side, his bony fingers bumping into my arm.

Roderick stood in front of me. "You were in the hospital today, right before the lockdown. Correct?"

I shrugged. "And if I was?"

He looked up into the leaves of the oak tree, reached up and plucked one. Rolling it in his fingers, he pitched his voice low. "Then you saw what happened there. Which is why I would like to hire you for a job."

My eyebrows shot up so high they about flew off my face. "Pardon?"

"Yes, I realize it may be hard for you to believe I would hire you, but this is not a job I can do myself since I'm on the council." He looked me in the eye then, and for just a moment I thought he was trying to . . . get into my head? Was that what he was doing? I squinted back at him.

"You have some nose hairs you need to trim." I reached up as if to pluck them myself.

He waved me off, then shook his head slightly as if I were a toddler to be kept in line. "Before you start asking questions, which at this point I know you will, let me explain as much as I can. Then I hope you will decide to help."

Robert bumped into me faster now. "Maybe friend," he whispered, his voice strained. Anxious.

His worry did not bode well for whatever Roderick was about to say.

"Okay, go for it." I motioned for him to speak.

"The council cannot know that I have hired you," he said. "That is where we'll start. I implored them to hire you directly as our own people have been unable to pin down the influx . . . of new supernaturals. Or why they are coming here now. And what ties they have to the undead that are popping up all over Savannah. But they refused."

I held up a hand, pausing him. "You want me to be a go-between?"

"Not as such." He shook his head, still rolling the oak leaf in his fingers. "The council wishes to force the supernaturals they *believe* are the problem back out of Savannah as they have done in the past. For various reasons that don't truly matter as they are all false. It is why they tried to take Mori. You met him in the hospital, yes?"

I nodded even as indignation rippled through me. The council had either allowed me to be imprisoned for Alan's murder or arranged for my lockup themselves, so I knew what it felt like to get a raw deal. "Dr. Mori didn't seem like he was one of the bad guys."

"He isn't," Roderick said softly. "He is an old friend of mine. I . . . encouraged him to stay here when the others of his kind were cast out. He did, and I helped keep him hidden for the last twenty or so years. The council believes he's part of the problem, but I'm unconvinced." That last word seemed to cost him. As if admitting that he didn't know something had opened a literal wound in his body.

I waited for more as Robert all but vibrated by my side.

Roderick let out a heavy sigh. "The council is barely able to keep the undead contained. There are more of them every day, and they are stretching our resources to the limits."

Crash had been talking to someone from the council. Someone who maybe helped set up the zombies at the hospital. So did that mean that the council members were all acting on their own, like Roderick here?

I held up a hand, stopping him. "The undead are slow and stupid. They are not like the Tonton Macoutes in New Orleans."

Roderick's eyes locked on mine, and again I got the impression he was trying to worm his way into my head. "The problem is they are fresh. The longer they are moving, the faster they get. And the hungrier. Tonton Macoutes don't innately want to eat. They are directed to kill and all it takes is a single bite to spread the disease. It takes time for the bite to truly turn the bitten into the undead, but it will happen. These undead . . . they are like unleashing a plague on the city."

I put my hands on my hips while at the same time internally clapping. Because Roderick was filling in some serious blanks for me. Maybe I wouldn't have to talk to stupid Louis after all.

I held up a single finger. "Let me think a minute."

An idea was forming, one that I didn't want to derail. The spell we'd been trying to stop, the one with the angel wings and the fairy cross was meant to be massively destructive to the city. Maybe even to the world.

What could be more destructive than a bunch of zombies rising from their graves and flooding the streets?

"Could it be the spell?" I didn't realize I was pacing until Roderick put a hand out and stopped me.

"It is not . . . the spell of which you have been learning about." Again, the words seemed to cost him. Like he didn't want to say too much.

"You sure?"

He nodded and I breathed a sigh of relief. At least we weren't on the chopping block with that again. I stared up at Roderick.

"Okay, so whoever's behind this needs to be found?"

"And stopped, as quickly as you can," he said. "I do believe there will be a city-wide spell unleashed in a matter of days."

I held up a single finger again, stopping him. "A city-wide spell that would raise the dead? And you're sure it's not the big-bad spell with the fairy cross etc.?" He nodded, and I held up a second finger. "In a town where there are so many buried beneath streets, parks, and houses that there is no telling the numbers?" He nodded once more, and I held up a third finger. "Undead that will gain in speed and ferocity as they get hungrier, and they'll attack anything and everything? Is that about it right?"

Roderick's jaw tightened, and he spoke through gritted teeth. "Correct."

"Shit."

"Exactly," Roderick said. He held out a hand to me, palm up. I carefully placed my hand against it because that seemed to be the thing to do.

He locked eyes with me.

Before he could ask a question, I beat him to it. "How do you know all of this?"

His fingers wrapped tightly around mine, and Robert slapped his bony fingers on top of ours and some sort of power flared between the three of us.

Death to death to death.

For just a flash, Robert was the man he'd been in life, blue eyes snapping with a fiery heat. "Yes, *do* answer that question, Roderick."

Roderick looked at Robert, who had gone right back to his bony self. "Does he do that often?"

"Answer the question," I said.

The councilman looked me straight in the eye. "Because I have seen it before, a long time ago. There are three signs that the spell is coming. One is the undead popping up here and there, still wobbly, still uncertain. The second is a green moon. And the third is a blood storm."

I blinked a couple of times. "Sounds like fun."

He leaned in closer. "The humans are predicting a green moon tomorrow night due to a comet flying by. But it is no comet that will make the moon glow like a cat's eye." His fingers pressed harder into mine, and his eyes were more than a little mesmerizing. I squinted up at him.

"Why don't you go and deal with the person who is doing this since you know so much?"

He drew back and rolled his eyes. "Because I cannot. That is why."

Sarge laughed. "That's a non-answer if I ever heard one."

I had to agree with my wolf friend. "Yeah, I'm with him. Give me a reason—"

"Because the only person that could drum up enough power to raise all the dead of Savannah is . . . ." His face scrunched up with an emotion that I couldn't place. Fear? Sorrow? A mixture of both maybe.

"Like a Band-Aid, spit it out," I said. He looked at me. Yes, the analogy wasn't quite right.

"My older brother. I believe he is behind this. I cannot come at him directly, though, because then he will know that I am on to him. Which will only make him more dangerous. As of right now he is being bold, and that can give us an edge." Roderick sighed and tried to take his hand from mine, but I found myself hanging on.

"You didn't want to tell me all this, but you did," I said. "Why?"

He placed his other hand over our joined fingers. "The council believes that Mori and his kind are behind the plague of undead. I know it is not true, but I cannot tell them that my own brother is involved, or they will believe I am working with him." He sighed. "As I said, I petitioned them to hire you but was outvoted. And so, I came to you on my own. In the hopes that you can stop the one I cannot."

I put a hand to my forehead as if I could rub away the wrinkles that were forming there. From where she sat hidden in my hair, Kinkly whispered a question to me, and I repeated it to Roderick.

"Spit out what you want me to do, Roderick, and what you are offering in payment." Because if he wanted me to kill his brother, I wasn't so sure I was down. I mean . . . killing monsters was one thing. Demons? Sure, you got it. But even the Tonton Macoutes had been hard for me because they were still soul bound. I had killed Sean O'Sean, but I'd done it unintentionally, and O'Sean Senior? Well, he'd totally deserved it.

He let the oak leaf fall to the ground. "I want you to . . . find my brother and stop him. Whatever it takes, whatever the cost." Yup, that definitely sounded like a possible murder. Maybe I could just tie the guy up? Let Roderick do the deed?

I waited for the next part. Because the payment was important if I was ever, ever going to get my own place, which hopefully would be Gran's house. If I could convince Crash to sell it to me. I had some money from Alan's life insurance. But I doubted it would be enough.

Roderick gave me a sad smile. "Half a million."

I couldn't have heard him right. There was no way he'd just said . . .

"As in five hundred thousand?" I may have shouted that out.

From his position by the front door, Sarge yelped as though he'd been swatted on the ass.

Kinkly tightened her hold on my hair, and even Robert slowed his swaying. They all knew what it would mean to me to have that kind of money.

I'd finally be able to buy Gran's house.

But that big payout meant something else too.

"So, it's pretty dangerous then? I mean . . . " I squinted an eye up at Roderick. "You wouldn't be offering me that kind of money if it was some easy walk in the park. Like your brother is a really bad dude then?" A thought hit me before he could speak. "It's not more demons, is it?" Jaysus on a three-legged donkey, I did not want to deal with demons again.

Roderick smiled sadly. "I wish it were."

I didn't know if he meant he wished it were easy, or he wished it were demons. Either way, his words confirmed this job was not to be taken lightly.

"When do you need an answer?"

"Now. You would need to start immediately. As I said, the second sign comes tomorrow night. The clock is truly ticking on this."

I snorted. "I would start in the morning, after I get some sleep. *If* I take the job." A thought jogged slowly through my brain, limping on the left side just like me. "Wait, why don't you get your Savannah supernatural police department to do the dirty work? Surely there is someone—"

"They've been disbanded," Roderick said. I raised my eyebrows, but he didn't comment on why the council's police force was no more.

Roderick stepped closer, looking down at me even as Robert pushed his way between us. The tall man acted as though he couldn't see the swaying skeleton with the long hair and raggedy clothes. Roderick's intense eyes locked on mine. "Savannah's future depends on you taking this job, Bree. I am offering you money because I know that you wish to stay here, and I hope that for the sake of our town that you do. But even if I did not offer you anything, I believe you would take the job. I believe you would try to save this town from this new threat. From my brother."

Damn it, I didn't like that he knew me that well. "Because?"

"Because you cannot turn away from those in need. And Dr. Mori and his kin are in danger because the council is hunting them, even as you take on this task for me." His eyes narrowed on me, and he stepped back. "I need your answer. If you will not help, then I have another I could ask."

"Anything else you can tell me?" I asked.

Roderick thought a moment. "It is most likely he will have a central to him place. Large enough for the undead, and also private enough that he would not be bothered as he works."

I looked over my shoulder at Sarge, Feish, Suzy, and Eric standing in the doorway, very obviously listening in.

I was going to make him sweat on this. "Let me confer with my associates. You wait here."

I made my way back up the steps to the porch and lowered my voice to address my friends. "How much of that did you hear?"

"Big money," Sarge said. "That will mean big danger, but you already know that. And if it's his brother . . . here's the thing. No one really knows what Roderick can do. Obviously, he has some magic and necromancer abilities, but otherwise we don't really know what you'll be up against."

"I can't do it on my own," I pointed out. "I know it, and you know it. I'm not taking the job if you all aren't on board with helping."

Suzy shrugged and flipped a hand through her long blond hair. "We're a team, aren't we? Gran's Girls. We help solve the mystery and get a cut of the winnings. That's how this works."

I grimaced. "I know, but this one is dangerous—"

"Clovis wasn't?" Eric asked quietly. "Or O'Sean? Or that fool of a goblin king, Derek?"

I couldn't quite put my finger on why I felt like this was more dangerous than the other jobs we'd pulled off. Maybe because the other big bads we'd dealt with were still around. Like Clovis. Like Karissa. They'd likely circle in on us while we found ourselves more trouble. I sighed. "It feels . . . more dangerous, I guess. I mean, yes, we're only going after one person, but he potentially has a whole town of hungry zombies at his disposal."

"You're going to take the job," Eric said, keeping his voice low. He pushed up his spectacles. "Roderick's right. You aren't one to turn away from need. And from the sound of it, this Dr. Mori is being framed by the council. They're so busy framing him that the real culprit—Roderick's brother—is still out there, causing trouble and death."

Eric was the reasonable one of the bunch of us, and he saw that this was going to happen one way or another too.

"Plus," Feish added, "if we do nothing, maybe zombies show up and we have to deal with them anyway, but then no money. That's a terrible idea. Money would be good for you. You could move."

A quick look at her revealed her face was far too smooth, as if she were trying to look innocent. "What do you know about the council's goings-on, Feish? Anything?"

I wouldn't have thought it possible, but her face went even blanker. "No idea what you're talking about."

And then she let out a burbled burp and swallowed hard. No idea, huh? Yeah, right.

"We're in then?" I wanted to make absolutely certain.

One by one, my friends nodded. Kinkly tugged on my hair and whispered a very good idea into my ear.

"Kinkly, that is brilliant."

"I know," she said through a yawn, "let me go to sleep now."

Back down the steps, I made my way to the oak tree and came to a stop in front of Roderick. "Okay, we're in." I held up a finger stopping Roderick before he could leave. "But we need one thing if we are going to make this work."

"If it is in my power, I will make it happen," he said.

I grinned. He might regret that by the time he heard what I wanted.

7

There were not a lot of hours left in the night after Roderick left, and I found myself feeling far more awake than was sensible. My friends all made their ways to bed, and the house was left to just me and Gran, who sat next to me at the kitchen table as I stared at my phone. I wanted to call Crash. I wanted to ask him what he knew about Joseph.

Joseph was Roderick's older brother.

But I also wanted to ask Crash why he'd walked away from me like that, and right after he'd said he wasn't going anywhere? Or had his hormones been talking at the time? I sighed heavily and spun the phone on its back.

I'd tried to get Robert to tell me what he knew about Roderick and his brother, but he didn't give me his blue eyes, just his swaying self.

Nothing was falling into place for me.

"You should sleep, honey girl." Gran patted the table, and while there was no sound, my memory filled in the sound from my childhood. The pat of her hand when she was trying to make a point.

I sighed. "Gran, Crash thinks I slept with Corb. He thinks that I was having a miscarriage of a baby that doesn't exist, all because he heard half a conversation without context. And I've checked the forge. It's cold. I've never seen it without at least some kind of fire going on. He won't answer his phone. And . . ." And that dream about him was rubbing me the wrong way.

Don't believe me. Those were his words. But they didn't make sense. Don't believe what, exactly?

Gran sighed and leaned forward, reaching out and touching my arm. The ghostly tingle of her presence on my skin was better than her not being there at all.

"Bree, my girl, Crash is being a fool. If he chooses not to see that you have been honest all this time, you can't fix it for him."

I sighed. "But shouldn't I at least try to explain? I want to."

"You said that at the hospital, you did," she pointed out.

I frowned. I had tried to talk to him, and he'd stormed out before I could finish telling him that he was hearing things wrong. That I'd worried I'd been impregnated *without consent.*

A shiver ran through me just thinking about that.

"I did, on the phone."

Now it was Gran's turn to sigh. "I've known him a long time, honey girl. A long time. I can't say I've seen him like this before. Certainly not over Karissa, not even when he caught her cheating. He just wished her well and walked away."

Frowning, I stared at the table. This was stupid. Crash had chased me for the better part of a month. He'd waded through a cemetery full of Tonton Macoutes, armed only with two swords, to save me. Said he would always be there for me.

And now he was walking away because of a misunderstanding. Maybe that's what the dream was about? I wasn't sure. But I knew one thing for certain.

"I'm going to kick his ass the next time I see him." I pushed to my feet. "But you're right, I need to sleep so I have the energy to really give him the tip of my boot."

He was an idiot.

Or maybe I was the idiot for letting my heart fall for a man I didn't really know.

My bed called to me, and when I laid my head down, I found myself wishing that things weren't so damn complicated. That Crash was there with me—not even for the nooky, but just to hold me. And so I could press my face against his chest and breathe him, and the comfort that came with him, in.

Closing my eyes, I tried not to think about anything at all as sleep sucked me down again. Of course, my luck being what it was, I didn't dream about Crash. Nope, I ended up dreaming about Alan, a.k.a. my ex-husband.

To be more exact, I dreamed of Alan's soul stuck in a dead body that was animated by Marge and Homer, the voodoo queen and her man back in New Orleans.

His stolen body was as tall and lanky as he'd been in life. Only it was scrawnier and had no pot belly. And this body had straggly hair instead of being bald. All and all, it could have been seen as an improvement if not for the fact that the body was dead.

Alan waved his flopping gray hands at me, the wrists limp as he motioned me closer. In the dream, I was dragged toward him.

He flopped his hands together and went down to one knee. "Bree, you have to get me out of here. I swear I'll be good. I won't be a pain in your ass. I could handle being a ghost after this. Please. Please don't leave me like this. Take me back with you. That Marge lady said you could, and I *know* you could. Please, just—"

There was a snap like that of a whip, and then his mouth locked shut. From the shadows stepped the Amazonian Marge. Jaysus, she was a big woman. She could have made a slam dunk without more than a little hop of her legs. She smiled at me, her face with the lightly tinged blue skin filling my field of vision.

"Well, hello. I see Alan figured out how to reach you by phone?"

"What?" I shook my head.

"That's what we call this dream talking. Phoning."

"Doesn't that get confusing when—"

"No," she spat the word at me. "I don't want him anymore. You take him right now."

Alan's face sagged with relief, and he held his begging hands over his head as if he'd won a race.

"What?" I shook my head, and I was sure I could feel the movement in my sleep. "I don't want him."

"Well, neither do I," she growled. "He's a complete and total whiner, and I can't get him to shut up! He doesn't even follow orders that well!"

My lips twitched. "You wanted him. You gave me a choice between Robert or Alan. I chose Robert." My grin widened. "No backsies."

Alan lifted his head and stared hard into my eyes. "Bree. You take me with you right now!" He flopped the hand that didn't truly belong to him, smacking it into the other palm. But it was like watching a puppet flip flop around. Not particularly graceful. "You have to! Please, I'm begging you."

"No."

Alan and Marge spoke together. "YES!"

What was a girl to do? I rolled my back to the two of them and settled into a deeper sleep, one that took me away from their 'phone call.' I was not taking Alan back. I hadn't wanted him when he was alive, and I surely didn't want him now that he was dead.

Between that 'call' and the long day preceding it, the next day came far too soon. Like ridiculously too soon.

And because I didn't have enough going on, when I rolled out of bed and opened my eyes to a ghostly Alan, I didn't hold back—I didn't even try to filter my thoughts.

"WHAT THE ACTUAL FUCK?"

Alan smiled at me. "I don't think you actually had a choice. And you didn't shut down the line properly is what Marge said. So typical of you not to do the job correctly. That is something you could work on, you know."

I covered my face with my hands as a pit opened in my stomach. "This is not the way I want to start my morning."

"I'll be good. Helpful. I said I would."

"You turned on me in New Orleans," I snapped as I opened my eyes and stared hard at him. "I don't know how in the world you think I could ever trust you again!" Yup, I was yelling by the end.

Gran came barreling in, and rage flashed in her eyes when she saw Alan. "You good-for-nothing cur! How dare you come back here!" She chased him around the room, out onto the landing, and then—by the sound of it—downstairs, their voices floating back to me.

Kinkly zipped into my room, ignoring the battling pair of ghosts. "Oh, my gods, he did it! Bree, come and look at the package Roderick sent to us!"

Eyes closed again, I forced my body out of bed and to the bathroom, where I peed, thought about it, and peed some more. All those IV fluids were finally making themselves known, thank you very much.

"Hurry your old lady bladder up!" Kinkly yelled.

"I'm only forty-three!" I barked back, still with my eyes closed.

"You might be dead tomorrow at that age!" she squealed and then flew away as my eyes opened and I glared at her.

Yawning and stretching, I made my way downstairs. The others were gathered on the front porch with a cardboard box at their feet. Sarge turned around, a badge pinned to his chest.

"We're officially members of the Savanah Supernatural Police Department!"

A department that had been disbanded. Which was why we were able to get the badges.

I grinned up at him and held out a hand. He placed a badge into my palm, and I looked it over. Typical shape, gold on black with SSPD etched through the middle. The little eyeball symbol etched behind it was not lost on me. Being watched much? "Don't get too excited. I doubt Roderick actually made us official. I just asked for the badges so we'd have more sway in the shadow world."

And hopefully in the human world too.

"We need to break up into teams," I said as Suzy pushed a large cup of tea into my hands. "That's going to help us cover the most ground. Roderick can't tell us where Joseph is hiding out, only that he's probably living and working in the same place."

Gran and I had discussed that for a long time last night. How to find Roderick's brother and fast. I had a few ideas and was going to employ them all.

"Suzy, you and Eric head to the outlying areas. Start at Eric's place and circle outward." I looked at each of them in turn. "If anyone stops you, just tell them you are looking for a new place to settle down."

Suzy nodded. "I am a swamp siren, so it makes sense. What should we be looking for? Anything in particular?"

I frowned. "Clues?"

Sarge laughed. "Let me help. Look for anything that doesn't fit. Anything that wasn't there before. Anything magical. And be careful. If we're looking for answers, then this Joseph will be out there too, expecting someone to come after him."

Suzy saluted, and Eric mimicked her. "Got it. We'll come back only if we find something. We can stay at Eric's."

I grimaced. I was going to miss Eric's baking. "Maybe head back every other day. To be on the safe side."

Eric smiled shyly at me. "I froze a lot of my baking, Bree. You won't starve."

A sigh slipped out of me. Thank Jaysus.

Feish looked at me. "Obviously I'm with you."

I smiled and felt a twinge of guilt. Not because I didn't trust her but at the same time . . . something was definitely going on with her. Crash had known about what was going to happen, I was sure of it. Feish had stayed out a long time with him, and he'd left and sent her back to me. But as a friend? Or as a spy?

A funny twinge started in my chest. Had he really known and chosen to leave me there?

"Can you keep an eye on Crash?" I asked her, and Sarge grunted as if I'd kicked him in the gut.

Feish frowned. "Why?"

"Because . . ." I wanted to believe him, to trust him. But things kept happening that pushed us apart. Why? Was it him, or was the shadow world just ducking with me?

Feish clasped her webbed hands together. "He will be in the fae lands. That's where he goes when he is upset. I'll find him there, bring him back to talk to you."

I spluttered, but she was already off and moving. I tapped a still sleepy Kinkly on my shoulder. "Go with her, please."

Kinkly spun out in front of me. "You sure?"

Again, I struggled to put my finger on it, but something was up with Crash, and I wasn't so sure that Feish would tell me. He'd taken the opportunity to run from me like I'd lit his oh-so-fine ass on fire. And since Feish's loyalty to "the boss," as she called him, was absolute, another set of ears and eyes were not a bad thing. "Yeah, I'm sure. Thanks."

I watched as Feish and Kinkly disappeared from sight.

"That just leaves us." Sarge draped an arm over my shoulder. "Can you be good cop, so I can be the bad cop?"

I pushed at him. "I'm going to get dressed, then we're heading to the police station. And to be clear, it won't be just us. Alan is back, and I can't trust him to stay here on his own."

Sarge raised his brows. "No, for reals, where are we going?"

"The police station!" I called as I climbed the stairs to my room. I threw on some clothes and grabbed my handy, seemingly bottomless bag. In it, I tucked my shiny new badge and saw the one book I still had. *Black Spells of Savannah and the Undead.* My finger brushed over the binding, and I pulled it out. The urge to flip through it and find this spell that was going to raise so many dead was strong.

"Stop dawdling!" Sarge bellowed. I stuffed the book down to the bottom of the bag.

"Coming!" As I ran down the steps, I called for the one last thing I needed to take. "Alan!"

"Yes?" He popped into view by the door, and I grabbed him by the ear, stuffing him into my bag with a good deal of force. Could he feel it? I didn't think so.

Did it make me feel better to stuff my cheating, lying, piece of shit ex-husband into a dingy dark handbag? You bet it did.

"I don't want to—"

"Too bad." I gave an extra hard shove and pushed him down.

Sarge raised his brows. "Alan slowing you up?"

"Always," I grumbled.

"Did not!" Alan shouted, but I didn't have to hit the bag—Sarge did it for me. I grinned up at him and then slowly my grin faded. I still felt . . . naked.

"I don't have my knives," I said. "I lost them both in New Orleans."

"We could go to Death Row?" Sarge offered.

We could, but the weapons sold there were crap. Maybe there was something left in the forge? Couldn't hurt to look. Surely Crash wouldn't begrudge me borrowing a weapon, would he?

"Just give me a minute." I jogged—yes, jogged with only a slight hitch in my giddy-up—around the side of the house to the outside entrance to the basement and Crash's forge. I let myself in and flicked on a light. Dead silence, not an ounce of heat. His forge was out completely, just like it had been last night.

I didn't like it, but I didn't know how to make him pull his head out of his ass.

And after wasting twenty years trying to make a dysfunctional relationship work, I was done chasing a man. Any man. Even a man as bone-meltingly hot as Crash.

"Stand firm," I whispered to myself. "He can get over his own shit and come find you. No more saving him."

Also, it was not lost on me that Crash might be in a little more of a hurry to find me if I took one or two of his knives. I made my way to the back of the forge and looked for any weapons he might have left behind.

The forge was eerily empty. No swords, no big axes or raw steel ready to be melded into something new, no flames. I scoured the room, stopping in front of the big anvil I'd been sitting on the day before. A black leather sheath sat propped on top of it, beckoning me.

The dagger had a shiny, smooth handle that perfectly fit my hand. As if Crash had made it for me. I scooped it up and pulled it clear of its sheath. The blade was etched with some sort of writing, but the light was too dim for me to examine the symbols.

I rolled the knife in my hand, feeling the balance fit me nicely. "Thanks," I whispered to the air, then turned and headed out past the forge. Maybe he wasn't as pissed as I thought if he'd left me this dagger. Or maybe he knew something I didn't?

A glimmer of bare steel caught my eye as I turned.

The forge had been cleaned.

Frowning, I looked over where the coal fire had burned so very hot, was it just the day before?

When we'd . . . burned the feathers from the angel wings. I swallowed hard and ran a finger over the forge and held it up. Not a speck of coal dust.

Surely that didn't mean the ashes of the feathers could be used, did it?

"Are you coming? Or are you reliving your moments in there from yesterday?" Sarge barked, yanking me out of my thoughts. I shook my head.

One problem at a time, one ducking problem at a time.

"Yeah. I mean. Yes, I'm coming, and no, I was not," I said, taking a closer look around the room—there was no clothing now, every tool was in its place, and only one weapon had been left behind. As if he'd known he wouldn't be here to give it to me.

"Damn it, Crash," I grumbled. "You could have at least said goodbye."

Sarge poked his head in the door. "I thought you wanted to go after this Joseph dude?"

I waved at him to go ahead of me, my heart breaking a little, as if I were letting go of Crash. I didn't want to, but what was I supposed to do? "Yeah, let's go. There's nothing here."

I paused at the oak tree and the swaying Robert. "You coming with me, Robert?"

"Friend," he said and then collapsed down to a single finger bone. I scooped it up and tucked him into my bag too.

Through the front garden and out the gate we went, the flowers drooping here and there from lack of water. Note to self, I had to make time for the garden. It was looking a little rough around the edges, and the last time we'd let the garden suffer, it hadn't gone well for us. The strength of Gran's spells woven through the plants and earth had faded.

It made the house less secure, less safe.

Sarge had his Harley parked on the street, and I hopped on behind him. "Are you sure you want to go to the police station?" he grumbled. "Things didn't go so well for you the last time you were there. You do remember I had to drag you out?"

I patted him on the shoulder. "I'm hoping they might have made some connections—you know, like following a serial killer's patterns on a chart or something. If we can figure out where the undead have been popping up, it'll help us pinpoint Joseph."

See, look at me making my binge nights of Crime TV work for me.

"Okay, but don't be surprised if they won't even talk to you."

Sarge started the bike, and as we pulled away, I felt the weight of someone's eyes on my back. I turned to see who was watching us, but no one was there. Or at least no one that I could see.

I leaned my head back, letting the wind pull through my hair, and enjoyed the ride to the station, not caring that I wasn't wearing a helmet for a few minutes.

Of course, it looked like I'd back combed every strand the second we stopped.

Sarge burst out laughing. "Ain't nobody going to take you serious like that, girlfriend."

I grinned and pulled out a ponytail holder from my back pocket. "Never leave home without it."

Hair suitably tamed, I headed for the front of the police station. With our shiny new badges, I hoped we'd be able to walk right in and ask to speak with the detective in charge of the case. Case #6666, to be exact.

"You sure you want to do this?" Sarge said out of the side of his mouth. "You don't actually think they will have forgotten you, do you?"

I gave him a wink. "Actually, I'm counting on them not forgetting me."

8

Sometimes it was great being right, other times not so much. As I stepped through the doors of the police station and made eye contact with the person at the front desk, I suspected this was going to be one of the 'not so much' times.

The cop sitting there was none other than Officer Cuffs, the fellow who'd shoved me into a cell after I was arrested for Alan's murder. He was a total dick, but it appeared he'd been demoted, hopefully for his role in my unlawful imprisonment and ensuing escape.

I smiled at him as I stepped through the doors. "I'm surprised you still have a badge. Nice that they kept you in a job at least. Answering phones."

Sarge gave a quiet groan. "Maybe not the best way to get in."

Officer Cuffs's face tightened until I could have bounced a pebble off it. "Get out."

Oh, this was going to be good. I fake fumbled my shiny new SSPD badge out of my bag. "Actually, I'm here on official business." I slapped the badge on the lip of the desk so he could see it.

He picked it up and then threw it back at me. "Making yourself a badge don't mean shit."

I glanced at Sarge. "They don't know what this is?"

"You really thought they would?" He shook his head. Of course, he could have said something *before* I tried to use it to get into the police station.

And honestly, yes, I had thought the local police station would have had some run-ins with the supernatural division of the police. Well, damn. I blew out a sigh. "Fine. I'm here to speak to Officer Burke. I saw her yesterday at the hospital."

I didn't think that Officer Cuffs's eyes could have narrowed further and remained open, but they managed it. "What were you doing at the hospital? Do they know you were there?"

Gawd in heaven save me from men who thought they could intimidate me just because they gave me a big angry frown. I put my hands on the desk and leaned forward over it. "Listen, dumbass, I just said that Officer Abigail knew I was there. But as for the rest, I don't have to answer a wee little secretary."

I leaned over the desk further to read his badge. "Kevin? Nice. Suits you."

His face blanched, and I tapped a finger on his nose, making him recoil. "Let Officer Burke know I'm here. *Now*."

I stood up and tucked my badge into my bag, ignoring a snickering Alan. Damn it, that was why Roderick hadn't argued with my request for badges.

They were freaking worthless.

Kevin picked up the phone. "Burke, I got a perp here to see you."

I rolled my eyes. As if being called a perp was going to bother me.

Sarge was quiet beside me, thought I could feel him stiffen and drag in a deep breath. I glanced at him over my shoulder, and he gave the slightest shake of his head.

What had he picked up on?

I didn't get a chance to ask him, because Officer Burke strode out from the glass doors to the back. Her stride slowed as she took me in.

"Ms. O'Rylee. I'm surprised to see you here."

I gave her a tight smile. "Can we talk in private? I have a couple of questions."

Kevin looked from me to Officer Burke and back again. "What have you got to talk to her about?"

"None of your business," Burke said, and I smiled.

"A recipe I've just got to have. You know, women talk." I wiggled my fingers at him when Officer Burke motioned for me to follow her. Sarge made a move to come with us, but she held up her hand. "Just Ms. O'Rylee. I don't need her bodyguard leering over my desk."

Sarge looked at me for confirmation. "Yeah, it's fine. I doubt she's going to suddenly turn into a zombie or anything."

Kevin grunted, his disdain for me and Burke obvious. I did not like Kevin.

But it was Officer Burke's reaction that interested me. And from the way her body tightened, and her throat bobbed in response to that word, she was completely aware of what had really gone on down at the hospital.

How many of the other police officers recognized what they were dealing with? How had they covered up what had gone on given dead people had been running amok biting everyone? Of course, Officer Burke was the fill-in for Officer Schmitt, who'd worked with my gran for years. So maybe she understood a little more than the rest just based on that.

I followed Burke back to the same tiny office she'd occupied the last time I'd been here.

"What are you doing here, Breena?" She dropped the professionalism the second the door shut behind her.

Might as well cut straight to the heart of it. "You and I both know that what happened yesterday is not the only incident of the undead walking about." I lowered myself into a chair, feeling a twinge in my back. Panic coursed through me at the thought of another ovarian cyst bursting, but the twinge faded, and I breathed a sigh of relief.

Officer Burke sat on the other side of her desk and faced me. "I have no idea what you're talking about. There was a gas leak that sent a number of the hospital's patients into an induced dementia like—"

"Bullshit and you know it." I held up both hands. "But for the sake of your job, let's say that was true. How are you going to explain when there are similar issues in places where there's no potential gas leak? Say at a playground? One set over unmarked graves?" Like right next to Centennial Park Cemetery.

Officer Burke stared at me, her face paling. "Is that . . . possible?"

I spread my hands wide. "Someone is . . . leaking gas . . . all over town. Or will be if they haven't already. I'm trying to find that person or persons and stop them. I was hoping you'd have some information that could help. You know, like a list of places that the . . . leaking gas . . . has happened so far?"

There was a pause in the conversation, and for a moment I thought she'd give me some info. Then she shook her head. "All the police files are closed to civilians. I can't help you." She leaned forward. "As you'll recall, the last time I tried to help you, it didn't work out well for either us. I ended up losing my job and you ended up in the clink."

I shrugged. "Everything turned out okay in the end."

She stared at me as if I'd lost my marbles. Maybe I had. "Barely. And only because one of my superiors gave me my job back."

I took a stab in the dark. "Jacob?"

Her mouth dropped open. "How do you know Jacob Black?"

Oh man, how original was it for a necromancer to be named Jacob Black?

Yes, I know that the answer is "not at all."

"Wait, isn't that one of the kids in that vampire book?" I blurted out. "Is he looking for fame now trying to market on that?"

Her face closed down and I wasn't sure if she was trying not to laugh or trying to be serious. "Look, you could get me fired again," Burke said. "And I'm not willing to go that route. I let you come back here so I could say it to your face and not in front of that gossip Kevin out front." She stood as a knock came on the door.

Another officer poked his head in. "Burke, you're wanted in the conference room. STAT."

Officer Burke glanced at me. "You know your way out." She put a hand on my arm. "But if I were to look, I'd check the bodies around the gas leaks. They all have the same sort of . . . stuff on them."

She left me there in her office, staring after her. Bodies. I needed to look at the bodies of some zombies. I took a quick glance at the files open on her desk, but there was nothing pertaining to the hospital, and I knew that I didn't have a ton of time before someone came looking for me.

Her tip about the bodies having the same kind of goop was something though. It would have to be enough.

Now what? I opened my bag and crooked my finger. Alan climbed out and shook himself.

"What?"

"You get a sense of anything dead around here? Gran said it's possible for you to talk to each other."

Alan frowned and rubbed at his bald spot. "I . . . maybe? I don't know." He did a slow turn as if he might find the answers looking back at him from the far wall. I sighed and reached into my side bag to pull out Robert's finger bone. I closed my eyes for a moment, warmth spilling along my spine and to the hand that held him. A split second later, Robert was swaying at my side.

"What do you think, anything dead but kinda alive around here?"

Robert slowly pointed to the floor and whispered, "Friends."

Friends. Maybe some zombies in the morgue?

"Alan, do not leave my sight," I whispered. "Let's see what we can find." I opened the office door, peering through the glass doors at the end of the hall, and Sarge glanced over from the desk and met my eyes. I put a finger to my lips. He touched his head and then leaned over the desk toward Kevin as he put on a blinding grin and . . . was that a wink?

What a friend! He was flirting with the jerk of a cop to keep him busy.

I hurried down the hall in the opposite direction. The stairwell at the end of the hall led not only to the cells—or what remained of them after my friends had busted me out of jail last week—but also to the morgue. When I reached the bottom, I turned right and followed the arrows to the morgue.

With each step I took, my guts tightened, and the air grew heavier. "You picking up on that too, Robert?"

He growled low under his breath.

Alan tucked his hands in his pockets. "Yes, definitely something here. This is very strange, Bree, very strange. Different than the ones in New Orleans."

I glanced over at him. "Yeah, they are different. No souls in these bodies."

Breathing shallowly, I stopped in front of the big metal door with "MORGUE" printed across the middle in bold letters. There was a tiny square window, and I got up on my toes to peek through it.

No movement that I could see, and considering what we were dealing with, that was a very good thing. Maybe there would just be the regular dead bodies down here, no up and moving ones.

The handle turned easily under my palm, and I let myself and Robert through into the room, Alan stepping up on my left. The room was chilled, and my breath billowed out in front of me as I took the space in. The walls were all metal, covered with tiny doors. Tiny doors just big enough for a body to be slid in and out of.

I grimaced even as my heart picked up speed. The room was quiet, there was no reason to be scared necessarily. Right?

"Alan, scout around and see what you can see."

"Fine," he grumped. "Not like I have anything better to do."

I put my hands on my hips. "Listen. Marge might not want you, but maybe I can give you to someone else? I don't want a single bit of whining out of you, not one little bit. Or I'll find a way to make you move on."

Alan's shoulders hunched. "I don't want to move on."

"Yeah, I picked up on that," I muttered.

Step by step, the tension in the air notched up. Besides the little squares in the walls there were four body bags around the room, two on the floor and two on the only two tables. They looked suspiciously . . . full. Why would they have left bodies out? Were the little body holders full?

"Robert, you think they ran out of room?" I whispered the question and immediately wished I hadn't.

The body bag on my left crinkled. As in something inside of it moved, a fingernail scratching along the inside of the thick plastic.

I backed up a step and bumped into Robert. "Friend," he whispered.

The bag to the right of him flopped and *sat up*.

Alan jumped. "Yeah, they aren't dead."

"We can do this," I said. "We have to open one of them and take a look. See if there are any marks or .

. . signs of what Abigail was telling us. There has to be something that ties them together. Okay?"

"Friend," Robert said. Almost like a tired sigh.

"What do you want me to do?" Alan asked. If I'd thought Sarge could see him, I would have told him to go get the werewolf for backup. Just in case.

"Just warn me if anyone is coming, okay?" I said.

"On it." Alan sounded as if he'd forced that last bit out, and I was sure he had. Helping others only worked for him if he was making a ton of money on their case, as their lawyer.

Clenching my hands, I did my best not to take note that the four body bags in the room were all moving. Then again, the zombies inside them couldn't get out. Right? That had to be the case. They were newly dead, not starving yet, so hopefully they were still nice and slow.

I moved over to the one on my left, the one that was just kind of twitching around. I unzipped the bag and immediately wished I hadn't.

The reason it was only twitching? The body was in bits and pieces. Whoever had tried to stop it had resorted to hacking it up like chunks of sushi.

Fingers wiggled around the bag like worms, and an eyeball rolled up at me. "I really need Gran's book of spells." Because I had no idea how you were supposed to kill a zombie. The movies all suggested head shots would do the job. But this one was literally hacked to pieces and still moving.

So how did you kill it?

I mean, really, how did you kill something already dead?

Taking an instrument off the sideboard table—I had no idea what it was, but it looked like a quacking duck when I squeezed the handle—I poked around in the body bag, moving bits and pieces here and there, looking for something that would identify where the zombie had come from.

A waft of stink rolled up out of the bag as the torso rotated, gas squelching out of it.

I waved a hand in front of my face and blew out a sharp breath. "Duck me, that is nasty."

Props to me though, I kept digging. "Robert, you see anything?"

"Friend." It was delivered in a worried tone, but I kept on moving parts around. I flipped a chunk over and paused. There, on a piece of the back, was something interesting. A design maybe? A tattoo or something that had put on after the person was dead? Better yet, it was glowing.

"I think I found something!" I yelped as I grabbed a piece of flesh with my handy tool and pulled. The torso piece wriggled, but the design I'd noticed was there on its back, right at the base of the spine above the tailbone.

A glowing tattoo was not a real thing, which meant I'd found a clue. Go me!

"It looks like maybe a rune? I'm not sure. Kind of shaped like a crescent moon but sloppily applied, like the paint dripped."

Robert grabbed at my arm, and Alan cleared his throat. "Bree. I think you need to see this."

I finally looked up. "What is it?"

"Friend." Robert's whisper had some serious urgency to it, and if not for the stench around me, I would have sucked in a sharp breath.

The body bags were all empty, and the zombies? They were opening the doors to the little wall chambers and letting their friends out. Eight zombies, seven not counting the bits and pieces at my feet.

"You should leave now," Alan said. "I think it would be in your best interest."

No shit, Captain Obvious.

"Okay, time to go," I said as I backed up, taking Robert with me.

I grabbed the handle of the door and turned it. Only it didn't turn. I scrambled with it, jerking and yanking.

"No. No this can't be happening!"

We were locked in the morgue with a bunch of zombies that, while slow and not yet hungry, were pretty much impossible to kill.

Damn it, this was not how I wanted to start my day.

9

I wiggled the door handle of the morgue again, because it wasn't the type of door that was supposed to lock from the outside. Unless, of course, someone was trying to kill you off and make it look like a zombie had done it.

At that point, I had so many people who didn't like me the list wasn't what I'd call short and to the point. But if I were to guess, I'd say that Joseph already knew we were after him.

The only person who knew I might come here was Burke. Was she working with Joseph? Shit.

"Double shit!" I spun and faced the zombies coming at us. Three from the body bags, four more from the wall chambers.

Robert growled, and I pulled him to the side with me. "Don't fight them yet, Robert. Alan, go and see if you can get Sarge's attention."

"He can't see me!" Alan snapped.

"Just try damn it!" I snapped right back. Rolling his eyes, he left, walking through the door.

Maybe *I* could get Sarge down here? Shifters had superior hearing, but could he hear me through all the floor levels?

I screamed his name as loudly as I could, and the zombies picked up speed. As in they went from shuffling to running, mouths open and hands outstretched. Like I'd rung the dinner bell.

Whoops.

Yelping, I grabbed a wheeled table and pulled it in front of me, keeping space between me and the dead things.

"Friend!" Robert snapped, and I could almost hear what he was trying to say. I could stop them. Maybe.

Gritting my teeth, I tried to find that spot in me that held power over the dead, the same place I'd tapped into when I'd seen Eleanor. When the fog had risen up. More and more, it was like looking through a cupboard inside my own body, opening doors until I found the right one. Because that power didn't just sit still, it kind of floated around.

"Stop!" I yelled, pointing a finger at the closest zombie—a flaccid-faced man with jowls that hung low and shook violently as he snapped his teeth at my finger. I recoiled and he lunged, throwing himself against the table, which in turn pinned me to the wall.

Yelping, I shoved back, but he was a big boy literally using his weight against me.

Another zombie joined him, leaning into the table and just about cutting me half.

How the hell was I supposed to focus on any sort of power inside of me when I couldn't breathe? Yeah, I couldn't.

I grabbed the new knife at my side and yanked it free, feeling a tingle of power zip through me and straight into the handle. I slashed at the arm closest to me, and the blade cut right through the flesh and bone like a hot guy makes panties drop. Magic. It had to be magic. But was it *my* magic or Crash's?

Because the arm fell and stopped moving. The blade did what not too many things could—it made the things it cut off dead again.

I slashed again and again, taking off arms and then a head, which slowed fat boy down considerably. Robert helped me shove the table off, and then we worked our way back to the door.

"SARGE!"

Behind me the zombies kept coming, so I turned and faced them with a grimace. I wasn't afraid so much as disgusted by what I was going to have to do.

"Okay, let's rumble," I grimaced and went to work as my forearm burned along with my muscles.

The knife that Crash had left for me did the trick, and fifteen minutes later, covered in guts, slime, and the rotting flesh of the zombies, I surveyed the carnage while breathing hard. I noted that Robert had stayed put behind me like I'd asked him to.

I spat to the side, cringing. "Gross. This is just . . . this is awful." I could only imagine how I looked. I was going to need a shower with a fire hose.

Since I was already covered in goop, I might as well have a look at the things on the floor and see if there were more glowing tattoos.

I flipped a body over to look at the back, then another and another.

Nothing. Not even on what I thought was the first one. With all the gore, it was hard to see if they had any other commonalities.

I wanted to put a hand to my head but resisted, remembering what I was covered in. "Was I seeing things?"

I was sure that rune had been shaped like crescent moon. Sloppy, but the shape had been undeniable. I mean, how often did you see a glowing tattoo on a zombie? You didn't. Plus, there was something else about that image . . . something familiar. I frowned. "The crescent moon, dripping in blood, I've seen it somewhere else too."

Where, though?

I wiped the dagger on the pants of one of the zombies and put it away. Robert flinched from me. Was that the real reason he'd stayed behind me? "Would this hurt you?"

"Friend," he whispered and cringed a little more.

"Robert, I would *never* use this on you." I held out a hand, and he tentatively put his bony fingers in mine. "I promise."

He gripped me tightly as I turned toward the door and wrenched the handle. It slid open as if it had never been locked. Huh. Alan came down the stairs, meeting us part way. "I couldn't get his attention."

"It's fine."

"You look terrible." His eyes scanned me up and down.

"At least I'm not dead," I said. Alan snorted and pouted.

After I trudged up the stairs, the first thing I did was poke my head back into Officer Burke's office. She looked up from her desk, saw me, and looked back at her paperwork or whatever she had going on there.

"I told you to leave." Then she did a long double blink at me. Yeah, that's right, take all this mess in.

"Shouldn't keep zombies in the basement," I said. "It's a terrible idea. And you shouldn't lock people in either. It's not nice."

Her eyes slowly widened and then, of course not only did she get a good look at the guts all over me, but I was pretty sure the stink of the undead was filling her office.

I stepped through the door and shut it behind me. "You going to tell me why you were keeping them there? Or who you're really working for?"

Her lips tightened. "Get out, before I throw you back in a cell."

I laughed. "Oh, my friend, that did not work out so well for your little station last time. Tell me, how are the repairs going to the wall we blew out?"

She stood up, and her hand settled on the butt of her gun. Wow. She was super-duper sensitive about all this apparently.

"You know what happens when they bite someone?" I asked. I didn't, but I was hoping maybe she'd seen it happen.

Her face paled, which told me she *had* seen it happen, and her hand slid away from the butt of her gun. "This is my case."

"You realize that I could help you? We could work together on this," I offered, even though she was being a right touchy bitch.

"Get out." She dropped her gaze to the paper in front of her, effectively dismissing me as she shuffled things around on her desk. "And do not come back."

I sighed and let myself back into the hall. Zombies in the morgue, what a damn morning.

A wave of foul air like a bad dog fart rolled up from my clothes every time I took a step. I wrinkled my nose. "I stink, Robert."

"Friend. Stink," he agreed.

Alan strode ahead of me and passed through the glass doors.

Making my way back to the front desk, I was caught off guard by a peal of male laughter. As I stepped into the main hallway, where I could see out the glass doors, I noticed Sarge was still leaning over the desk toward the officer.

I wasn't limping, but my back ached and the pinch point where the table had slammed me against the wall was not happy. I made my way out through the glass doors, deliberately smearing them with my bloody, gut-covered hands as I went.

Sarge looked up, smiling, and then his mouth dropped open and he recoiled, plugging his nose. "Umm. You stink."

Officer Kevin turned around, the faint blush on his cheeks suggesting he wasn't immune to Sarge's charm, but his smile faded rapidly.

"What the actual hell have you done?"

"There's a mighty mess in the bathroom." I waved a hand in front of my nose. "That time of the month does terrible things to my guts."

And I continued on, walking right out the front doors with Sarge trailing along behind me.

"Seriously, are you going to tell me what happened? You smell like dead things. You found zombies? Why didn't you come get me?"

"You didn't hear me screaming for you, I take it?" I rolled my eyes up to him, and he shook his head.

"Sweet baby Jesus. I'm sorry, Bree! I didn't hear a thing." He looked down and to the side, ducking his head like a dog that had been scolded.

"I don't think it was your fault, Sarge. Someone or something locked me and Robert in the morgue and then, you know, zombies. I sent Alan to get you, but you can't see him." I waved a hand at my body, encompassing the absolute mess I'd made of myself, and took Alan in at the same time.

He wasn't covered in anything but irritation and obvious disdain. Par for the course with my ex.

"Don't take this the wrong way, but I really don't want to ride with you back to the house smelling like that." Sarge wrinkled up his nose again and swallowed hard as his skin went a wicked shade of green. I nodded and sighed.

"I'll walk. It's fine." I motioned for him to go on. I could use the time to figure out just what had happened back there. If Joseph or one of his underlings was on to us, how had they found out? Was it Officer Burke? I just couldn't say for sure.

Behind us, the police station was suddenly rumbling like an ant's nest that had been poked repeatedly by a small boy with a stick. The small boy being me.

Sarge left, and I picked up my feet a little and hurried across the square closest to me. As I drew close to a garbage can, I peeled off my long-sleeved button-down shirt and tossed it in. That got rid of some of the stink, but it also showed off my knife and sheath. I took them off and tucked them into my handbag.

"I don't know, Robert. What do you think happens if you get bitten by a zombie?" I asked the question of my shuffling friend, wishing he could be the blue-eyed, eloquent man that he sometimes showed himself to be. "You up for being a little more substantial today?"

"Friend." He shook his head as he swayed alongside me and then collapsed down to a single finger bone. I sighed as I scooped him up and tucked him into my hip bag. So much for that.

Alan glanced over at me. "Why don't you ask me that question?"

"Because you don't know anything about the shadow world," I said.

"I lived with Marge and Homer for a week. I learned some things." He shrugged all casual like.

I found my feet taking me down toward the waterfront, toward River Front Rd.

Factors Row all but beckoned, and I let myself go there. If for no other reason than it was more than a little sentimental to me.

I'd met Crash here.

I'd met Jinx and Feish here.

I'd dodged bad guys.

"Okay. Why don't you go ahead and tell me what you know about zombies. They are not the same thing as having your soul being stuffed into a dead body."

"If they bite you, the infection can take a long time to kill you, but it *will* kill you," Alan said.

"Marge seemed to know something was going to happen in Savannah."

Convenient.

My feet slowed as I drew close to Factors Row, but I ended up passing the hidden alley and heading right to the other side of River Street. More than a few tourists eyed me up and down—I was quite sure I presented a lovely image.

I did a slow turn and found myself looking up at Vic's Restaurant. I'd met Karissa, queen of the fae, in their ladies' bathroom. On a whim, I pointed at the bag and gave Alan a look. Sighing heavily, he did as he was told. With both of my companions in my handy bag, I made my way across the street, picking up speed as I hurried through the doors to Vic's Restaurant, strode across the lower floor, and then up the stairs to the bathroom on the top level.

Mind you, the last time I'd been there, the bathroom had exploded.

But as I stepped through the door to the bathroom, I could see that hadn't been the case, not at all. In fact, it looked exactly the same down to the crack in the floor. Which meant the explosion had been all smoke and mirrors. An illusion then?

I flicked on the water and grabbed some paper towels. Might as well get clean while I was in there. I scrubbed the worst of the gunk off me, washing my face, arms, and neck.

I didn't bother doing more than a cursory glance in the mirror because let's be honest, I wasn't going to reverse the damage with a little soap and water.

What I didn't expect was to hear a voice I knew all too well coming from the other side of the wall. I couldn't make out her words, but I would know Feish's voice anywhere.

"What are you doing here? You were supposed to be watching Crash?" I mumbled to myself as I pressed my ear to the wall, just as a woman let herself into the restroom with me.

Her eyebrows went up, and I smiled. "I think my husband is cheating on me."

Jaw dropping, she patted me on the back as she went by. "Clean him out, darling, clean him out and never look back."

With a now wry grin on my lips, blocking out Alan as he bitched, "How about you just kill him and be done with it?" I pressed my ear closer to the wall. For sure I could hear Feish, but where was Crash's deep rumble? Just thinking about his voice made me want to cross my legs—even when he was being a dick, he was still smoking hot. I still wanted him.

Nope, that was not the voice I heard.

The dulcet tones of the queen of the fae answered my fishy friend. I stood upright, and the woman in the bathroom came out of the stall and washed her hands. "Who is it? One of your friends shagging him?"

I looked over at her. "No, his ex-wife."

The woman shook her head, clucking her tongue. "Worse and worse."

"You could say that again," I said wondering just what the hell I was going to do with this info. Of course, it could be innocent. Feish could have been cornered by Karissa, that was possible.

I let myself out of the women's restroom and looked around at what was next to it. The men's restroom?

"In for a penny," I muttered as I shoved open the door to the men's room, "in for a pound."

10

The men's washroom was just as nice as the women's, only it had two guys at the urinals.

"Hey! Wrong room!" the guy closest to me yelped, trying to tuck 'it' in and peeing on the floor in the process.

"Calm your tits, I'm not even looking at you and your little pencil." I waved a hand at him as I walked to the far wall connecting the two restrooms and put my ear against it, which happened to be right next to guy peeing number two. I didn't even peek, promise. After being with Crash and seeing what he had . . . well, I doubted there would be much reason to try and compare him to someone else.

"Lady, get out of here!" the second guy yelped, doing the same hopping, freaking out dance that guy number one had done.

I closed my eyes and focused on listening.

Feish's and Karissa's voices, now sounding like they were in the women's washroom.

"Lady, are you on drugs? You can't just come in here—"

I did glance over at that point, fumbling out my shiny new badge from my bag and flashing it at them. "I'm working. Hush your faces!"

"Showing us a fake badge ain't going to get you anywhere," said guy number one. "My kid has a badge just like that. Got it out of a vending machine for a buck."

I glanced down at said badge. Which was now plastic and etched with a cartoon police officer.

"Gawd damn," I whispered. Roderick had played me. Son of a bitch, but why? Didn't he want me to deal with Joseph?

"Yeah, so get out of here," said guy number two.

I narrowed my eyes at the two of them, put my hands on my hips and channeled a little of my gran. "How's about you two leave, seeing as you've finished your business and I haven't started mine?"

For good measure, I pulled my sheathed knife out of my bag and just held it. Not because I would have pulled the dagger on them, but I thought it looked good. Strong. Or maybe just weird enough to make them wonder what I was capable of.

Apparently so.

"Crazy ass bitch," peeing man number one threw at me before he turned and left. Peeing man number two shook his head and backed out.

"Crazy."

I shrugged. "I've been called worse."

With the two men gone, I put my ear back to the wall. The two voices were still there, so how the hell did I get through to them?

Behind me came the shuffling of feet, and I cringed as a man cleared his throat. "You looking for a way in?"

I slowly turned.

This was an unexpected meeting indeed. Stark, the literal oldest member of the council, the one everyone pretend to defer to yet didn't listen a whit to in private. The one who didn't speak, and yet he'd spoken to me. Twice now.

"Stark?" I blinked several times just in case my vision was giving me some sort of hallucination. "What are you doing here?"

His smile was slow. "Same as you, I suppose."

"Peeing?" I offered.

His laughter had a rusty sound, as if he didn't laugh often. "Headed into the walk-through. I'm going to get a drink; would you like to join me?"

Now this was . . . interesting. "You're headed into a fae bar? Is that what I'm hearing?"

He nodded and continued shuffling toward the stall at the end of the room. His long white hair was pulled back from his face, and his beard reached down to the middle of his chest.

There was one teensy problem. The fae world had a tendency to warp time—go there for an hour or two, and you might find out days had gone by. Even weeks. "How long are we going to be stuck in there?"

"An hour," he said. "Just an hour on both sides of the door. Otherwise, I'll be missed, and we can't have that. This is my little secret. You speak the time you wish to spend before you step through."

He tapped the side of his nose and then stepped through the stall door with the out of order sign on it, silence following him. I quickly pulled it open again, fully expecting to see a toilet and the back wall of the restaurant.

The dim lights of the fae bar beckoned me, the smell of incense and musk curled up my nose. Chocolate, I was sure I could smell chocolate as I stepped through after Stark. He shuffled his way to a back booth and slid in, tapping the table three times, pausing, and then tapping three more.

As I walked toward his table, I looked around. The bar was fairly empty, and I hoped to catch a glimpse of Feish and Karissa. They had been here; I was sure of it.

But they weren't anywhere I could see.

I slid into the booth across from Stark. "You come here often?"

He let out a sigh as a waitress arrived, a glowing, steaming mug of something in her hands that she set on the table in front of him. "The usual." She smiled and turned to me. Her long blue hair, woven in long intricate braids that fell to her waist, moved independent of her body, fascinating me . . . and then I saw the tips of the braids had eyes.

Look away, look away! Lawd only knew if those eyes could put some sort of spell on me. For all I knew, she was Medusa reincarnate.

I blinked and shook my head. "Nothing for me."

Stark tapped the table with two sharp raps and then the flat of his palm. The waitress gave him a nod and winked a heavily lashed eye at him. "You got it, one bursting volcano for the new girl."

I held up both hands, remembering how ill I'd been the last time I'd made the mistake of drinking something in a fae bar. "No, seriously I don't want—"

Stark put a hand on mine. "It's a safe drink, even for one like you."

My brain brakes slid on with a solid screech, and I forgot that I didn't want a drink. "One like me?"

He took a sip of his drink and then let out a sigh. "Lovely. Just what I needed after the day I've had. The council arguing is always tiresome."

His fingers tightened on mine, and his eyes were intense as he looked at me. "This is as safe a place as any to discuss what I can discuss with you, and *only* you. None of this can be passed on to your friends. Roderick especially cannot know that we spoke. I am aware of his concerns."

I stared hard at him. "Seeing as everyone thinks you're a mute, I don't think that should be a problem."

His turned his cup in his hands, over and over. "You aren't like any of the other supernaturals here in Savannah, Ms. O'Rylee."

My heartbeat was speeding up. "My gran is a witch, and my grandfather was fae."

"Is fae," he corrected me, and my jaw hung open. "Pardon . . . *what*?"

"Is. He isn't dead. Though perhaps Celia believes otherwise." Stark spun his cup faster, but the liquid inside didn't so much as slosh a single droplet. "That is neither here nor there at the moment. More concerning is your father's bloodline. Have you guessed at it yet?"

The blue-haired waitress reappeared and slid a steaming cup in front of me. "Let me know if you need anything else, darling."

Stark nodded, and I didn't so much as look at the drink. "Something to do with the dead," I said. I wasn't going to label myself seeing as I wasn't even sure.

He took a sip of his drink. "Yes. But he too was far from pure. You carry four bloodlines in you, Sentinel, which makes you uniquely qualified to tackle the problems our beautiful home faces."

"Like the zombies."

Stark grimaced. "Like the zombies, though they are just a symptom of the disease."

"Why wouldn't the council listen to Roderick—"

Before I could finish my sentence, he cut me off. "Because the council answers to a higher power, one that does not like how things have been done for the last few hundred years. One that does not like Roderick or his kind."

A strange tingle ran over my body, and I turned in my seat to see a few people step into the bar. None that I recognized, but their magic was running on high if I could feel it from this far away.

"Fae," Stark said softly. "They don't hold their magic back here. And that side of you will always respond to powerful fae."

I nodded and kept the newcomers within sight. "Keep going."

Stark didn't look away from me. "I do not know what exactly your father was, though everyone has their pet suspicions. Necromancer perhaps. Ghost whisperer. Death."

My eyebrows shot up. "As in *the Death*?"

"Possibly. He kept his cards close to his chest. We know your father was mortal because he died. But it is possible that he gave up mortality for a reason." He waved his hands in front of him. "Listen to me. As I said, the zombies are a symptom, they are not the disease. You must look past them to find the cause and root it out."

"I know that, and that's exactly what Roderick asked me to look into," I said.

How much did I tell Stark? Was he trustworthy?

Stark sighed. "Yes, well . . ."

I waited, but he didn't continue. Without thinking, running on habit, I lifted the steaming cup to my lips. The liquid was warm and tasted of vanilla and a spice that made my tongue tingle. I tried to speak around the tingle, but my speech was slurred in a split second, even though I felt fine. "The thombiezz

. . . one of them had a crethent moon on the thpine." I shook my head. "Thamn it."

"Give it a moment, the tingle will pass." Stark sighed. "You have the book of curses still?"

I blinked up at him. How the hell did he know about that? "Yeth." I cleared my throat. "Yes, I still have it." I pushed the drink away. I did not need that today.

"There is information within it that can guide you. That is why I placed it in your path." He tapped the table, and the waitress appeared. He handed her a pair of gold coins while my brain tried to make sense of the fact that he was the one who'd arranged for me to find that book.

"Each of the four bloodlines will call to you, Breena," he said quietly as he stood. "When you decide which one to follow, that is when you will find out who you really are."

I sat there watching him go, but my gaze caught on the person he crossed paths with at the door. Stark tipped his head at Crash, going so far as to put his hand on the blacksmith's arm.

Now there was someone that I needed to speak with, and I wasn't about to let the opportunity pass. I slugged back another swig of my drink for good measure and a little bit of courage.

Fae king or not, he was going to listen to what I had to say.

11

I got to my feet and was immediately glad I'd only had the two sips of the 'bursting volcano,' because my legs wobbled as if my knees had come unhinged. I didn't feel drunk, not at all, but something in the drink was slowing me down.

Crash hadn't seen me yet, and he was moving away from the door, away from *me*. I had to move fast. Except I could hardly move at all.

I tapped the table the way Stark had, and the blue-haired waitress appeared as if she'd never left. "Can you bring Crash over to me?"

Her eyebrows went to her hairline. "Umm. I can ask him. But—"

"Tell him that if he doesn't come on over here, I'll be forced to come and get him, and he doesn't want that. I would end up making a terrible scene, I'm sure." There, that sounded tough.

Her jaw dropped open. "I can't—"

"It's fine, Lulu," Crash's deep rumble stopped her. "I'll speak with her."

Lulu backed away, blushing a deep purple across her pale cheeks. "Of course."

Crash did not sit down.

And I wasted no time, cutting straight to the heart of the issue. "You actually think I slept with Corb and lied about it? Are you out of your damn mind?"

His face hardened. "Do you want the entire bar to know your business and who you are sleeping with?"

"Business would imply that Corb and I had any outside of the fact that we worked together. Which we *didn't*." I found my anger rising rapidly with my voice. "And if you'd done more than just left me in that *ducking* hospital, if you'd given one damn shit, you'd have listened, instead of jumping to conclusions. And then leaving me there to deal with a bunch of zombies! Or worse, be caught in a trap you clearly knew about!"

He slapped his hands on the table and leaned forward, blue-gold eyes sparking with anger. "Maybe if I thought I could trust you—"

I didn't know I could move that fast. I slapped him so hard my hand stung with the impact and there was an audible gasp that rolled through the room.

"I'm not the one who is lying!" I hissed the words out and forced myself to my feet, clinging to the table for support. "I'm not the one who knew the council was up to something before they wrapped the hospital up in some sort of trapping spell! I'm not the one who won't give a straight answer to anything! I'm not the one playing games!"

Damn it, I did not like the way my eyes were tingling. My anger was spilling into tears, hot, angry tears. In the back of my head the questions I couldn't quite formulate roared through me.

Why was he doing this? What had changed? It could not possibly be Suzy's throwaway comment about Corb. Crash was not like that. He'd never been the one to make an assumption, to cut me off without letting me explain. It was totally out of character for him.

He grabbed me around the wrist and dragged me upright. I could have fought him, I could have stabbed him with the knife he'd so obviously left for me, except I wasn't afraid of him. So, I let him drag me across the room to a door that was not visible until we were on top of it.

Through the doorway we went, and he slammed it shut behind us.

With a snap of his fingers, a fire roared to life. No, not a fire, his forge.

It looked almost exactly like his old forge on Factors Row.

I turned to him, planning to yell at him and maybe kick him in the balls.

He caught my face and kissed me, hard, desperate, even as a tremor ran through his body. To say I was caught off guard was no small thing. I pulled back and stared up at him.

"What—"

His breathing came in deep drags as though he'd been running. "Darkness comes, Bree. And I am fighting not only for you but for the safety of my people. The goblins are my responsibility, too, thanks to that dumbass, Derek." His thumbs were gentle against my face.

"What darkness? You mean Joseph?"

He jerked as though I'd stabbed him in the side with a knife. "How do you know—?"

I let my fingers slide up over his biceps to the back of his neck. "I want to trust you, Crash. I want to tell you everything. But you . . . you're treating me like I've done you wrong, and let me be clear . . . even if I *had* slept with Corb, you and I were not an item. As far as I know, you've made no promises to me."

His eyes fluttered closed. "I thought to use it as a clean break. To—"

"Protect me? Jaysus gawd in heaven, man. Have we not been down this road before? I love that you want to protect me, and I might even need to be protected once in a while"—okay, maybe more than once in a while at the rate I ran into trouble—"but cutting me off? You think that's the best way?"

Crash's fingers skimmed down my arms to my hands, lacing our digits together. "Yes. I am tied to darkness, Bree."

"You mean like you were with O'Sean?"

He shook his head and lifted our joined hands to his mouth, pressing his warm lips to my fingers. "No, it is . . . deeper than a simple spell."

A solid wash of desire slid through me. "Crash, tell me now if this is going to work. Are we worth fighting for?"

His jaw ticked, and he swallowed hard. "I want you with all my body and soul, Bree. I want every feisty, brilliant, complicated, sensual part of you in my world. In my bed."

I went up on my tiptoes to press my mouth to his, and he turned his face, so I landed on his cheek. He hadn't said the 'but', and yet I heard it loud and clear. My guts twisted up into a knot so big I was sure I could feel it at the back of my throat.

"But I can't ask you to be tied to me," he said, finally looking me in the eye. "I can't ask that of anyone. No matter how much I want you."

Sure, he'd tried to push me away before, but this felt different. Something had happened between our time in the forge and when he came to me at the hospital. Hours had passed, sure, but what had happened in them to turn him so hard from me? "Did you know that you were going to have to do this, when we started this dance?"

He shook his head. "No. I thought I was finally . . . that I could finally have the life I wanted." He untangled his fingers from mine and cupped my face. "I was wrong, Bree. I can't give you anything. I will always do my best to protect you from the shadows, but I have to let you go. I have to."

A kiss landed on my forehead, and I tried not to think about the tears tracking down my cheeks. "Are you even going to tell me why?"

He shook his head. "I . . . I have to take Feish with me. Not yet, but soon. I'll give her a few more days with you."

Another stab straight to my belly.

"And if I won't let you go? If I chase after you?" I asked quietly. "If I fight for you?"

"Then I will have to be the asshole you saw in the hospital." He swallowed. "And I don't want to be that man to you, Bree. You don't deserve it. You deserve someone who can give you the world. Not a man tied to the darkness."

My chest was shaking with unspent sobs as I stood there and stared up at the man whom I'd thought . . . whom I'd thought was going to be the guy in my life.

I didn't know what to do.

Crash made the decision for me. "Back out into the bar we go. They'll think we've been gone only a few seconds." He paused at the door, turned and grabbed me.

His kiss was as fierce as the last one, more so because I kissed him back with all I had. The taste of salty tears only added to the urgency, to the need between us. Because we both knew this had to be the last kiss.

His fingers buried into my hair and his mouth didn't leave mine. "I'm so fucking sorry, Bree. You cannot know how much I wish this were different. How I wish—"

"Then we make it different," I whispered back.

He leaned his forehead against mine. "I . . . can't. There is no way."

No way.

Crash flung the door open and dragged me out with him while I was still covered in tears, my lips bruised from his mouth. He spun me out, all but throwing me from the room.

Then he stepped back, out of reach. "I don't answer to you, Ms. O'Rylee. I suggest you remember that in the future should you wish to stay in the shadow world. In one piece instead of many."

Yup, jaw dropped. This was the asshole side of him. And this was all I was going to get now.

I forced my legs to get under me so I could slap him again. If he wanted it to be like this between us, then I would oblige.

"One day that will change, blacksmith," I snapped, letting hurt fuel my words. "I think one day you will answer to me." Let's see how he liked them apples. I was trying desperately to change my hurt into something else. Anger. Indignation. I considered slapping him again for good measure.

Maybe he saw the look in my eye. Maybe he wondered just what I was going to do. His jaw tightened and his eyes narrowed until there was nothing of the gold glimmer I loved.

However, I didn't get a chance to hit him again.

A hand grabbed my arm, and I was spun away from Crash. "Time to go," Feish burbled.

"I knew I'd heard you here!" I yelped even as she dragged me away. I turned to see Crash watching us go.

There was no anger in him.

Resignation. Sadness. A bone-deep sorrow that I felt all the way to my center. But no anger.

Gawd damn him and his secrets.

Feish dragged me through the bar and out a back door, which tumbled us into an alley somewhere on River Street.

"Feish, what in the hell is going on?" I tried to pull free of her, but my legs were only just recovering from that bursting volcano drink.

"Hell is exactly what is going on." She didn't look at me but glanced left and right as if she expected we were being followed.

"Feish!" I snapped her name.

She turned to me and fisted her webbed hands up by her face, pressing them hard into her cheeks. "I can't . . . I can't tell you." She covered her thick lips with her hands and spoke from between her fingers. "You have to get out of here. It's dangerous and—"

I took her hands and held onto her. "Feish, you can tell me anything. We're friends. Aren't we? If you tell me, then I can help."

Because suddenly it truly hit me that Crash wasn't the only one slipping away from me—Feish was too. I was going to lose my friend. My heart was pounding out of control, bouncing around in my chest. Maybe I could blame that on the drink, but I didn't think so.

"I'm trying to keep you safe," she whispered, and a tear tracked down her face. "Boss too."

"I know he is, but I can help keep us all safe if you'll just trust me enough to tell me what in the world is going on." I lowered my voice and pulled her closer. To an outsider we probably looked like a couple having a heated conversation. I didn't care what anyone thought.

Feish shook. "I don't want you to die. Someone has threatened to kill you if you stay with Crash. When you're with him . . ."

Her lips pressed together as if she were in pain.

I tried to think of why someone would care if Crash and I were together. Karissa maybe?

"Boss trying to keep you safe." She scrunched her eyes shut. "Go to Eammon."

And then she pushed me away as she backed up. "I don't want to be your friend anymore. Get away! You a bad person," her voice hiccupped on that last bit. "Very bad! Very weak!"

Holy shit, this was really happening? I knew that she didn't mean what she was saying. Crash had said he'd have to take her away too, but I hadn't thought it would be this quick.

In the space of just a few hours, my world had been turned upside down. Feish turned and ran from me, dodging back through a doorway that was barely etched into the wall. I ran after her and put my hands on the same stone.

The wall was solid. There was no doorway for me to follow her through.

Shaking, I leaned my head against the cool stone, the sounds of the street and the tourists washing around me. The world was just going on as usual while my life fell to pieces at my feet.

I turned and looked out across the water.

"Ten of swords!" a scratchy voice screamed out from above me. I looked up to see a big colorful blue and green bird staring back at me. A parrot? The bird was perched on a lamppost above my head.

"Ten of swords!" it screeched again and dropped something from its claws.

A card fell to the ground at my feet, and the bird flew away, screaming "ten of swords" over and over again.

I didn't pick up the card. It was exactly the same as the one I had in my hip pack.

Besides, I didn't exactly need a reminder that things were as bad as they seemed. No kidding.

I could have beaten myself up for screwing up the best thing that had happened to me in a long time—a.k.a. Crash. I could have told myself I was a loser, a failure, a washed-up hack of a bounty hunter. That I was too old, too soft, that my knees and back wouldn't let me keep going.

In the past, I would have. Instead, I took a deep breath and stepped on the ten of swords at my feet. "Nope. Not today, Satan, not today."

Of course, I hadn't counted on the screaming to start immediately after I said that.

A shriek went up from a group of tourists down by the candy shop, and I was running toward the sound before my brain caught up with my instincts. Maybe this was a terrible idea.

Maybe it was more than I could handle.

Maybe I needed a really good distraction from the hurt of losing my friend and the guy I was falling for, and this—whatever this screaming was attached to—would do the trick.

People spilled out of the candy shop, falling over each other to get away from something that was currently roaring like a wounded animal.

I grabbed the edge of the doorway and looked in to see—surprise, surprise—a pair of zombies slamming their fists and heads onto the back wall of the candy shop. Bits of flesh flew out with every blow, splattering across the freshly made chocolate and candy pieces.

I grimaced. "Well, that's a waste." I reached into my hip bag and pulled out Robert's finger bone, and Alan spilled out with him, yawning widely.

"What now?" Alan froze. "Are those Marge's?"

"No, you twit, they're someone else's creation."

Dropping the finger bone to the ground was all it took, and then Robert was there next to me, swaying slightly. "Robert, look, more zombies! How fun!"

"Friend," he growled and shook his head. Maybe my sarcasm was lost on him. That was possible.

"Yes, I know, I know. Dead things seem to like me."

He grunted, apparently picking up on the irony.

I let out a whistle, trying to get the attention of the two zombies. But that didn't work. I chewed the inside of my lip, feeling the eyes of the tourists and workers on me. We didn't need a panic, right? Roderick wanted this all kept quiet, no doubt.

Stark seemed to think I could handle it.

"Thank you all for coming to our impromptu show today!" I waved a hand in the air.

There was a faint smattering of applause, uncertain laughter following it.

Doubt, I just had to give them some doubt and hope no one had videoed it with their phone.

The zombies were still hammering their heads against the stone, oblivious to the people, which was interesting. Weren't they supposed to get hungrier? Not that I was complaining.

I slid sideways toward the opening that led into the backroom and kitchen. Snapping my fingers at the two zombies, I tried to get their attention. If I could get them into the halls that led to Death Row—what was essentially an open-air market for magical bounty hunters and others in the shadow world looking for magical goods—there would be no human eyes to see what happened next. There was a secret little entrance back here, and I planned to use it.

"This way, boys!" I hollered, and one zombie finally turned his face toward me. His eyes hung out of their sockets and rested on his cheeks, but he still tried to blink, which was unsettling. Robert was all but glued to my side, bumping hips with me and cracking his knuckles over and over.

I snapped my fingers again, then clapped my hands together as I whistled a second time. A rush of recklessness rolled over me. "Come on, boys, here we go! Off to the next gig!"

Now I had the attention of the other zombie.

I grimaced as he turned to me.

Sean O'Sean was not someone I had ever wanted to see again, certainly not as a zombie.

He lifted his hand, and magic began to pool at his fingertips.

Ah, duck me.

Only one choice now. Time to run and hope they followed. I spun and sprinted through the kitchen of the candy shop, praying they'd follow. A blast of magic slammed into a table on my left, flipping it up and at me. I ducked, barely missing the corner of the table.

"You need to work on your flexibility," Alan said. "You almost got impaled there."

"Shut your face!" I snapped but didn't put any real heat into my words. I was saving my energy for the running.

A quick look over my shoulder showed me the two zombies were at least following now. I slowed a little, staring at the magic pooling in Sean O'Sean's undead hands.

"Shit." I looked ahead and sprinted hard—which for me was not all that fast—and tried to zig-zag.

That wasn't the worst of it, though.

No, the worst of it was that Sean O'Sean's magic slammed right into the middle of my back and sent me flying ass over teakettle. I closed my eyes.

Damn it, this day was just not going to cut me a ducking break.

12

My thoughts as I flew through the air were only a little scattered. Someone had raised Sean O'Sean specifically to come after me, I was sure of it.

Because the bastard no doubt hated me still, even after death, even if his soul was no longer attached. I mean, could you blame him? I'd really screwed up his plans, stopping him and O'Sean senior from wreaking havoc on the shadow world. I'd stopped them from getting the fairy cross that would have helped with the spell that they—and whoever they were working with—was trying to build.

The wall came up fast, and I slammed into it, shoulder and hip first. O'Sean's magic felt . . .

different than the last time I'd dealt with it. Not necessarily weaker but more out of control. Wilder.

Even as the thought occurred to me, the purple streaks of his magic slid off my body and skittered over the walls, crawling like spiders on the hunt—little bolts of power reaching out as they searched for something to destroy before fading.

"Breeeeeeenaaaaaa." His voice was thick as he reached for me, his hand still coated in magic. "You . . . . arrrrrrrre . . . . . deeeeaaaaaaaad."

No soul, so just an echo of the past?

I rolled over and scrambled to my feet, Robert helping me up with a bony grip on my belt, and then fumbled behind me for the door I knew was embedded in the wall. Somewhere. "Actually. *You* are dead. I'm alive and seriously plan to stay that way."

The wall slid sideways under my palm, and I stepped through, drawing the two zombies into the shadows with me.

The door slid shut behind them, and although I wasn't exactly relieved, this was the best I was going to be able to do to keep them away from the humans.

The darkness was absolute, and I stumbled over Robert, hit the floor, and rolled, wincing as my back took that moment to spasm.

Alan started laughing. "I do not know how you have survived all this. It's ridiculous. You're like Scooby-Doo, stumbling around in the dark."

Before I could yet again tell him to shut up, a charley horse seized up my back, in the middle of running for my life, while my ex-husband called me

Scooby-Doo. I bit down on the shriek that bubbled up to my lips as I flopped like a fish out of water. Robert reached down and grabbed my wrist, dragging me away from the two zombies.

His hold on me only intensified the spasm, and it shot down my legs so that they kicked and flopped on their own. "Robert, stop!"

"Friend!" he grunted. The floor under me disappeared. At first I didn't understand. Robert still had a hold of me, the zombies were all lit up with O'Sean's magic, eyeballs dangling, but the floor . . .

"Stairs," I breathed as we dropped and bounced. If I'd thought being pummelled into a stone wall with O'Sean's magic was bad, it had nothing on this. The wind was knocked out of me, my left arm was twisted so hard the elbow popped loose, and I smacked my head on the corner of the bottom step before finally rolling to a stop.

But you know what? That wasn't the end of that.

Zombies apparently weren't any better with stairs than I was.

O'Sean and his buddy came flopping down the steps, grunts and thuds echoing in my ears a split second before they landed on top of me and Robert.

I did the only thing I could think of—"Help!" I squeaked out.

With one good arm, a throbbing head, and three hundred-plus pounds of dead weight on me. I was well and properly trapped.

The idea of them biting had me thrashing. An incurable infection that would take months to kill me.

No thank you.

"Friend!" Robert grunted, but he was under me and the best he could do was hold the snapping mouth of O'Sean's friend from my face.

"Help!" I screamed the word this time, hoping someone from Death Row would hear us.

What I didn't expect was for it to be my arch nemesis.

A golden glow filled the room, and the zombies were dragged away from me by a hundred small fairies.

I sat up and turned to see Karissa, her hands raised, sparkles dusting off her fingertips. As always, she shone like the midday sun, her bright blond hair and stunning blue-green eyes holding me hostage.

I didn't dare thank her and owe her a favor.

Her eyes flicked to my face. "I will never understand what he sees in a mutt like you when he could have me."

Unable to keep the groan in my mouth, I pushed to my feet with my one good arm and struggled against a wash of stars behind my eyes.

"Well, he doesn't see anything in me. Not anymore." Bitter, yup, I was feeling it even though I'd seen plenty of regret in him. The thing was . . . regret could only take you so far in a relationship. If you kept making the same mistakes, pushing the person you say you care for away, then eventually they would get the message that you don't want them. Even if you do. "Yeah, so, we can clink glasses and commiserate that he wants neither of us."

I pulled the black-handled knife from its sheath and stepped up to the first zombie, ready to chop it up into pieces.

"The heart," Karissa said. "That dagger through the heart will do the trick."

Okay, why was she helping me?

What did it gain her? I nodded and faced the zombie with the dangling eyes as it wobbled to its feet and lunged for me, barely held back by all the little fairies. O'Sean was also held back, his hands jerked up high behind him. I stepped closer to dangling eyeball zombie and shoved the blade into its heart. "Be at peace."

The critter let out a fetid blast of air and then crumpled to the ground. The fairies holding it up flitted away, and I thought for a second I saw Kinkly in the group, but the flash of autumn colors was there and gone before I could be sure.

O'Sean stared at me, his eyes almost . . . knowing. "You still in there?" I asked.

The Tonton Macoutes I'd dealt with in NOLA had souls in them. So far, the undead I'd encountered here in Savannah were not driven by souls but by some sort of magic that had to be . . . "Cut out of you?"

"What?" Karissa asked.

I held the black-handled knife up to O'Sean and watched as his eyes tracked it. "You know what this is?"

His eyes slowly went from the knife to me. "Deeeeeaaaaaath."

What I hadn't expected, because I'm a damn fool, was that Karissa wouldn't continue to have her fairies hold him back.

Nope, they let him go, and who did he come straight for? Yup. Yours truly.

O'Sean's cold hand shot toward my throat, grabbing me tight. I fell backward—again—as I got my good arm up between us, snapping his hold on me.

That dislocated elbow of mine? Yup, it flopped, and I screamed as my vision wobbled along with my knees. But I kept up my resistance because if I went down again, I wasn't sure I'd be able to get back up.

"Ducking hell!" I kicked out, catching him in the knee and sending him facedown onto the floor. Stepping onto the back of his neck, I turned to Karissa. She was gone, along with all her ducking little fairies.

Gawd damn.

O'Sean began to laugh, the sound wet and thick with phlegm.

"What's so funny?"

"Watching you run in circles," he said, his voice surprisingly cultured. Educated. I frowned.

"Dr. Mori?"

"I've been watching you since you came back to Savannah, little one. You intrigue me. Perhaps we will discuss how we can be of . . . service . . . to one another."

Hell, this had to be Joseph. Roderick's brother.

Another laugh, and then the body convulsed and went still. Whatever magic that had been animating it was gone.

But that voice stayed with me. The slight accent—not Dr. Mori, more European. There was a cultured refinement to it. I put my good hand to my head and stumbled back until I had a wall to lean on. "Robert, are you okay? Where were you? I could have used some help."

I looked around to see that Robert was gone. Frowning, I fumbled a flashlight out of my hip bag and swept the area for him or even his finger bone.

Nothing.

"Robert?"

This was not like him.

Not one bit. I turned again to see Alan right behind me. "Where did he go?"

"I think that beautiful woman took him, though why is beyond me." Alan shrugged, even as he gave a heavy sigh. "Damn, she was . . . so pretty."

"Eloquent as always," I muttered even as my mind raced to figure out what the hell Karissa wanted with Robert.

Why would she take him? I knew that it was unlikely she could hurt him, and Robert had always been able to find me when I was in trouble, regardless of whether I had his finger bone. I had to believe that was still the case. Given the amount of trouble I seemed to find, he'd be back in no time.

"Robert?" I called for him. But he didn't pop back to me. Breathing out a series of curses that made Alan blanch, I shook my head. Karissa had come for Robert, that was why she'd helped. But why Robert?

I'd go after him. But I had a few things to do first. Like deal with my injuries.

Leaving the zombies' now *dead*-dead bodies, I made my way down the dark narrow hall to the entrance to Death Row, cupping my dislocated arm and moving gingerly. Stepping into the narrow marketplace, I gave it a once-over.

The vendors were always the same. Weapons on the left, Gerry and her leather armor on the right, everything in between, well, in between. Still holding my upper arm to protect my elbow, I made my way over to Gerry as Alan drifted away, looking at stuff.

Her eyes swept over me. "What in the hell happened to you?"

"Stairs, zombies, fairy queen." I grimaced. "So pretty much the usual." I motioned to my bad arm. "Can you help me get this back in?"

"Maybe?" She took my hand. "Let me see if it's actually out."

"Oh, it's out—"

She gave my arm a quick twist and shoved as I hollered as a loud pop filled every sense in my body. This time the world did wobble, and I ended up sitting on the floor with my head on my knees. The blond twins at the weapons table—Tweedle Dee and Tweedle Dum—hooted and hollered.

I blinked up at Gerry, ignoring the jabs from the young pair. "Thanks."

"No problem. Always works better when you don't know it's coming." She shrugged and looked me over. "You got roughed up?"

"Two zombies in the passageway." I pushed up to my feet and grabbed the edge of her table for balance as I took stock of my very unhappy body. My arm ached. My head throbbed. I was covered in zombie goop.

But my back had stopped spasming, so yay me.

"Dead?"

"Yeah. *Dead*-dead," I muttered.

What I needed was a stiff drink and a quiet place to look over the book of curses that Stark had told me to go through, to consider what O'Sean-slash-Joseph had said, and to in general catch my breath. Maybe nothing connected all of what I'd learned so far, but I doubted it.

Gerry snapped her fingers. "You two, go clear the passageway."

Surprisingly the twins did as they were told, and Gerry shoved a stool toward me. "Have a seat." Then she shoved a flask at me. "And a drink."

"Will you marry me?" I asked as I took the flask and then snapped back two long pulls. The fire-laden whiskey raced down my throat and burrowed into my belly.

"You know, I get that a lot." Gerry laughed and pulled a stool up next to me. "But the answer is no. I'd never be stupid enough to do that again."

I held the whiskey flask out to her. "Amen to that, sister." And took another pull for good measure. Because seriously, what the duck had just happened?

I blew out a breath and could think of only one person who might be able to help me—Penny, the witch who had known my grandmother and taken me under her wing. The only problem? The plan was that she was going to live with another witch who hated me with a passion.

"You leaving so soon?" Gerry stood with me, and I knew what she saw. A wobbling middle-aged woman who looked as though she'd been pulled through a knot hole repeatedly—and with some serious force.

"Work calls." I clutched the whiskey flask and smiled at her, feeling the much-needed buzz coursing through me.

"Wait. Before you go, try this on. I have a feeling you're going to need extra protection." Gerry pulled a piece of leather armor out from under her table. Stitched in a variety of colored pieces with buckles here and there, I couldn't tell what it was at first.

Gerry slid it around my shoulders and tucked my arms into it. With three-quarter-length sleeves, it was kind of like a shawl that buckled across my chest, making my boobs pop. "Hey, that fits you good." Gerry nodded. "And these." She handed me a pair of leather gloves. I slid them on. Like the other armor I'd purchased from her, they were lightweight, but I knew from experience they'd hold up to a lot. You know, like gator teeth.

"Thanks, I'll bring money. Later." I bobbed my head at her, and she made a shooing motion.

I turned to see Alan at the end of the row. "Alan, let's move."

I snapped my fingers, and he scurried back to my side. "There is a leprechaun at the other end of this market, I'm sure of it. A leprechaun! Do you think he's got a pot of gold?"

I ignored him and moved to hand the flask back to Gerry.

She shook her head. "Just bring it back full, that's the rule."

I tipped it toward her, winked, and wobbled my way out of Death Row heading toward the Victorian district.

"Straight into the cranky lion's den," I whispered to myself.

Straight to the witch who hated me the mostest.

Missy.

13

Drunk on borrowed whiskey, I stood in front of Missy's house, confused. Was I really hearing shouting, or was it the whiskey talking? Pots clattered. Glass shattered. A burst of rainbow sparkles shot out of one window, drawing my eyes.

Magic spells being flung around probably didn't mean much good.

"Alan, am I drunk or are you seeing all that too?"

He rolled his eyes and put his hands on his hips. "You *are* drunk, but that noise and all that garbage coming out of the house *is* happening."

I took a pull on the whiskey flask. "Damn," I mumbled. "Empty." I fumbled but managed to get the flask back into my bag. Must return later. Full. Okay, maybe half full.

I probably stood there too long, but truthfully I wasn't with it enough to make good decisions.

Until Penny stuck her head out of the door and saw me, her dark eyes wide, her white hair all mussed up. "Damn it, girl, get in here and help us!"

I managed to give her two thumbs up as I stepped onto Missy's property. A tingle of magic washed over me, and a certain witch screeched from inside the house, "I do not want her help! I do not want her here!"

"You need it!" Penny shrieked back. "We both do! The dead like her!"

I blew out a raspberry and stumbled up the walkway, wobbled up the stairs, and put a hand on the door. "Dead shmed." Locked. The door was locked.

Feeling brassy, I lifted a foot to kick it in, only as my foot contacted the door, I didn't give it enough force to actually break anything. Which meant I ended up stumbling backward. My butt hit the railing around the deck, and I flipped right over and into the bushes. Twigs and branches jabbed at me, and I couldn't help the giggling that followed.

Alan stuck his face through the bushes. "Jesus, you're a mess."

"I'm not Jesus," I stage-whispered. "Though he was like . . . undead too, right?" Oops, that was probably super sacrilegious. Forgive me father, for I have sinned. I giggled and stared through a foggy, frowning Alan.

"Marge is going to want to know about this," he muttered. I blinked up at him.

"What?"

He shook his head and moved out of my line of sight.

There was another burst of magic that shot out above my head, this one a deep green that shimmered and writhed like smoke come alive. I held a hand up to touch it. "Pretty."

"Breena!" Penny's voice snapped me like a whip, and I was up and moving before my brain really engaged. The front door opened, and three zombies stumbled out, saw me, and came straight for me.

Three against one. This should be no problem. Except for the flask of whiskey I'd downed . . .

"Hey, stop it! Go back to sleep." I pointed a finger at the one closest to me, and he snapped his teeth, barely missing me.

The three of them lunged for me together—faster than any of the other zombies I'd dealt with so far—and tackled me to the ground. Rotting flesh, the creak of bones, and then a set of teeth burying into my shoulder. All of it happened so fast. Or maybe not, maybe I was just too under the influence to keep up.

Incisors cut deep into the leather of my upper arm and shoulder, gnawing at me. Thank gawd for Gerry's armor.

"Doesn't hurt," I grumbled as I kicked and struggled under the weight of the three undead buggers. Maybe it wasn't just the whiskey affecting me.

Because I felt far more sluggish than even a good dram would do for me.

There was more screaming in the background. Lots and lots of screaming. Penny and Missy for sure, but as I rolled to the side, I was sure I saw Feish and the flutter of Kinkly right along with them.

What in the hell was going on? Feish had run away from me, and Kinkly had been with Karissa. I think. Thought. Thinked?

I forced myself to my feet, fumbled for my knife, and managed to get the point into the heart of the first of the three zombies.

I wobbled, and the second zombie all but impaled himself on the dagger next, which left only one. The woman turned her head to the side to look at me, then spun and sprinted—ducking sprinted!—for the road.

"Yeah, run while you can!" I shook a fist after her.

I turned to see Penny and Missy on the battered-up porch. Penny smiled.

Missy glowered.

"You're welcome." I gave them a cocky, mostly drunk bow.

"For what?" Missy snapped. "That last one had the book!"

The last one . . . I turned around. The last zombie was long gone, and I slumped in place. She had Gran's book. "Maybe you shouldn't have taken it from me then, huh?" I threw at her.

Missy's glare didn't ease off, even as Penny hobbled down the steps. "Girl, are you okay?"

"Nope." I grimaced and squinted one eye. "Drunk, fell down the stairs, though to be fair that happened before the whiskey, and my friends are not my friends anymore." I turned toward the place where I'd seen Feish and Kinkly, but they were gone.

If they'd actually been there in the first place. Maybe I was just seeing things.

Penny patted my arm. "Bad day, huh?"

"Going to get worse if the moon turns green," I mumbled, and her face turned ashen, a spectacular look on a woman whose skin was a deep brown to begin with.

"What?"

"The moon is going green tonight, then tomorrow is a blood storm. I have to stop Joseph, but I have to find him first!" I burbled it all out. "Crash is off again, Feish can't be my friend anymore, and I've lost Robert to that bitch Karissa!" I was wailing now; the drink having undone any control I'd had left.

Penny pulled me with her up onto the porch. "Sit."

I did as I was told, flopping into a wicker chair, hunching over myself. "This day could not get worse," I said.

From inside the house, Missy let out a shriek. "Do not say things like that, you fool!"

I rolled my eyes, then leaned forward and put my head in my hands. "Penny, nothing is going right. I need help. I need . . . I need someone on my side."

Her hand was gentle as she pulled my fingers away from my face. "Girl. You have lots who love you, who will help you. You know that."

I sighed. "I do. I'm just sad. I couldn't even get the police to tell me where the zombie activity was happening. I thought I could find, like, a central place to look for Joseph."

Penny frowned. "Who is Joseph exactly?"

"The older brother of Roderick from the council. Dear old Rod hired me to find and stop him." I rubbed my face again. The whiskey was burning off too quick. I wasn't sure I was ready for sober yet.

Missy banged through the screen door. "Are you going to go after that zombie and get my book?"

I blinked up at her. "*Your* book?"

She didn't even flush. Nope, she just rolled with it like she hadn't pretty much stolen the book from me in the first place and continued to glare at me, hands on her bony hips.

Penny kept her eyes on me. "What do you need to know?"

"The green moon, that freaked you out. Is it real then?" I asked. To my surprise, Missy was the one who answered.

"The green moon is a sign of the uprising. If a blood storm comes tomorrow, then yes, we will be dealing with all the dead crawling from their graves and coming after us." Her eyes flashed with anger. "It is a very old spell, one that has only been used once before."

"Like the one that needed the angel wings and the fairy cross?" I blurted out. "Is it that one?"

"No." Missy snapped the single word, sharp and hard.

"There will be a single person at the center of this spell," Penny said, her voice low. "But there will be many others helping that person. I believe . . . I believe what we've always feared has come to pass."

Oh, this was new. "What is that?"

"The Dark Council is active," Penny said even as Missy hissed at her. Penny ignored her. "The Dark Council is supposed to be a myth, a legend even in the shadow world. While our council here in Savannah works to keep the shadow world in check, the Dark Council . . . they wish to unleash the shadow world on the humans. To take over wherever they can."

I stared at her as the words sank in. "Are you serious? Why haven't I heard of this before?"

"Because it is not talked about!" Missy slapped her hands on the table between me and Penny. Penny didn't jump. I didn't have the reflexes to jump.

"Like so many things, there is a fear that if it is openly discussed others might seek them out and side with them," Penny said. "Like the shadow witches of New Orleans. Like Derek the goblin king."

I stared hard at her. "Like Clovis."

She gave a slow nod. "It's possible they are all connected. That they have been sending their people in one at a time to test Savannah's defenses."

Sweet baby Jaysus in a paper manger. I couldn't help the way my face twisted up. "That's . . . not good."

"No, it isn't," Missy growled. "Because they have many, many more people than we do, and they are recruiting more!"

"The council is making a mess of things." Penny nodded. "Hunting their own kind."

"Like at the hospital?" I offered, thinking of Dr. Mori. Sure, he hadn't been all warm and fuzzy, but he had seemed like a good sort. Plus, he had a connection—a strong one—to the dead. His talents would have come in useful, and instead the council had turned on him.

Penny smiled. "Like at the hospital."

I stood; thinking of Dr. Mori had given me an idea. "I've got to go."

"You know where to find us," Penny said.

"I don't want her back here!" Missy shrieked. "Not one foot on my property. You'll ruin my grass! Not unless you have my book!"

Ruin her grass, would I? Let's just see about that.

I stepped out onto her lawn.

"Skeletor, you up for a ride?" The ground in front of me heaved, and the lawn split even as Missy let out a belly scream. I smiled and waved at her. Yup, totally worth it.

My undead ride lurched forward and got his hooves under him as he dragged himself out of the soil. The horse was like Robert—dead but not—and he'd given me a ride out of trouble more than once. Also, like Robert, he always seemed to be there when I needed him. There was one key difference—Skeletor became more lifelike each time he answered my summons. Now, he looked like nothing more than a great big black stallion with a flowing mane and tail, not a single speck of rot on him. Well, that wasn't entirely true.

His eyes were pretty much empty black holes.

He took a step forward, and I grabbed his mane. "I'm going to need help, friend."

He went to a knee and I scrambled up, wincing as I used my recently reassembled elbow. He lurched up and bounced me onto my belly. Oh, that didn't feel good.

The whiskey poured out of me, all over what was left of the lawn.

"Oh, you little bitch!" Missy screeched. "You did that on purpose!"

I blinked up as I stopped puking, waved at Missy and Penny, and then urged Skeletor forward.

"Can you find a man connected to the dead, goes by Mori?" I asked my horse.

He flicked his head up and down, mane flowing, then leapt out of the yard, hooves clattering on the cobblestones as he tore away from the Victorian district and the screeching Missy.

"Easy, boy, I'm wobbly!" I struggled to get upright as Skeletor dodged around vehicles and tourists, heading straight toward River Street.

He gave a buck that threw me up into a sitting position, and I clung to his neck. "Easy, I said! We don't have to go so fast!"

Skeletor snorted and only picked up speed as he approached the river. With a grunt, he jumped into the water. I closed my eyes as we went fully under before bobbing back to the surface. I'll be honest, this was not what I'd expected. Not at all.

The water sloshed up and over my hips as he swam hard, blowing great billows of steam from his nostrils. I wiped my face and my jaw dropped.

"Boats, there are boats coming!" This was the problem with the horse under me. There was no steering him, and he, being already dead, was oblivious to mortal danger. You know, like the bigass steamer paddle boat bearing down on us.

I jerked to the side, trying to get off Skeletor's back. Nope, his magic held me tight, and I was good and properly stuck.

The only option left was to try and help him go faster. Like the fool I was, I paddled with my one good hand. The one that I'd popped out of the joint didn't want to help, so it kind of just splashed.

"Shit, I'm turning us in a circle!" I yelped and stopped paddling. So much for that idea.

I looked up again as the steamboat continued toward us, the big paddles splashing as it came closer and closer. "I said take us to Dr. Mori, who is connected to death, not to kill us!"

The boat captain up in the wheelhouse didn't even look down our way, which wasn't altogether surprising because my mount was invisible to most people, along with anyone on his back. Still, I waved a hand just before the first wave off the chugging boat hit me and Skeletor, rolling us underwater. I held my breath as we tumbled and came back up, closer yet to the boat.

"This was a terrible idea!" I yelled at the horse. What in the world had he been thinking? What in the world had *I* been thinking?

I kept waving, hoping the captain would somehow see us. "Hey. Hey!"

But the captain didn't notice us, of course, and another wave knocked us under. We bobbed back up, and I gasped for air.

I lifted my hand limply. Then found myself staring down the side of the boat, where people had lined up and were pointing in our direction. Wide eyes. Open mouths.

They were looking at us.

The people on the boat saw us down here?

"Help!" I yelped the word as one of the boat's paddles thundered so close poor Skeletor had to fight to keep us above water. I held my breath as we were pushed down and then bobbed back up again.

Ropes were flung down off the sides of the steamer boat. No, not ropes, more like nooses. One caught around my hand in the water, the other flipped over my head to my middle. Either there was a master wrangler aboard that ship—unlikely in the middle of Savannah—or they were guided by magic.

"Oh, shit." Did I need the help? Yes, yes I did. But also, did I want to get strangled and dragged up for a meet and greet with unidentified magical people? Not so much.

I fumbled with the one on my good arm—actually, fumbled was the best verb to describe what I'd been doing for the past two days—but it was no use.

The noose tightened, and I was pulled up the side of the boat as Skeletor went under the next paddle and didn't come back up. I knew he'd be okay, but it still felt wrong to leave him like that.

My legs bumped the side of the boat, and the noose around my middle tightened until I couldn't breathe, the rope cutting deeply into my abdomen. But I wasn't being pulled up, just being held there, at the water's edge as I the ropes kept me from doing more than a shallow gasp.

One thought kept me moving, digging for my hip bag.

My knife, I had to get to my knife. Based on the whole rope thing and the passengers' ability to see me and Skeletor, I was betting they were part of the shadow world, and there was a pretty good chance they weren't friendlies.

Maybe going under the boat wasn't such a bad option. Surely I could hold my breath that long? I looked at the size of the boat, the length of the hull.

Yeah, who was I fooling? I was no Phelps. I had to hope that they pulled me all the way up and that I was ready once I reached the top.

My bad arm the only one left to me, I reached for my knife as the ropes continued to tighten. My legs were being pulled under the boat, which only intensified the tension.

I couldn't breathe.

Just as I got hold of the knife handle, I was yanked so hard that I flew up to the edge of the deck and found myself looking into the faces of what to anyone else would be just a bunch of humans. Hands grabbed at me and pulled me over the wooden railing. The rope around my waist loosened, and I sucked in a deep breath, keeping my face down and my hand holding my knife hidden underneath me.

"You don't need that here," said a familiar voice. I slowly raised my head to look into the fathomless dark eyes of Dr. Mori. He didn't smile down at me. "What are you doing here, Ms. O'Rylee? I thought I made it clear that I did not want to see you again. Not ever."

The ropes that had loosened on me were suddenly wrapped around my arms, pinning them to my sides. I rolled and kicked, taking someone out at the knees.

"Robert!" I yelled for my friend—the one person I'd been able to depend on since my life had taken a left-hand turn at the Hollows. What I got was Alan spilling out of my hip bag.

"Where are we now? What trouble have you found?" Alan did a slow circle, and Dr. Mori raised an eyebrow.

He could see Alan.

"Your friend Robert cannot find you here," Dr. Mori said, ignoring Alan. "None of your friends can find you here." His eyes drifted back over to my ex-husband. "And we don't like spies."

Hands twisted me around and held me so I couldn't look away from Dr. Mori. He scooped up my new knife and held it in the palm of his hand.

"Spies?" I stared hard at him, wishing I could turn and look at Alan. Alan was a spy? What had he said when he'd thought I'd been drunk? That he had to tell Marge . . . .

"I am not a spy!" Alan squeaked out in the same voice he'd used when he'd told me he wasn't cheating. Which he most certainly had been.

"I'll deal with you later," I said and then changed direction. "I know you aren't doing this, Dr. Mori."

His eyebrows climbed. "Doing what?"

"The zombies. I know that the council has it wrong." I also knew that I had to talk fast if I was going to get my ass out of this frying pan. This was not where I'd thought Skeletor would take me. I'd figured he'd bring me to a house, possibly the police station if they were holding Dr. Mori there. Not a boat out in the middle of the river where I had no easy way to escape.

His dark eyes flicked over the knife and then to me. "Then why are you here? I know that the council hired you." He crouched in front of me and spread his palms wide. The people around us were quiet and I had the feeling that he was the boss here. King. Leader. Whatever.

"No, the council didn't hire me. Roderick did. His brother Joseph is the one causing all the grief."

He smiled, though it was sad. "Joseph? Is that the name he is going by now? Interesting. But again, why are you here?"

"I was hoping you can help me find him."

Dr. Mori grunted and shook his head. "You do not want to find that one, Ms. O'Rylee. He is far more dangerous than anything you have seen in the shadow world so far. You'd be better off to stay far away from him."

"I've met Roderick, and they're brothers," I pointed out.

"Roderick has excellent control for one of his kind. Joseph"—he shook his head—"does not."

Perhaps I should have been more afraid, trussed up on an old steamboat ship that nobody else could see from the shoreline. How did I know that? In my peripheral vision, I could see about a dozen tourists at the water's edge, and every last one of them was looking right past us.

As if we weren't there.

"Ghost ship?" I asked, and Dr. Mori nodded.

"Here, even Joseph could not take us."

"He would try to control you? Is he part of the Dark Council?" I stared up at him.

Dr. Mori sighed. "Joseph is just a harbinger. What comes behind him wants nothing less than the power you and I hold. The power over death itself."

14

Now being told you have some power over death itself should actually be cool, or frightening, or something. But I was just pissed.

"Really? If I'm so powerful, why couldn't I save my gran? Why couldn't I stop Clovis on my own? Why—"

"Why can you call your undead friend Robert to you?" Dr. Mori said. "Why can you board this ghost ship that no one else can see? Why can you channel your abilities through this knife to end the undead?"

Alan was blessedly quiet.

Dr. Mori motioned at the knife. "The blacksmith made that for you."

"How did you know that?"

He sighed. "So many questions. You want all the answers for nothing. That is not how it works, Breena. There is a give and take in the shadow world."

I stared up at him. "The council thinks you are calling up the zombies. That's why they tried to catch you in the hospital."

He nodded. "Correct. But I felt their magic and slipped the bonds before they could settle the spell over the entire hospital. Just imagine if you'd been caught inside. You would have been held accountable for the mess that is rapidly growing."

I swallowed hard, letting the ramifications filter through my mostly sober brain. He was right. Hell, hadn't *I* considered the possibility that I'd risen the dead unintentionally? "It wasn't me, right?"

"Speaking to Eleanor before she died did not cause the other zombies to rise," he said, and I breathed out a sigh of relief.

"Wait, let me get this straight. If I am like you, and I'd been caught in there, then . . ."

"Then you would be at the council's mercy," he said. "They would pin the rising of the undead on you. As they have done to our kind in the past. They prefer to believe that the undead are an issue easily placated. Rather than face the truth that they are up against the Dark Council once more." He placed his hands on his knees but didn't rise out of the crouch. "Some of them are corrupt. Many of them are afraid. And all of them believe that there is nothing to fear." He paused and nodded, seemingly to himself. "Tell me what it is that you want, and I will . . . consider helping you."

I wanted to ask him why. I didn't. But he answered it anyway.

"I knew your father. And while we were not close, I respected him. I will help you if I can."

My legs were numbing, and I knew that the second I stood up I'd have pins and needles running up and down them. "Do you know where Joseph is?"

I'd have crossed my fingers if I could have.

"No."

I'd expected as much. "How about where all the zombies are rising?"

His eyes drifted closed. "I could help you with that." He snapped his fingers, and a couple of his people picked me up and took off the ropes. I rubbed my arms, wincing as my elbow reminded me it had recently been on a trip of its own outside its socket.

Yup, pins and needles like crazy down my legs, and I grimaced as I tried to follow him across the deck to a door that led into the ship.

Alan drifted to my side, and I glared at him. "You stay out here."

"I'm not a spy," he repeated, even though he was unable to look me in the eye.

"Just like you never cheated on me?" I threw back, and a few snickers rolled from the group of people on the deck. "They can see you. Why don't you go make a friend or two?"

Alan turned, and I could see his jaw drop as the realization hit him that he wasn't invisible to them.

These people were like Dr. Mori. Like me. A quick head count put at least fifty of them on the deck. But there were no scales, not snouts. No monsters. What was Mori? What was I? Was I going to end up scaly too? I wasn't sure I liked that idea.

Dr. Mori led the way, and I stepped through the door after him.

"The disease of the undead is spreading. In the past, we—" he lifted a hand and waved it to indicate the gathering on the deck, "—would have made short work of them. But we're being held culpable by those who do not understand. For our own preservation, we have chosen to sit back this time."

The ship was done up in a light oiled wood that caught the sun and glowed a lovely honey hue. I followed Dr. Mori to an enormous circular table bolted into the floor. It was easily twelve feet across in each direction. A gasp escaped me.

The entire city of Savannah was etched into the tabletop, all the way out to the surrounding areas with designs and details so intricate my eyes couldn't take them all in. From each square and the specific kind of flowers that bloomed there, to the fountain in Forsyth Park that had fairies dancing around it. I blinked.

The fairies were moving.

I blinked again and leaned over the table. "Is this . . . real?"

"It shows an accurate positioning of many of those in the shadow world," Dr. Mori said. "If you touch it you can move it, and you can tighten the frame to focus on a specific area."

I scanned the table, looking for zombies, and then glanced up at my host. "No undead?"

"This magic has its limits," he said softly. "What will you give me for the use of this map?"

I spread my hands. "What do you want?"

"I wish to train you."

Now that was not expected, not at all. "What?"

"You have multiple bloodlines running through you, Ms. O'Rylee. One will become dominant if it is trained. Then the others will fade. I wish to train the bloodline that would be most useful."

My mind flashed to Gran's attempts to teach me spells when I was a young girl. I'd been okay at them but not great. And then I'd left Savannah with Alan. What if I'd stayed? Would I have become a witch like her?

Stark's words about choosing a path rolled through me.

I glanced at the map, wondering how much help it would actually be. But the thing was . . . I'd always shown the most aptitude with this type of magic—the type wound up with death. And if I trained with Mori and the fae side of my bloodline faded, maybe my heart would let go of Crash?

I swallowed hard and then nodded. "Okay."

He tipped his head to me. "One week from today, you will begin training with me."

"Assuming we aren't overrun by the undead." I smiled at him. "Assuming I can stop Joseph."

Dr. Mori waved a hand at the table, and it flipped over, the mechanics so smooth it didn't issue a single creak.

Apparently, the map had only shown me the light side of the shadow world.

The flip side was . . . well, dark.

Savannah was covered in shadows, creatures moving in and out of them, creeping around buildings and through and into the water.

"This is the side of Savannah that few see. The side of the ill-intentioned. The side of the shadows that are truly dark." He brushed his fingers over the map. "It is both a blessing and a curse to have this."

I turned to him. "You can see which side of the map people are on?" Like people you thought were your friends but weren't?

"You can."

"Dare I ask?"

"You are on the other side." His smile was still tight. "For all your bungling, you are well-intentioned. It's why I didn't just kill you in the water and allowed you onto my boat."

I blinked a couple of times. "Thanks?"

But I didn't look down at the map. Because I was suddenly afraid of who I might see skulking in the shadows of Savannah.

"It is hard to see the truth about the people you thought were your allies," he said, ever so quietly, his eyes flicking to the table. "It is hard to know that not all of those you love have good intentions."

"I'm not sure . . ."

"The undead are not on here; they have no thoughts, good or bad, but perhaps there is a pattern to those who have ill intentions. I . . . do not look at this side of the table often. I prefer to study the other side."

I took a deep breath and looked at the table. The whole city was coated in darkness, shadows and bits of fog curling around some parts far more than others. Like Factors Row.

Like Centennial Park Cemetery that was across from Corb's apartment.

I bit my lower lip and tried not to notice the actual people moving around.

Forget it, I made myself look at the Victorian district where Missy lived. I touched the map and the image bloomed larger. There she was, sliding in and out of her house. Surprise, surprise. Penny was not with her, and I breathed a small sigh of relief. I'd felt a connection to Penny from the first moment I'd met her, and the idea that she could be out to get me churned my guts like butter.

I looked away from Missy and scanned the board quickly, too fast to see the details of the people as I slid my fingers over the map, manipulating the size here and there. The minutes ticked by as I kept scanning, keeping my eyes deliberately unfocused so that I was catching movement but not faces.

What if one of my friends was on here?

What if several of them were? Part of me knew it would be better to know. But I wasn't sure I could take much more heartbreak.

"Fool," I whispered to myself. I forced my eyes to search the shadows, looking for faces I knew. But at least where I looked, there were none.

"So, this doesn't show the dead at all? Like Alan wouldn't show up on here?"

"That is correct," Dr. Mori said, "though he is marked heavily by the queen of voodoo, so it is obvious to me that he is a spy. She is not inherently evil. Consider her more of a trickster, neither good nor bad, only looking out for something interesting."

My eyes locked onto an area that was not any darker than the rest, but there was a lot of movement around it.

"Is that the old Fort Jackson?" I asked. Mostly because it didn't look quite right. "Is it a five-pointed star?" The fort was a damn pentagram? How could that have been missed? Then again, the building itself didn't have that look exactly above ground.

Dr. Mori leaned over the table and looked closer. "That's the shape of the building's foundation. Much movement there, you are correct."

The old fort was at the edge of the river, outside of Savannah. Set up to protect the city from water invasion.

A shiver ran through me as I stared at it. "Then I guess that's where I am going to go."

"Take your friends with you," Dr. Mori said. "If Joseph is there, then you will need all the help you can get."

He turned my face to him with a finger under my chin. "You need to understand, Breena, that some of your friends *are* on this side of the table. Even if you do not see them now. No one has friends that are all on the light side of the table."

I swallowed hard. "I should look for them again?"

"To be safe, you should look for them. But another day, when you are not so busy. For even though two of them are not well-intentioned, they mean you no harm."

Like Crash and Feish. Telling me they were doing what they had to do. "It's okay, I know . . . I think I know who they are."

He removed his finger from my chin and stepped back. "Then I will see you in one week, at midnight. Meet me at the bank of the river outside of the Hollows."

I held out my hand, and he took it. For just a minute, his mask slipped and that black and gold scaled monster looked back at me.

A shiver of fear cut through me, but I didn't let it get me down. Nope, I had direction. I was going to stop one Joseph, brother of Roderick. Then I was going to have a long nap and eat a box of Oreos, chased with a handful of Advil to soothe the aches in my heart and hips.

We walked back out to the deck of the boat and the wind blew across my face, cooling a rapid burst of heat. Hello mini-hot flash.

Alan was chatting away, of course, but I snapped my fingers at him and drew him to me. Grabbing him, I stuffed him into my bag while he grumbled.

"You and I are going to talk about Marge later, but for now you can stay in there," I whispered. Alan situated, I turned to say goodbye to Dr. Mori. "I guess I'll see you next week. If things don't go too pear-shaped. And . . . thank you."

"Don't thank me yet," Dr. Mori said. "There is only one way off this boat. Consider it a first lesson from me."

"Wait. What lesson?"

Those were the last words I got out of my mouth before Dr. Mori lifted his hand, and it was like a stiff wind slammed into my middle out of nowhere, throwing me out over the open water of the river.

Screeching at the top of my lungs—"This is not how people disembark a boat!"—I managed a quick breath in before I hit the icy cold. Okay, so it wasn't *icy* cold, but it was still wet and full of traffic, and I had already been dunked once, thank you very much.

The water whooshed down over my head, the waves off the steamboat shoving me down into the depths of the river. Down where the dead things waited.

How did I know?

I could feel them—and no, I did not mean I could feel them in my head.

Hands grabbed at my ankles and dragged me further down, fingernails dragging through my jeans. I really should have put on my leather pants before I left home.

Jaysus, lord have mercy, I needed a ducking break!

Floundering in the water, I twisted around, my knife still in hand. I stabbed it into the fingers that were grabbing me, cutting them off, prying them away one by one.

Still, swimming was going to be tough. I had all my clothes on, one bum arm, and exhaustion was settling in heavily.

I needed help. Alan was useless. Robert was gone. And I wasn't sure I could trust the one person who showed up, swimming hard, gills flapping as she reached for me.

To drown me? Or to save me?

15

Feish's webbed fingers wrapped around my hands and clamped down hard as the undead grabbed at my ankles. I kicked out, but in the murky depths I couldn't see anything. What I knew was I was running out of air.

Fast.

Feish swam hard, pulling me upward, but the zombie below hadn't let go. Which meant she dragged us both to the surface.

I broke through, gasping for a breath, and then was pulled back down the second Feish let me go.

I folded in half and stabbed blindly at the critter clinging to me. I hit something and the weight on me lessened. Hands wrapped under my arms, and I was yanked to the surface once more.

"What you doing? I pulled you up!" Feish yelled at me.

"There's a zombie on my leg!" I yelled back, spitting out a mouthful of river water. Gross.

Fingers were still attached to me, but one more kick, and whatever was left of the critter fell away.

Holding the knife handle in my mouth, I swam for shore, Feish swimming ahead of me now. As if she didn't want to be seen helping me?

Finally, I touched bottom and stood up. Kinkly buzzed down around my head and landed on my shoulder.

"You look like a drowned cat," she said.

"Don't you mean rat?" I twisted so I could see her.

"Only one rat around here, and it isn't you," she whispered.

Shit. Feish? But hadn't I seen Kinkly with Karissa?

Clomping forward, I made my body work a little more. "Stay with me, Kink."

"On it," she said and settled herself more fully on my shoulder.

Feish stood on the shoreline, her arms crossed and her body shedding water at a speed that was anything but natural. "You trying to die?"

"Not today," I said. "Thanks, Feish. I mean that. You've always been a good friend to me."

Her eyes went wide and teared up. "No. I am not your friend."

"Then why did you save me?"

Her mouth hung open, like the fish out of water she was, and her lips flapped for a moment before she finally spoke. "I don't know."

I took a step, then another and another, until I was walking briskly away from her. "I'm sorry you feel that way, Feish." At the top of the slope leading away from the river, I let myself look back at her. "But if you ever need my help, you know where to find me. I'll always be your friend."

Feish's eyes closed, and I turned away. I didn't want to see her cry. I didn't want to hurt her more than she was obviously hurting.

Her ties to Crash were making her step away from me.

"What's happening?" Alan mumbled from my bag, and I flipped it open, so he spilled out.

Kinkly fanned her wings against my cheek. "Why did you open your bag? Oh no . . . is your ex back?"

"Yes," I said. "And he's spying on us for Marge and Homer, so be careful what you say around him."

All the way back to my gran's house I clomped. Yes, clomped. I was hurt, angry, tired, and freaked out all at once. That last bit was mostly because I knew where we had to go—the old fort—and I'd seen the bustling of dark activity there.

I needed to gather the troops and try to stop Joseph.

At the foot of my gran's porch, I stopped. Because attached to the door was a large yellow envelope. A shot of fear cut through me.

Yellow envelopes and I had a bad history. Divorces. Evictions. Shitty spells.

I took the steps carefully, as if one of them might fall out from under me.

"What are you doing, sneaking up on the door?" Alan barked.

"Gawd, if I could kill you dead a second time I would," I barked right back at him.

The door swung open, and Sarge stuck his head out, oblivious to the envelope. "Hey, what took you so long?" He frowned as he looked me over. "What happened?"

I all but pulled myself up the stairs. "Can you call Eric and Suzy? Tell them to come back. I know where we have to go."

Sarge took his phone from a back pocket and dialed them while I stood in the foyer, swaying. The open door next to me mocked me with its yellow envelope. Crash's handwriting was clear as day on the exterior.

I couldn't do it. I couldn't read another notice ordering me to get out of Gran's house. Not if I was going to tackle a big bad in a few hours.

"Aren't you going to read it?" Kinkly asked.

"Nope. I'm going to get changed, shower, and have something to eat." Up the stairs I went and did all that. No excitement. At least that was the plan.

The water poured over my body, soothing away some of the aches and pains.

Maybe I cried a little. Because if I was going to cry, that was the place to do it, where no one could see me.

"Damn it all," I whispered into the water. I'd lost Feish, Crash, and Robert all in one day.

My three closest friends. Another hiccupping sob escaped me as I let myself consider that one of my closest friends was a dead guy.

The heat loosened my muscles, though, and I slowly regained control of myself. Flicking the water off, I reached blindly for a towel, and my hand bumped up against a body.

Eyes flying open, I turned.

Crash stood in my bathroom, his eyes roving my body. The moisture in my mouth dried up as I took him in. Dirty, blood flecking his bare chest, coal smudges running up his arms almost to his elbows like he'd been working and disturbed, more coal dust speckled over his face.

"Crash?" I grabbed a towel and wrapped it around myself. "Crash, what happened? Are you okay?"

His jaw ticked, and his blue-gold eyes looked away. "Get dressed. You need to come with me."

He left me there in the bathroom, shivering from the intensity of his gaze. Shivering and shaken to the core that he was here.

I'd laid out clean clothes on the counter—the leather pants Gerry had made for me, a white tank top, underwear, bra, socks and my boots sat beneath them. I slid them all on, and then topped it all off with the leather shawl thing she'd given me. I tightened the straps across my chest, slid my hip bag on across my body, then pulled my hair into a high ponytail before I looked in the mirror.

For just a moment I didn't see myself. Not my forty-three-year-old face or body. Not the wrinkles I was earning every damn day or the increasing laxity of my skin. Not the failure I so often saw. Certainly not the girl who wondered if she'd ever get it right.

No, I saw someone else. I saw a damn boss bitch ready to take on the day. I saw a woman who had earned her scars. I saw a woman who faced each day with all the energy she had left. I saw a woman who loved with all her heart, even when it hurt her.

I saw a woman I liked very much; a woman I'd like to see more of.

My jaw trembled, and I clenched my teeth together. No more tears.

Taking a deep breath, I stepped out into my bedroom. Crash stood looking out the window.

"I'm sorry for everything, Bree," he said without looking at me. "I thought . . . I thought I was away from it all. But there is no getting away from my past. It's come back to haunt me now, and I can't escape."

He turned then, and my eyes dropped to his hands.

A pair of iron shackles stared back at me. "Are you fucking kidding me?"

His eyes bored into mine and, like with Roderick, I could feel him trying to bend me to his will. And my heart broke right there.

"No," I said.

"I'm sorry," he whispered. "I am so, so fucking sorry. I tried."

The door was smack in the middle between us, wide open, and I knew it was my only shot. Although I didn't believe Crash would hurt me, I knew he wasn't acting of his own volition anymore.

And whoever he was working for had it in for me.

I leapt for door, diving through it as he reached for me. His fingers slid over my boot, and I kicked out as I fell, shoving him backward even as I half rolled, half lurched down the stairs, hitting the bottom and then running at full speed. "Sarge!"

A muffled grunt turned me around to the living area. Sarge was bound in a chair, his eyes wide and sparking with anger. Kinkly was bound up and laid in his lap, her eyes closed, wings still. The tiniest of metal bands were wrapped around her—they looked like twist ties.

I ran to them and turned so they were between me and Crash. Scooping Kinkly up, I put her in my hip bag.

The blacksmith stood in the doorway to the living room. "Do not make this harder than it has to be," he said. "I don't want to—"

"Hurt me?" I offered as I ran my hands over the iron holding Sarge tight, trying to find a latch. "Too late."

His jaw ticked. "I never meant to hurt you."

He took a step, and my gran was suddenly there, between the two of us. "Get away from her!" She flung her hands up as if casting a spell. "I said away!"

He shook his head and held up a hand. "Celia. You can't stop me any more than she can." And gawdamn if his voice wasn't wrecked with sorrow and resignation.

"You have to go," Sarge growled to me. "You can't break this iron."

"I won't leave you," I whispered.

He grunted. "I'll be okay. You know how I know?"

I shook my head and gripped his shoulder. He smiled up at me. "Because I know you'll come back. I know you'll save me."

Okay, now the tears did spill. I hiccupped a sob and turned toward the only way out.

Through the pane glass window. I ran, hopped up, and slammed my body into the single pane, shattering it as I fell through. Did I land gracefully? No, I did not, but I managed to get to my feet with only a few cuts on my upper body.

"Skeletor!" I screamed for my horse but kept running. Because I could hear Crash behind me. And he was gaining.

I didn't dare look back. I put my everything into the run ahead of me.

My lungs were on fire, my legs were weak, but I didn't slow down as I bolted across the first square, hopped a bench, and made a beeline for a square halfway across the city. I wouldn't make it without Skeletor, but I had to try.

A brush of Crash's fingers in my hair gave me an extra spurt of energy.

Long enough to hear the hooves on the pavement.

My undead black horse came racing down a side street, and in a moment of pure magic, I grabbed his mane, pushed up off the ground, and somehow pulled myself onto his back.

Only then did I look back.

Crash stood in the middle of the square, watching us go. I couldn't resist. I blew him a kiss.

If he wanted to be on the opposite side of the table, then so be it.

"To Forsyth Park," I leaned forward and whispered to my horse.

Because if there was anyone at all I could trust in this world, it was Robert, and the fairy queen had taken him.

16

Unlike the other times I'd visited the land of the fae, it was night. The sky was a deep purply black, and the stars were brilliant flecks of colors, radiating not just white light but various shades of pink, blue, green, yellow, and red. Every color you could think of scattered across the sky. But using Stark's trick, I'd spoken that I wanted only to be gone an hour before we leapt through the doorway.

Please gawd let it be a real trick that worked. Because the time crunch I was on was real, and I couldn't afford to lose a day. Even for Robert I couldn't afford to lose a day.

I found myself turning to the right, what felt like south. "That way." I bumped my heels into Skeletor's side, and we bounced off at a rocking gait. This was better than the bouncing trot. As we went, I dug Kinkly out of my bag and held her in one hand while I untwisted the metal ties from her body. I put them back in my bag—no littering here—and then touched her back with a finger.

"Kink, you okay?"

She groaned and rolled over, stretching her arms and wings before her eyes flew open. "What happened? Crash was there and then . . ." She shot into the sky, flying around my head. "He tied me up! Sarge too!"

"I know," I said. "We're going to find Robert first—"

Skeletor slid to a sudden stop, tucking his bum down hard until he almost sat in the long grass.

Ahead of us stood one very amused-looking fairy queen.

I blew out a breath. "Look, you took Robert, and I want him back."

Her head tipped to the side. "Do you understand now why I was trying to stop you from shagging my ex?"

I frowned. I doubted her motives were pure, but sure, I'd play along. "Yes, he's one of the bad guys. And, to be clear, we never actually shagged, as you so delicately put it." Just saying that felt disloyal.

She shrugged. "Close enough." I didn't know if she meant the shagging, or my comment about him being a bad guy. Did it matter? Not at that moment.

It couldn't matter. Whatever was driving Crash's behavior, he had still turned on us.

"Why did you take Robert?" I asked. "He doesn't mean anything to you."

"Insurance." She smiled and threw Robert's finger bone at me. I caught it in mid-air and clutched him hard in my hand a moment before sliding him into my bag. Insurance. What the hell was that supposed to mean?

A wave of her hand at us, as if she were shooing away a fly. "Go. Do what you must and understand that I am not the bad one here."

I snorted. "Shades of gray, my friend, shades of gray."

Skeletor flipped his head, and as we turned, I noticed that the flowers we'd come through were dead in the spots where he'd planted his hooves.

Interesting.

I urged him forward, and we galloped back the way we'd come, Kinkly easily keeping up with us.

"I can't believe he bound me!" she shouted as we reached the exit and plunged through, coming out in the middle of the fountain in Forsyth Park. Skeletor clomped through the water as if it were nothing, and not one tourist so much as looked at us. I mean, a goblin sitting on a bench gave me a bit of a look, but that was it.

"Hey, what time and date is it?" I shouted at the goblin. He blinked up at me. Of course, he'd just seen me come out of the land of Faerie.

"Seven in the evening on the eleventh of June."

One hour, almost to the second. Good enough for me. I gave him a wave in thanks.

"We need to get a hold of Eric and Suzy," I said. "And tell them to meet us at the old fort."

"Why there?" Kinkly buzzed. "What did you learn?"

"Joseph has set up camp there," I said. "And maybe we can stop him before he knows we know where he is."

She bobbled in front of me and finally landed on Skeletor's mane.

"If we fail tonight, then we still have tomorrow to try and stop him," I said.

"Assuming you're still alive and not chopped up into pieces," she pointed out. I grimaced.

"Nobody is getting chopped into pieces," I said.

Urging Skeletor forward, I pointed him in the one direction I was pretty sure was safe.

To the Hollows.

At the speed Skeletor could travel, it didn't take us long to reach the hidden cemetery.

The gates were cracked open, and I slid from the horse's back and stepped through, pushing them the rest of the way open so he could follow. Snorting, he kept pace with me. I tried not to look at his undead eyes. Despite him being a friend, he still had a good creep factor going on.

Picking up my pace, ignoring the aches in my lower back the best I could, I made my way to the entrance to the Hollows.

"Eammon? Tom?" I hesitated and then called the other name. "Louis?"

Please don't let Louis be here.

A shuffling of feet, and then I breathed a sigh of relief as Eammon poked his head up out of the stairwell by the statue of the angel with the broken wings.

"Lass, what do you be doing here?"

I sagged where I stood. "I don't know where to start. But it's bad, Eammon. Really bad. Do you have a phone?" I held my dead one out. "I soaked mine."

"You came here to make a call?" He squinted up at me, but did offer me a cell phone. An old flip phone, no less.

I opened it and dialed Eric's number. He picked up on the second ring.

"Where are you?" I blurted out.

"Almost back to Celia's house."

"Don't go there!" I shouted. "Come to the Hollows, Crash . . . turned on us. He has Sarge."

Eammon sucked in a sharp breath that was followed by an explosion of curses that made me raise my eyebrows. Perhaps he was part sailor and not just a leprechaun.

"Oh no," Eric breathed out. "Okay, we're on our way."

He hung up, and I handed the phone back to Eammon.

"Crash . . . went back to his roots, did he?" Eammon wiggled his way up onto the edge of the statue's base.

I sat next to him, my whole body slumping. "Said he didn't have a choice."

Eammon harrumphed. "Always a choice. You just might not like the choices you have is all."

In a matter of minutes, I spilled out the last day and a half. I told him about the zombies at the hospital, the job we'd taken for Roderick, Dr. Mori's table and what I'd seen on it, Feish and Crash turning away from me, and Karissa stealing Robert.

Of course, the core of it was one thing that just had me reeling. "The Dark Council is a real thing then?"

Eammon nodded slowly. "Yes. Though I thought it be disbanded a long time ago. Maybe the members just scattered long enough to gather power."

That did not make me feel any better.

A beep of a car horn turned us around. Suzy and Eric came skidding along the path to us, the brakes coming on at the last second as they slid to a stop. Eric stepped out first, and while he adjusted his glasses and bowtie, he seemed otherwise unbothered by the fact that Suzy drove like a damn maniac.

Once more, I told the story of what I'd learned and all that had happened.

"And you think he's part of this council?" Eric asked gently.

"Makes sense, doesn't it? I assume that the Dark Council has some sort of order that they are all a part of? Like they have to make an oath or something?" I asked.

Eammon nodded. "Yes, exactly."

Which was why Crash could never get away from them. I rubbed my face with both hands. He'd left me the knife to keep me safe from the undead. I knew he cared for me. Maybe even loved me.

But we were on opposite sides now. Maybe we always had been.

"What are we going to do now?" Suzy asked. "You know where this Joseph dude is, but do we know anything about him? Like is he a siren or a necromancer? Or what?"

I shook my head and looked at Eammon, who mimicked me. "I don't know, lass. Roderick and Joseph have always kept their cards close to their chests. Best guess is he's some brand of necromancer."

"We have time," Eric said. "Should we go now?"

I had no plan. I had no idea just what we were supposed to do. "Give me a minute." I pushed off my spot against the statue and walked away from my friends. I found my feet taking me to Eleanor's grave. Not Eleanor from the hospital, but Eleanor that was somehow attached to Robert.

When I reached her gravestone, I pulled his finger bone free of my handbag and set it on the ground. "Robert, you still with me?"

"Friend," he murmured.

I closed my eyes before I could see his swaying skeletal figure. Because I needed all of Robert. Not just the part that so loyally called me his friend. That feeling of warmth started in my hips this time and traveled up through my torso to my arms, cooling as I reached out.

Robert set his hand in mine and curled his fingers tightly, weaving them between mine.

I opened my eyes, and he was standing there, as solid as I'd ever seen him.

"You're getting better with your connection to the dead." He smiled at me, blue eyes watching me closely.

"You know the situation?" I asked.

He nodded. "I do."

"Do you know what Joseph is?"

"Yes and no," he said, rubbing his thumb across the base of mine. "Like you, his bloodlines come from multiple places. Necromancer is one of them. Shinigami is the other."

I blinked. "What?"

"Shinigami. A death walker," he said. "They escort the dead to their resting places. Amongst other things."

"And that's it?" I asked.

"No, there is something else kicking around. He and Roderick are not full brothers." Robert frowned and pulled me a little closer. "Crash should have fought harder."

His words were a kick to the guts. "Yeah. Probably."

"Corb should have fought harder too."

He lifted a hand, and I stepped back, remembering the dream I'd had in New Orleans. Robert—well, the non-skeletal version of him—had kissed me. "Robert, are you making a move on me?"

From the other group, I heard Eric choke a little.

Robert smiled. "And if I am? I may be dead, but as you know dead isn't truly dead in our world."

"How about we focus on the danger at hand?" I said. "How about that? And then after—"

His smile widened. "There is never going to be an 'after' with you, Bree. The trouble you find is always there. You need someone who is okay with being with you in those brief moments between bouts of chaos. But yes, for you I will let it drop."

He tightened his hand on mine. "For now, yes, let's focus on the danger at hand. You want to go after Joseph tonight?"

"You think we shouldn't?"

"From what I know of him—" he pulled me to sit on the edge of Eleanor's tombstone with him, "—he is pretty cocky. He won't think of you as a threat. And he won't expect you to come to him."

"Then we go?"

"What about a recon mission?" Robert offered. "If you can get Penny to disguise you, you could slip in and snoop around and then slip back out before Joseph and his cronies know you're there. See how many people he has with him. Crash knows you, and he knows how you think. He won't expect this."

I sat there quietly. "You mean he knows I'd normally run in with a full head of steam?"

He chuckled. "Something like that."

"Thanks, Robert," I whispered. "You're a good friend."

"Always." He lifted my hand to his mouth and kissed the back of it. And then, between one blink and the next, he slid back to being the Robert who was with me the most.

Bony fingers released my own, and he stood swaying at my side.

"I wish you could stay with me," I said softly.

"Friend," he sighed out.

Yeah, me too, Robert, me too.

We walked back to the others, Eammon, Eric, Suzy, and Kinkly all staring at me expectantly.

"I think . . . I think I have a plan. One that Robert came up with. Joseph won't expect it. And more importantly, neither will Crash," I said, then I grimaced. "There is just one problem."

Everyone waited, and I looked at Suzy. "We have to let her drive."

17

Suzy's driving was, as always, nothing short of terrifying. But we did make it to Missy's house in very good time.

"I thought you said we needed Penny?" Eammon grumbled from the front seat. "Why are we sitting out here?" He claimed he got carsick in the back, though after riding with Suzy I suspected that he would no longer want the front seat.

Knowing you were going to die one day was one thing.

Seeing it come straight at you through the windshield was a whole other ball of wax.

"Kinkly, you're going to slip in there and bring Penny out. Okay?"

I rolled down the window, and Kinkly shot out, heading straight for the house. She zipped through the garden, and a moment later she was through an open window.

"We can't go in there," I pointed out. "Missy is not one of the good ones."

"She's not so bad," Eammon said.

Only I'd seen her skulking in the shadows on Dr. Mori's table. She was as bad as I'd always thought. My hand went to my hip bag, and I peeked in and pulled out the tarot card. Alan blinked up at me, and I pointed a finger at him. "Not a word, Alan."

He shrugged and rolled so I was looking at a piece of his back.

The card in my hand was the same as before, only . . . was there more blood on the dripping crescent moon?

Crescent moon.

Like the marks on the back of that one zombie? My breathing grew shallow. The shape *was* the same, but how were they actually connected?

A fluttering of wings, and I looked up as Kinkly zipped back to the car. "She's coming. Said she had to pee first."

Eric—sitting behind Suzy—reached forward and put a hand on her shoulder. No words between them, just a simple touch. They really were sweet together. So much so that I had to look away. I didn't begrudge them the bloom of love they had going on. Not for a second.

But it hurt to see something I wasn't sure I'd ever get. I'd never had anything approaching love with Alan, and although I'd seen glimmers of it with Crash, we clearly weren't meant to be. The whole Corb flirtation had also gone down in flames.

Maybe I just had really bad taste in men.

"Hey, Eammon, if one day I make it to old and gray, and I'm still single, want to marry me?" I blurted out.

Eammon twisted around and burst out laughing. "You're a fool, girl. You'll find him, whoever he is. Don't fuss it."

And just like that I was smiling again. Because he was right. I'd find him. Whoever he was. Maybe I'd just needed a little practice with the fools who'd come and gone.

Of course, the thought of one of those fools cut deeper than the others, but I breathed through the pain.

Penny stepped out onto the porch, cane in hand as she shuffled down the steps and then along the path to where we waited. Letting herself in the backseat, she sat down next to me.

"Girl, what are we doing now?"

I grinned. "We need you to whip up a spell. Think you can do that?"

She thumped her cane against the floor. "Well, of course. What kind of spell?"

I leaned over and whispered in her ear the idea that I had been building on.

Penny gave a low chuckle. "Oh, Eammon isn't going to like that. Leprechauns don't like cats."

"Cats? What have cats gots to do with this spell?" Eammon barked.

Penny tapped her cane on the floor of the car. "I have a place we can go. Suzy, take us to Brick Street."

I frowned at her. "Why are you staying with Missy if you have another place—"

"I was trying to get the spell book back." She leaned back in her seat. "You know, the one the zombie girl ran off with? And I didn't want Missy to know that Celia and I had a backup place here in Savannah."

I groaned and leaned back with her. "Right. Add that to our to-do list."

Of course, I had my own little spell book. I put a hand to my hip, thinking about it. Stark had told me to look through it, but I hadn't had the time.

"How long will a spell like that take to make?" I asked.

"Couple hours," Penny said. "And it'll last about an hour once you've been covered in it."

That gave me time to peruse the *Black Spells of Savannah and the Undead* for clues. Maybe I could find something in there about this undead spell?

I closed my eyes as Suzy drove. Prayed to whatever gods, god, deity or supernatural that might be listening that we'd make it there alive.

Penny laughed with glee and thumped her cane onto the floor of the car. "Like a rollercoaster!"

Eammon groaned, and Kinkly stayed steady on my shoulder, her wings fluttering as she balanced herself.

When the car came to a lurching stop, I opened my eyes but had to wait for Penny to get out before I could escape the death trap. I mean, generally speaking, it's bad form to crawl over an old lady to get out first.

The house was two stories and the windows were boarded up. The garden around it was dead, dry, as if it hadn't seen any attention in years. Penny led the way, and the rest of us followed her up the steps.

I let everyone else go first and found myself rubbing the back of my neck. Turning slowly, I looked out at the quiet streets around us.

Someone was watching us. But who? Crash?

I lifted my chin and thought about the badass woman who'd looked me in the eye in the mirror earlier. I was her. I could be her. "I know you're out there. You going to come out and say hello, or just skulk?"

The silence was heavy, but the feeling of being watched slid away. Fair enough.

I headed into the house after the others. A dull glow illuminated the empty front room. Well, almost empty. An wooden table with thick legs and a worn top sat in the center of the room, its surface covered in candles at various heights.

"Eric, you go up to the attic and bring down the big plastic tubs. They have all my spelling equipment in them." Penny motioned at him with her cane, and off he went. She looked at Suzy next. "You go out into the back garden and pick me some sage, belladonna, larkspur and nepeta."

Suzy grinned. "I know what all those are."

"Good, then you won't bring me the wrong one." Penny took a stabbing motion with her cane at Suzy, who dodged her easily.

Kinkly fluttered about. "What about me?"

"Think you can get me some fairy honey? A good amount now, no scrimping."

I grimaced. That stuff made me feel amazing, but it had a hell of a kick back.

"We'll use that for the delivery system of the spell," Penny said, glancing at me. "That way you'll also have an extra boost to get the job done."

Kinkly saluted and was gone in a flash of orange and red sparkles.

"What about me?" Eammon asked.

"Can you cook?"

"I've been known to whip up a meal or two." He puffed out his chest, and she patted him on the shoulder.

"Then go make us some food. There is a pantry down in the basement with dried goods."

I glanced at her as she shooed them all away. Finally, she looked at me. "You got that book of curses still?" I didn't ask how she'd known about it in the first place. Did it matter? No, because I trusted her.

I pulled it out of my bag and handed it to her. She sighed. "Good thing too. My memory isn't what it used to be. I'd hate to get a step wrong. I'd never hear the end of it from Missy if you all ended up as toads instead of cats."

She flipped the book open, did some more flipping, and then stared at a page a moment. "Excellent. There you go, have it back."

I took it from her and backed up to the wall, sliding down to sitting. Part of me wanted to watch her work, but I knew that I needed to see if I could find the spell Joseph was using to raise the undead.

I mean, it had to be massive, right? I started looking through the book for spells that required a large number of ingredients—because the connections between the spells' names and functions were far from obvious.

Fromgato Bushton
Latinia Vocalus
Gorgondian Bashium

For all I knew, they could be fancy pasta dishes in an Italian restaurant. The words weren't Latin, not really. And they weren't any other language I could figure out. More like made up words, or a language that was long dead. There wasn't even a description under each of the titles. You just had to know what you were looking for. Almost like you needed a key to read this book.

Still, I kept at it as the world around me moved. Penny was at the mortar and pestle, then Eric stepped up to help her. As a cook, he was a natural with spellwork. Suzy helped Eammon, and one of them brought me a grilled sandwich—I wondered where the hell Eammon had found bread—and a large glass of something cold. I barely noticed as I sunk deeply into the book, reading, trying to understand.

Feeling that what I needed was just out of reach.

Like the part of me that was a witch really wanted to help. I chewed on the inside of my lip and thought about tapping into that ability. What would it mean to call forth my witchy powers? What would it feel like?

My connection to the dead ran warm and then cool.

What did my connection to my witch magic feel like? I closed my eyes and thought about working spells with my gran and the feelings it had pulled forth in me.

We'd often practiced in the garden of her house, under the shade of her wisteria. It had always smelled like flowers back there. I'd assumed the scent was from her garden, but what if it was more than that? What if my connection to my gran's side was more earth-based? I drew in a breath and focused on that memory. Moments later, my nose filled with the scent of fresh herbs, sage, thyme, mint, lavender, basil, and rosemary. The smell of wisteria clung to me like a thick perfume, drawing a smile from me.

"What are you doing?" Penny asked.

I didn't open my eyes, just kept my thoughts and feelings focused as I answered her. "Trying to connect with my witch side?"

She tapped something on the table. "Well, girl, you see what you can do with that."

I opened my eyes after a few minutes of feeling my skin tingle, and the smell of an herb garden still surrounded me. I opened the book of curses and stared at the first page.

Horatius jay trachaias.

"To steal someone's voice," I whispered and then grinned. Now we were onto something.

I flipped through the book, scanning the strange titles, amazed when they were translated inside my head. "You could have helped, Penny."

"Then what would you have learned?" She didn't look up from her work. "You don't lead well, Bree. Best to let you fumble through and figure it out."

I scanned what had been strange words before and now made perfect sense.

Drying up a river.
Creating a fire that can't be quenched.
Turning someone against their lover.
Stealing another's will.

The further into the book I got the more I squirmed. Near the back of the book, I stopped.

Leviathan mort.

To raise the undead.

I ran a finger over the spell.

There were the three markers, two of which were still to come. The green moon. The blood storm.

I scanned the process and the ingredients. There was no fairy cross. No angel wings. No strange rhyme to the process.

A lot of different herbs, some gems and minerals. But that wasn't what caught my eye. No, what caught my eye was that this spell required more than the efforts of a single witch.

It needed a necromancer.

And it needed a fae-made cauldron.

Just like the one Crash had been asked to make that very first day I'd met him by Sean O'Sean himself.

18

My fingers trembled as the truth came crashing—no pun intended—down on me. The broken pieces of my heart shattered on what was left of my hope. Penny kept on working the spell, Eammon kept on cooking, and Suzy and Eric kept helping where they could. Only Kinkly noticed something was wrong. She fluttered to my face, fanning me.

"You look like you're going to pass out," she said.

"Crash has been working for the Dark Council all along," I breathed out. "That's what Feish meant when she said he was talking to someone from the council yesterday. Not the council that Roderick and Stark are on. The council that Joseph is on." My guts twisted up. The short guy in front of the limo. He'd been from the Dark Council. Shit, he could have been Joseph.

Kinkly swung back and forth, her face twisted up. "I'm sorry, Bree."

I looked at her. "Did you know?"

She shook her head. "No. He was always . . . the bad boy. But I didn't know that he was working on the Dark Council."

I leaned my head back and closed my eyes. When I'd dreamed of him, he'd told me 'don't believe me.' What did that mean?

The tiniest part of me wondered if he could be a double agent, like a spy who has gone too deeply into the enemy's camp.

"He's been with them a long time." Eammon's voice cut through my musings.

I looked up as he dragged a simple footstool over to me and sat down. "They found him when he was young and alone. When the rest of the fae didn't want him because he was different. Not pretty and fluffy, but dark and dangerous without even meaning to be. The last of his line."

"You never said any of this before." I stared at him, wondering just how far his connection with Crash went.

He shrugged. "Didn't seem pertinent. We were friends once, he and I."

My eyebrows rose. "And?"

"And we had a falling out. Then the Dark Council disbanded, and I thought he was free of it. But that didn't heal the rift between us." Eammon sighed.

"I'm sorry, lass, I know you had feelings for him. And maybe I hoped a little you were what he needed to pull his boots up."

I looked at my hands clutching the book of spells in my lap. "I know from experience he has to want it for himself. Change, that is."

I wanted to ask more questions, to pepper Eammon for information, but I couldn't get the words out. Nor did I feel the need to. The situation was perfectly clear to me. Crash was on the wrong side of the tracks, and it didn't matter that he might not want to be there, or that he was maybe even fighting not to be. It *couldn't* matter.

I couldn't trust him anymore, and that meant I couldn't trust Feish either.

"Almost ready here," Penny said and clinked a spoon against a steaming bowl. The clink turned into a chime that resonated through the room, humming and twisting until it sounded like the meow of a cat.

Eammon frowned. "What be that noise for?"

I tucked the book back into my hip bag and stood up. "How long?"

"About ten minutes," Penny said. "It needs to steep, and then it will be all ready."

We waited in silence, and the ten minutes seemed more like an hour by the time Penny clapped her hands over the still slightly steaming bowl.

"You'll drink it now. It'll take thirty minutes to affect you." She looked at me, Eric, Suzy and Eammon one at a time, pointing at us with her cane. "I would suggest you four take it. I'll drive you to a drop-off point not far from the fort. Kinkly can act as a watch."

Suzy tipped her head. "Can you drive a stick shift?"

Penny rolled her eyes. "Child, I'm going to show you just how to make that car of yours hum."

Eammon slid off his stool and took the proffered drink from Penny. He slugged it back like it was nothing. Eric went next. Suzy offered me a hand and helped me to stand up.

"Are you okay?" she asked in an undertone.

I knew she wasn't asking because of the way I winced as I stood, my back still protesting, my elbow aching. No, she meant my heart. I shrugged. "Could have been worse, I guess. I could have actually slept with him and then found out he was off limits."

Suzy squeezed my hand. "You let me know when you're ready, and I'll set you up on a date with someone I know. I think you'd like him."

Lawd Jaysus, a blind date. I forced a smile. "Maybe after we deal with the undead rising around us."

"Oh, for sure." She waved a hand. "He's human, so this would be a bit of a shock and all."

Penny handed her a cup, and she tipped it back. "Hmm. Taste's lemony."

"Just enough left for you, girl." Penny spooned the last of the liquid into a final cup and handed it to me.

I'd had fairy honey before, and the thick liquid was nothing short of epic, with just the right amount of sweetness. This drink had that same sweetness, but there was a sour after kick that had to be the spell.

Suzy was right, the honey faded to a lemon quality. I said so, and Penny replied, "That's the nepeta." Then she grabbed her cane and headed to the door. "Come on now. We're on a time crunch."

A few minutes later, we were in the car. Penny was driving, and I no longer thought Suzy the worst driver ever.

When the car tipped on two wheels for a second time, Penny squealing with laughter, I glanced at Suzy to find her wide-eyed and gripping the sides of her seat.

"Penny, we need to not be noticed if possible!" I yelped as she wove around cars, driving down the center lane of the road.

"We also need to hurry. Once you take the shape of your animal, you have one hour to get in and out and back to the car." She glanced in the rearview mirror, and I grabbed the back of the seat. Penny was not looking forward, and a car was headed straight for us.

Suzy grabbed the wheel and cranked it hard to the left, saving our bacon.

"I'm sorry, I'll do better," Suzy breathed out. "I promise never to drive like that again."

I would have grinned had I not been biting back a serious dose of nausea from all the weaving in and out of traffic.

What I will say is that Penny got us out to the old fort in about half the time it normally took.

Probably a good thing it was after midnight and there weren't many people on the road.

As we approached the long road stretching out toward the fort, swamp on both sides, she pulled over. "This is where I'll wait. I can feel a boundary line up ahead. In animal form, you won't trip any alarms, not if you cross it one at a time. Spread out. Be cagey. Like a cat."

Her wink at me was not lost on Eammon.

"What shape are we taking?" he barked. Though it might have been a bit more like a meow.

As he was talking, I got a serious twinge in my guts to let out a fart. Like the cramping, bloated feeling of air trying to push its way out of your body, and you cross your legs in the hopes that it doesn't escape you and, if it does, no one notices.

Suzy leapt out of the car, and apparently, I wasn't the only one struggling. A fart tore out of her that sounded as though it could have ripped her pants.

Kinkly giggled.

Eammon laughed. Only when he laughed, it came out both ends. He was still in the car. The noise was not lacking in smell.

Gagging, Eric and I tumbled out of the car at the same time. Again, my guts grumbled, and a squeaker snuck out.

"That's the spell activating in your body," Penny said.

"I'm going to use that excuse the next time I let one slip." I leaned on the trunk of the car as a chorus of rumbles worked its way out of all of us.

Kinkly squealed and flew to the other side of the road. "I swear there is a green fog rolling from all of you!"

Eammon had been the first one to drink the spell, and he was the first one to shift.

Into a fluffy, white, stub-legged cat with a long tail. Blue eyes blinked up at me, and I fully expected him to meow as he stepped out of his clothes that were now piled on the ground. Kinkly flew down and caught them all up and tossed them into the back of the car.

Nope, Eammon didn't meow. He spoke. "What do I look like?"

"A cat." Suzy groaned as she bent at the waist.

"A what? Damn it all, Penny, you know I hate cats! I though you just needed a cat for the spell, not that you'd turn me into one!" He spun around and tried to jump back into the car, but his legs were too stubby, and he bounced off the step instead and flipped over.

I shouldn't have laughed. A fart tore out of me, and the cramps doubled down. I struggled to breathe over the snickers as Eammon cussed Penny out and she shushed him.

"Don't be a pussy, Eammon," I said.

He shot a look at me. "Don't you start with me."

Suzy gasped and took a short, sharp breath. "Gods, this is terrible! Penny, you should have warned us!"

Cat Eammon and Eric bobbed heads in agreement.

Eric stumbled and slid onto his knees, his body shimmering and then disappearing in a little puff of smoke. Out of his shirt peeked a cat with big hazel eyes, all scrawny and leggy with a whip-thin tail. His coat was a simple brown coat, slick to his body.

"How do I look?"

"Like you. But as a cat," I said, hit by another cramp that I breathed through. Really, I didn't know what they were all whining about. Then again, I had just dealt with the ovarian cysts the day before.

Suzy's cat form was peach-toned with blue eyes. She was petite and just super cute as she was on two legs. Eric slunk over next to her, Eammon joining them with a sigh, and they waited on me.

As far as I could see, everyone's cat coat was close to their hair color, so I expected to be blond.

Nope.

After I crumpled to the ground, I looked down at my legs and saw I was a deep gray cat with black paws and, I looked over my shoulder, a black tail.

"Your ears are black too. Cool markings," Suzy said.

"Get on out of here," Penny said. "You have less than an hour now, fifty-nine minutes."

"Okay, let's go," I said as we hurried off. "We need to see if there is any easy way in. What the layout is, who is helping them, all that. Gather information, don't get caught."

I bounded out in front of the others, feeling a spring in my step that hadn't been there when I was human. Of course, the fairy honey was also coursing through my veins.

The four of us raced toward the fort, bounding and leaping over clumps of bushes, splashing through bits of water.

"Sure hope there aren't any gators," Eammon spat out as we raced past some deeper water. I found myself scuttling to the side, closer to the road.

Ahead, I felt a low buzzing sensation. "You feel that?"

"I'd bet good money that's the boundary line Penny mentioned," Suzy said.

I flicked my ears, loving the way they moved on command. "I can feel it like an electrical charge. Let's split up to help keep us from triggering it."

She and Eric went to the right before I could suggest it might be better for us to go one by one. I sighed. Eammon and I raced to the left as we continued on our way.

"I'm impressed you can keep up with those little legs." I bounced over a downed log that had eyes.

The gator snapped at me but missed, and I howled as I ran a little faster. Yeah, that was not how I wanted to go out. Eaten by a gator while I was a pussy cat. No thank you.

Eammon grunted as though he hadn't just seen me leap through the jaws of death. "Easy with fairy honey. I'll be sore tomorrow."

"Me too."

"Assuming we're both still alive."

I laughed. "At this rate, probably not."

He laughed with me, and just like that we were having a good time. Sure, we were running into the vipers' den, and Eammon probably wasn't enjoying the whole cat thing nearly as much as I was, but we were friends on an adventure.

The fort rose up ahead of us, and we scooted across the bridge and in through the iron grated door that was closed, but the square grates were just big enough for us to slip through.

On the other side was the open courtyard showing us the ring fort in all its glory. The brick and stone structure was huge, a perfect circle on top of the ground, with the far side facing out across the mouth of the river.

But as soon as we were through the door, I could feel every hair on my little body stand at attention and I was no longer looking at the fort.

Of course, it didn't help that there was a row of zombies standing guard all the way down the path. I backed up, a low growl rumbling from me.

Eammon, on the other hand, hopped left and right like a prize boxer, his back arched as he spat and hissed. "Go on, I'll keep the beggars busy!"

He dodged to the left, and the zombies lurched after him. Once they got moving, they weren't the slow dawdling zombies of yesterday. These undead were quick. And they were snapping their teeth as they reached for his fluffy little ass.

"Go!" Eammon hissed as he zipped across the courtyard, his bright white fur all but glowing in the darkness. My gray and black coat blended into the shadows, serving me well. I raced forward, following the tingling sensation through the fort. Thanking my stars that my gray and black coat blended so well with the darkness. There were other zombies shuffling, and I easily avoided them.

Two of them walked right past me as I crouched in the shadows.

I made my way around the ring wall that made up the fort, peeking into doors and snooping through jail cells as I followed the feeling of pressure. I paused at one of the slits that looked down at the underground bunkers that looked like the backs of whales bursting out of the ocean.

And who should I see walking down into one of them?

Crash.

I slipped through the slit in the wall, leapt for the ground, and raced across the open stretch. I could feel the weight of eyes on me again, but no one popped into view, and even if someone was watching, they'd only see a cat.

I made it to the steps that led down into the bunker in a matter of seconds.

There was no murmur of voices.

No light shining out of the dark space.

Swallowing hard, I slunk down the steps. A whiff of Crash's unique scent curled up my nose and my tail twitched. Damn him for smelling so ducking yummy.

My cat eyes were damn perfect in the dark. I could see the outlines and shapes of doorways even though there wasn't a speck of light. With nothing else to go by, I followed Crash's scent to an indentation in the wall that led to a hollowed-out room. A dead end.

Only I knew better than that. His scent circled around the center of the floor.

There was the slightest indentation in the floor, and I paced it. Jumped on it. "Open, damn it," I finally hissed at it.

Nothing.

Screwing up my nose, I thought about what I had on me.

I snooped around, pushing with my nose and paws on any bit of stone or wall that looked like it could be a hidden button. I tried jumping on the opening again.

"Open sesame!" I growled.

Tail lashing, I paced the tight space. How the hell was I going to follow him now?

Think, girl, think! Joseph has necromancer in him, right? Power over the dead. I had that. Maybe the door could be opened with a connection to the dead?

I perked up, ears flicking forward. Maybe that would get me in?

I wrapped my tail around my paws and sat still as a statue in the middle of the trap door as I reached for that warm power within me. There, in my left hind leg! I drew it up through me, and it cooled until it was nearly icy.

Bowing my head, I pressed my nose to the floor.

The circular lines cracked silently and slowly swung sideways. Well oiled, was my first thought.

A set of stairs led nearly straight down into the earth. I leapt to the bottom, landing silently and ever so grateful for my borrowed form. Who would have thought a little housecat would be so damn handy in a spying situation? Not me.

I was at the bottom of the stairs before voices curled through the underground tunnels. I let my ears lead me and hurried as fast as I dared. The last thing I wanted was to lose this shape and end up buck naked in the enemy's camp.

Jaysus, don't let my thoughts curse me.

The voices were a lot further away than I'd realized, the acoustics of the place skewed by the narrow hallway and solid stone walls.

Light finally flickered ahead, and I slowed my pace.

"What do you mean you couldn't capture her? I thought you'd gained her trust?" The voice was smooth and cultured and not all that different from Roderick's, to be honest. Right down to the accent. Just like what had come out of the zombie's mouth.

I wanted to get a look at him.

"She suspected something was off," Crash said, his deep rumble calling to me.

Crawling on my belly, I peeked into the room. Huge and circular with tunnels leading away from it in at least ten directions if I included mine.

Two for every point of the pentagram foundation.

A chill swept me, and I pinned myself even closer to the floor.

"Did you ever get her to tell you where it is?"

I turned to see Crash shake his head. The defeat on his face was obvious to me, though I wasn't sure his friend would understand what he was seeing.

"No."

"Pity." The person who had to be Joseph stood up from behind a hulking desk. I honestly hadn't noticed him before because Crash had commanded my gaze.

He was rather short. The man from the hospital in the limo, I was sure of it!

Short and perfectly manicured. His bright blond hair was smoothed back and tied at the nape of his neck in a fashion from a bygone era. I would have guessed his eyes to be a dark brown, maybe even black. His clothing was pressed and so clean I'd have laid money that everything was brand new. Black pants, shiny black boots, a deep red shirt, tie, and suit coat. That part was modern even if his hair wasn't.

He circled around the desk and leaned on it, looking up at Crash. "Have you grown soft, Crash? I wouldn't have thought it possible, but perhaps you do *love* her? I mean, I know you never really loved Karissa. She was a conquest, nothing else. A means to an end." He leaned back on his hands, which only made him shorter.

He didn't seem to mind.

Crash looked away from him. "She is unique, and I find her incredibly . . . intriguing. But that being said, I know where my loyalties lie. Do not question me, Joe."

Gawd. He might as well have stuck me with a knife.

Joe, as Crash had called him, grimaced. "Is the spell still running smoothly?"

Crash nodded. "Yes. The witch has made sure of it. The cauldron is holding."

Witch. Did he mean Missy? Come on boys, give me some names!

Joseph drummed his fingers on the table, then scooped up a sheet of paper and looked it over before setting it back on the table. "The plans are all laid out. We are still missing a few ingredients, but we have time."

My ears tipped forward. Was it possible their master plan was on that table? Thirty feet away from me?

Heart pounding, I knew I had two choices. I could run back to Penny and the others and tell them or . . . I could try and get that paper.

Yup.

Time to play the innocent pussy.

19

Think like a cat, think like a cat, think like a cat.
Cats were self-righteous, thought they owned the damn world, and took what they wanted.

I stood up, stretched with my black-tipped paws out in front of me and sauntered across the room, sniffing the ground here and there.

Acting for all the world like I belonged in the place.

I didn't look up at the two men.

Saw a spider. Chased it around the room until I caught it under my paws.

"What. The. Hell. Is. That?" Joseph said. "Did you leave the door open?"

"It's a cat," Crash drawled. "And I must have. Unless one of the other tunnels is open?"

Joseph grunted and threw a freaking bookend at me. I dodged the heavy item, stared right at him and hissed.

Motherducker thought it was cool to throw things at cats, did he? For good measure, I fluffed up and arched my back. Might have even hopped sideways and batted at the ground.

Come on dude, try me. Just try me. It's been a day, and I could use someone I don't like as a solid punching bag.

Crash grunted. "I don't think that cat likes you."

"They rarely do. Go check the doors."

I let myself de-puff and skulked through the room, drawing closer and closer to the table. I could do this. I just had to hop up on the table, grab the paper in my mouth and make a run for it.

There was no way they'd catch me. Not in the dark.

I'd run straight back through the tunnel, use my magic to open the door if it had closed behind me, and then I'd be good.

I was under the table now.

I let out a meow.

"Jesus Christ, get it out of here!" Joseph yelled, and he kicked at me.

Murder mittens were a wonderful thing. I slashed at him through his thin dress pants, feeling my claws dig into his soft flesh. He screamed and fell backward, and I used that moment to leap up onto the table. Where I couldn't help it.

I arched my back and hissed at him again.

Duck with me and my town, will you?

I didn't dare look at Crash. Because as far as I could tell, he still hadn't left, and what if he looked into my eyes and saw me? What if he saw through this shape?

Joseph was hopping around, fumbling for his leg. "Damn it, that ducking cat gouged me!"

I was on top of the paper. I could do this.

I bent my head as if sniffing, then grabbed it in my jaws and leapt from the table.

Only to be caught by a pair of hands I knew all too well.

A pair of hands that sent shivers of desire rippling through me. Didn't matter that I was a cat. A pitiful meow slipped from my mouth.

His fingers massaged my back, moving up along my neck. "Kitten, what are you doing down here?"

"Just kill it," Joseph snapped.

"Joe, it's a cat," Crash said.

I clutched at the paper with my front paws and mouth. I could see some of the words. The spell I knew they were using, *Leviathan mort*. Names that I didn't recognize. Was it a list of people on the Dark Council?

Crash tried to take the paper from me, but I held onto it. Another pitiful meow.

And then my guts rumbled.

"She's hungry," Crash said, and I just couldn't look at him. I couldn't look at the big, strong man who was being so soft with a stray cat. I couldn't look at him because *this* was the man I'd been falling in love with. *This* was the guy I wanted.

He was still in there.

And maybe that was what hurt the most.

"Kill it," Joseph snapped, and there was an instant change in the man holding me. His fingers tightened, and I realized there was some sort of compulsion involved. He took a deep breath and let it out.

"You can't force me anymore," Crash said, and I dared to peek at his face. "Not for something like that. Not any more than you could make me hurt Bree. I have my loyalty to the council, and I will do everything in my power to see our plans through, but I will not hurt her."

"Then she's a fucking liability!" Joseph roared. "She has it in her to stop this, and you damn well know it!"

Crash closed those gorgeous eyes of his. "I know."

Damn it. I wanted to hate him. I knew we were on opposite sides—truly on opposite sides. I tightened my paws on the paper, but I let him keep stroking my back, from the nape of my neck all the way down to the tip of my tail. The purring was unintentional. The drooling I couldn't stop. Crash pulled up a chair and sat down with me against his chest, his fingers working their way through my fur in ways that were truly melting me.

He tried to take the paper, and I hissed at him, all the melting gone in a flash. So, he'd softened me up to take the paper, huh?

"Okay, okay, it's yours," he murmured.

Footsteps echoed through the big circular room, and the two men turned toward the newcomer. I peeked over Crash's shoulder. I didn't recognize the woman. She had super long legs, bright red hair, and boobs that were in no way possibly real. She wore a leather catsuit as vibrant as her hair.

"There is a disturbance in the courtyard." I might not have recognized her appearance, but that voice . . . I *knew* that voice.

Monica the shapeshifter was on the Dark Council.

She was the one who'd helped Crash get Gran's house . . . and tried to have me executed for the murder of Alan.

"What kind of disturbance?" Joseph—limping, I gladly saw—made his way around the table and straightened up the papers I'd skidded over.

"The undead are chasing a bright white . . . something around the courtyard. I think it's a cat."

Duck. Me.

I felt all eyes land on me.

Crash's hands tightened around me.

I tried to launch myself out of his arms before his hold got too tight. Only my guts had other ideas.

My stomach rumbled, and I let out a rather loud kitty fart.

Crash chuckled. "A farting cat?"

Of course, that wasn't the end of it. Not by a long shot.

The change in my body was so swift and violent, accompanied by a fart comparable to the sudden deflating of a ten-foot balloon as I went from tiny little kitten to large-bottomed naked woman, that I knocked Crash backward and off the chair. As if the propulsion of the fart had compelled us.

His eyes locked on mine.

I had the paper in my mouth.

I may have grinned at him. Damn it, in for a penny, in for a damn pound of the man. I grabbed him and kissed him over the paper.

"Grab her!" Joseph yelled, and I scrambled up, paper still clutched in my now-human mouth, and ran for the tunnel. I didn't look back.

Hopefully my quick kiss had frozen Crash to the spot. I knew he was faster than me. The only reason I'd beaten him last time was because I'd had Skeletor to scoop my butt up.

The darkness enclosed me, and I ran the straight line until I jammed my toes into the bottom of the steps.

Lurching forward, glad that the fairy honey was still coursing through me, I hit the top of the stairs and then grabbed hold of my magic and all but shoved it at the door. It swung open as someone below brushed their fingers against the sole of my left foot.

I spun, slamming my magic back into the door and prayed it would slow my pursuers down as it closed on the person's fingers.

Monica's fingers, by the nail color.

Which meant Crash hadn't come after me yet.

Bare naked, I bolted through the tunnel, up and out into the night air. My skin was flushed, and I barely felt the cool breeze rolling in off the river. I did, however, see a very naked Eric running full tilt ahead of me.

And a naked Eammon.

"Run!" screamed Suzy as she joined in from the side.

Jaysus, what the hell was wrong with us? Could none of us keep track of time? It hadn't felt like an hour, but obviously the time had slipped by.

I started to laugh, I'll admit it. If for no other reason than the sheer ridiculousness of the four of us, buck naked, ending our covert mission by running for our lives. Did I mention that we were buck naked, bits flapping in the wind?

Yeah, good times had by all.

The only thing we had going for us was the fairy honey coursing through our veins. Eric busted us out of the main door next to the big iron grate.

"I got the zombies all locked up in a jail cell!" Eammon laughed.

From there, we ran straight down the road to where Penny was snoozing in the car.

"Start the car!" I yelled. "Kinkly, wake her up and start the damn car!"

Because I had no doubt there would be pursuers. Then again, we'd taken them by surprise and the worst of the guards—the zombies—had been taken care of by Eammon. I high-fived him as we ran.

Dared a look behind us.

The fort was lit up now, every light in the place looked to be on. But where were the bad guys chasing us down?

Where were the monsters that had to be working with the Dark Council? This felt too easy.

I had a single piece of paper gripped in my hands. But what had the others learned?

We tumbled into the car as Penny jerked awake, her hand on the ignition and gas before the last door was shut.

Cranking the wheel, she peeled the car's tires on the pavement, and we were away.

All in one piece.

Naked, but in one piece.

Go, team!

20

Penny drove a little slower on the way back. She kept yawning in between asking questions.

"Well, what happened?"

"I kept the undead busy." Eammon leaned back in the seat, and I looked away. Somehow I'd ended up in the front passenger seat, and I was immensely grateful for that fact. "I kept them running and herded them all into one of the cells. Just kept doing it till this bossy gal in a red leather suit showed up. That lass had a meanness to her."

"That's Monica," I said. "She's a shapeshifter. She was the realtor who sold the house to Crash and also the lawyer who was going to put me on trial for Alan's murder. She's on the Dark Council."

Eric shimmied into his pants and pulled a shirt on. Suzy seemed content to be naked up against him, but then again, she was a siren. "I found a few of the leaders running the show. And I saw Feish with them."

I didn't wince, though I wanted to. "That's to be expected. Where Crash goes, she goes."

Eric nodded. "True. I only recognized one other person."

"Who?" Eammon said.

"The bookseller," Eric said, and it took me a minute to put two and two together.

"The leprechaun?" I blurted out. "He was the one who sold me Gran's book. And he was the one who . . ." My mind raced. He was the one who'd led me to the book of spells and curses. But Stark had said *he* was behind it.

"He's working for Stark," I breathed out. "I'm sure of it. There is no way that they would have let that book out of their hands." I blinked and looked around the car. "Where is Kinkly?"

Penny hit the brakes, and since none of us had seatbelts on, we all slammed forward.

"Suzy, please drive," I said.

Penny didn't grumble but scooted closer to me. Eric handed me my clothes, which I yanked on as Suzy drove us back toward the compound.

Kinkly had gone in too, quiet as a mouse.

What if she'd been caught?

What if she'd turned us in?

"Hey, that spell only lasted forty-five minutes!" Eammon barked suddenly.

"I said about an hour!" Penny snapped at him. "Maybe it was an hour from taking it!"

I stared out the windshield as they argued, my hip bag slung over my shoulder. Barely registering what I was doing, I reached into it for Robert's finger bone. I just hung onto it a minute.

"You're weird," Alan grumbled up from the depths.

"And you're dead," I said. "So, I think I win here."

He grumped and disappeared into my bag.

Suzy leaned forward over the wheel as she drove. Squinted out the windshield. "What *is* that?"

"Pull over," I shouted, seeing exactly what it was. Kinkly. Kinkly carrying something way bigger than her little body.

Behind her came a string of goblins. There were the troops I'd thought we'd be dealing with. Just a little on the slow side.

I leapt out of the car and ran to meet the glittering, pissed-off fairy.

"You left without me!" she screeched as she dropped Gran's spell book into my hands and zipped around my head. And then she giggled. "But watching the four of you run away from danger, bare-ass naked, was worth every droplet of sweat. And you made a great distraction. Nobody was looking at me, because they all had their eyes on you."

I pointed behind her. "Except you brought goblins."

The goblins saw us and the car, and picked up steam, screaming and hollering. Controlled by Crash no doubt.

I thought about fighting them, I really did. But I was tired. "You all really want to fight me when I killed Derek not that long ago?"

There were maybe a dozen of them and they slowed, exchanging looks with one another. The leader stepped up. "Boss said to make it look good. Like we came after you hard."

Boss. Crash.

I sighed. "Well, good job. We're terrified!" I put a hand to my cheek and gasped. They grinned. Saluted one another and turned to go back to the fort.

Crash once more trying to protect me. I watched them go. "Tell him . . . tell him that I hoped he liked petting me."

They cackled, the humor right up their alley apparently. Let Crash chew on that.

Then again, I doubted we'd be as lucky if we tried to break into the fort a second time. We'd tipped our hand. That wasn't great.

I slid into the front seat and clutched the book to my chest. "Kink, you saved the day."

"Of course I did." She flipped her hair and smiled. I held up a finger, and she slapped her palm against it.

Once more we were on our way to the safe house.

"Suzy, what did you find?" I asked. "Anything?"

She shivered. "They have people in cages. All sorts of supernaturals." Her eyes shot to mine, and I could see her trying to find a way to soften whatever it was she had to say. "I followed a zombie down. The doors open for the undead from what I could see."

"Go on, it's okay."

"They have Corb," she said. "He's there. Sarge too."

I clenched my jaw even as my heart panged for my two friends. Well, for Sarge surely. Corb was kind of a secondary concern. "Okay. We'll get them out when we stop Joseph tomorrow."

Eric cleared his throat. "There is one other thing. The goblins are helping them, as you saw back there. They had only just arrived, and it looked like they were awaiting orders in the underground part of the fort."

The goblins that I'd helped Crash take rulership of. I just leaned over my knees. "Undead and goblins."

"Sounds about right."

They were all quiet a moment. Penny tapped me on the leg. "And what is this?"

My piece of paper crinkled, and I told them about the conversation I'd witnessed between Joseph and Crash.

Their questions were much like mine. What item had they been talking about? What was Crash supposed to find?

I finally unfolded the paper, spreading it out on my lap.

Of course, it wasn't as simple as "Plans to take over Savannah" or even "The who's who of the Dark Council."

Nope, there were names on one side. Corb and Sarge were on that list, both of their names crossed out. Other names I didn't recognize. "This side is a hit list of sorts, I think."

I showed it to Eric and Eammon in the back. Eammon let out a low whistle. "Your name is on there, Bree. Right at the bottom."

Yup, it was. I'd chosen not to mention that part out loud.

I flipped it over. It was a spell, all right, but not the one I'd expected. Not the one to raise the undead.

No. This was the spell that Clovis had been trying to recreate. There was no name, but I recognized some of the stanzas. The one with the fairy cross and the angel wings. I blinked a few times as I read the rhyme in its entirety, feeling my blood pound in my head.

Of demon skin and angel wing
Of stolen cross and healing spring
Blood of a ghost, and an unmarked grave
Soul of a witch, and a siren's cave.
Bound swiftly neath the darkest night
Those of the blood shall have their sight
Of death and power, of magic and pain
That which comes shall find those slain
Raised anew and given life
A waning once, this call is strife
One last line to lock this spell
A soul whose blood has tasted hell.
Thus shall the ambrosia be brewed and given life to death.

"They . . . they are looking for the pieces to this spell," I said as I held the paper out to Penny.

This was the master plan. They were looking for the ingredients to this spell. The zombies, were they part of it?

"Are you sure that this isn't the same—"

Penny shuddered. "No, this is not the spell they are doing now. *Leviathan mort* is bad but girl, this here," she flapped the paper, "this is worse. And I don't even know what it does exactly but the vibration coming from it is beyond dark."

I felt like it was there, on the tip of my brain, if I could just pull the pieces together.

The sky lightened as we drove.

Only it wasn't that close to dawn. I rolled the window down, and the night air rolled in. A flicker of green in front of us drew my eyes. The sky glowed a deep, thrumming green as the moon slid through its descent.

"The green moon," Penny breathed out. "Pray that we stop them tomorrow."

Ten minutes later, we were back at her place, and she had Suzy drive her old clunker into an equally clunky garage.

"They'll be looking for us," Penny said as she banged the garage door with her cane then turned to me. "Why don't you go get Celia?"

I paused between steps. "You think she could come with me?"

"Missy untethered her. So, she can come with you as surely as that ex of yours does." Penny gave me a wink. "Go on. But be quick. You know if Crash comes looking, he'll go straight to that house."

Still buzzing on fairy honey, I knew I could get to the house and back in time for a few hours of sleep. Good enough.

I jogged away from my friends. It hadn't been a good night, but it could have been worse.

I was Crash's weakness. The thought made me smile until my mouth slipped into a frown. I wasn't sure I could be that girl who used a man's feelings for her against him. Then again, he'd been lying to me this whole damn time. Sure, maybe he'd been hoping the Dark Council wasn't going to show up. But it seemed more likely that he'd been sent here to get Savannah ready.

As much as I wanted to moon over him and try to figure out his motives, this really wasn't the time.

"Let him go, girl," I muttered to myself as I ran. My body felt amazing, at least, all the aches and pains missing while the fairy honey did its magic.

Damn, that fairy honey was going to leave me hurting. I reached the Sorrel-Weed house and crept past it. Sure, the house ghosts were calmer now that the resident demon was gone, but the place still gave me the willies.

Slinking between the two lots, I let myself in through the back door of Gran's house.

Keeping the lights off, I made my way through the kitchen to the stairs and climbed up quickly. I peered first into my room first. On a whim, I grabbed a bag and stuffed it with a few clothes, and my favorite pillow.

"Gran?" I whispered.

"Bree?" Her voice echoed from her room, and I made my way across to her. She sat on the edge of the bed, her hands folded in her lap. "What are you doing back here? Its not safe!"

"Came to get you. Come on."

She held up her hands, and I noticed they were shaking. "I can't."

"You can. Missy untethered you."

She took a deep, shuddering breath. "I am afraid for you, honey girl."

I smiled. "Me too."

Her head snapped up, and I smiled a bit wider. "But gawd in heaven, Gran. What would be so bad about hanging out as ghosts and spooking the shit out of people if I get myself dead dead? We would be a team, even then."

Her bottom lip trembled, and she bowed her head. "You are the best of all of us, Bree. And you don't even know it."

I held out my hand, and she stood and took it. Like with Alan, I could hold onto her even though she looked insubstantial.

Down the stairs we went, and I paused at the front door, remembering the yellow envelope that had been taped there like an unexploded bomb just waiting to be detonated. Was it *still* waiting for me? I creaked the door open and peeked at the front of the door. Yup, my name glared back at me. Beckoning me.

Like a damn sticky trap for a stupid ant.

"You should take it," Gran said. "He was pretty torn up when he left here. And despite what happened, he is not a bad man."

I gave her an incredulous look. "Are you serious?"

"I've known him a long time, Bree." She sighed. "He . . . I won't make excuses. He has to figure it out. But at the core, he is not a bad man."

With a grimace, I grabbed the bottom corner of the manila envelope and tore it down.

I stuffed it into my hip bag and threw my other bag onto my back. "Out the kitchen door," I said as I led the way through the house. Just in case someone was watching.

Which, with my luck, they were.

We stepped out into the green glowing night, and I led the way across the yard, past the Sorrel-Weed house, and found my feet pausing. What we needed was some firepower for the next day. Some unrepentant crazy motherducker who just wanted to cause chaos. Someone or something that wouldn't mind going up against zombies and goblins.

"Gran, you ever hired a demon before?"

21

Gran stared at me like I'd lost my damn mind. Which was fair, all things considered.

"Honey girl. Are you feeling all right? You did not just ask me about hiring a demon, did you?"

I kept staring at the Sorrel-Weed house. "I mean. If we *could* hire a demon, even for a couple of hours, and set it loose on Joseph and his minions . . . it would be a hell of a challenge for them. Maybe we could hire a few demons even?"

I kept staring at the house, thinking about how hard it had been for me to deal with that critter.

A little chaos couldn't hurt, right? I mean, Joseph had Crash and his goblin crew and a whole bunch of undead zombies. And it's something Crash and Feish would never expect from me, not after my dealings with the bloodborn demon.

We were past the Sorrel-Weed house now, but I was still mulling the idea over. "Gran. Seriously, what do you think?"

She walked silently beside me, and I mean that literally—it wasn't like her shoes tapped on the sidewalk. "There is never a good reason to hire a demon, honey girl. Never. They can't be controlled. And the price is always too high. Even if the state of the shadow world in Savannah is worse than it has ever been."

Her words sent a chill down my spine, and I reached into my bag for the tarot card I'd been given. Alan came tumbling out. "What did I miss?"

I ignored him and held the card out for Gran. "Does this count? I mean, we both know what it signifies. I've been given two of them."

Gran sucked in a sharp nonexistent breath. "Ten of swords."

"Yup." I nodded.

Alan tried to grab the card, but his hand went right through it. "Is that a tarot card? You're ridiculous, Bree. Psychic readings are scams to sucker foolish people into believing what they want to believe." I'd heard that tone enough times during our marriage to know he was about to deliver a tirade on why we were wrong, and he was right.

I snapped my fingers in his face, then made a pinching motion with my fingers and thumb. "Not tonight, Alan. Not tonight."

"There is always a choice," Gran said, her words echoing Eammon's from earlier. "And a deal with a demon, any demon, is beyond dangerous. You barely survived the last encounter, and now you want to willingly go into business with one? No. It is a terrible idea." She crossed her arms over her bosom and tipped her head downward. "Let me think on what else might be done. You don't understand the shadow world like I do."

Her words cut me. I hadn't suggested the demon thing lightly, and I had a gut feeling it was one of the only things we could do to stop Joseph. I knew I didn't understand the shadow world like she did, but . . .

I cleared my throat and schooled my features.

"Well, whatever you come up with has to be quick, because of the whole blood storm thing, plus the raising of the dead all over Savannah. Kind of a big deal," I said as we walked along.

She waved one hand at me, shushing me without saying a word.

Damn it, I didn't like feeling at odds with Gran. Not after all we'd been through.

The green light from the moon was finally easing off. The sun rose early this time of year.

A sudden wash of fatigue rolled over me, and I stumbled, grabbing a fence for support, and had to fight to stay upright.

"Seriously, Bree, you need to work out more if a simple walk has you stumbling to your knees," Alan said.

"And you need to tell me why you're spying on me for Marge, but I don't see that happening," I threw the words at him.

"I'm not a spy," he said, but the lie was heavy on his mouth.

"Remember that I know you, Alan? I especially know when you're lying, you dumbass," I said. I could see the safe house ahead of us now, and I forced my tired legs to hurry.

At the top of the stairs, I almost went to my knees, but I managed to get to the door.

Of course, it was locked.

"Penny," I thumped a fist on the door. "It's me."

The door swung open, and I about collapsed through the space.

Penny grinned down at me. "Fairy honey wearing off?"

"Uh-huh." I used the door frame to wobble to my feet.

"Sleeping mats are over there." She pointed with her cane to the corner of the room she'd done all the spelling in. "You got Celia?" Gran strode in through the door, and Penny turned her head. "Oh, there you are."

"You can see her?" I limped over to the one mat not occupied. Eric and Suzy were curled up under a blanket, and Eammon lay flat on his back next to them, snoring.

The thin foam mat looked damn heavenly, but I knew that I was going to regret sleeping on it. I could already feel the points of my hips and shoulders as I lay down and curled on my side.

"Yes, your gran and I could both see ghosts," Penny said. "Go to sleep, girl. I'll keep watch."

I held a hand up with a thumb pointed to the ceiling, then tucked my hand into my hip pocket and closed my fingers around Robert's finger bone. I could almost feel him holding my hand back.

I closed my eyes and fell fast asleep.

Part of me had thought I'd dream about Crash again. That he would tell me it was all a ruse, and he was a spy like Oster Boon, the leprechaun who was obviously working with Stark.

But Crash didn't visit me in my dreams.

No, my dreams were not so simple as that.

I groaned as I looked around.

I stood in a patch of dark forest, the branches reaching high overhead. The trees blocked out the light of the moon, which I somehow knew was behind me. A green moon like the one that had lit up the sky tonight.

A figure stepped out from between the trees, so cloaked in shadows it was hard to see if it was a man or a woman or something else. Maybe a demon?

The figure crooked a finger and turned, cloak flaring out around muscular legs. So maybe a man? Or a really buff woman.

"Who are you?" I called out, not moving from my spot. "I don't follow strangers. Not even for candy."

The chuckle was low and decidedly male. "I will not harm you, Breena."

With the voice came a flare of magic that I recognized right away. Fae.

I tightened my hold on the bone in my palm, and a second later Robert stood next to me. This wasn't skeleton Robert, though. His eyes were serious and blue, and he held my hand as tightly as I held his.

"New adventure?" he asked.

"Stranger danger," I whispered.

"Come, Breena, there is limited time, bring your friend," the cloaked fae called back to me.

I took a step, then another and another, Robert right with me.

"You call me in a way no one else could," he said as we walked. "You shouldn't be able to make me manifest in your dreams."

"She is not so like you as you think," the fae said. He'd been twenty feet ahead of us, but suddenly, in the way of dreams, he was right there, three feet from my face. The cloak hid his features, and he didn't seem inclined to pull it back. "While she is a sentinel as you were, Robert of the Damned, she is not of the same blood."

My jaw dropped. "Robert of the Damned?"

"Another time." The fae held his hands out and flipped them over, and a ball of light began to spin and grow above his cupped palms. "The shadow world depends on sentinels to do what others will not. Celia does not understand that you have an innate drive to protect this town. You will do what you must, no matter the cost."

The spinning globe slowly lit up his features. A thick white scruff covered his lower face, but I got a glimpse of a crooked nose that looked like it had been broken before and eyes the perfect shade of blue. What bits of his hair I could see were silvery, likely blond when he was younger.

"What's your name?"

"The demon you need to contact is Stavros. He walks and moves about as a human. But he is the strongest demon that calls Savannah home. Tell him that Altin sent you." He held out his hand, and the ball of light floated between us. Altin. "Take it. Offer it in exchange for his help but not right away."

"Make him work for it?" I offered.

He smiled under the scruff and stepped back. "Make him sweat, Breena, and you will gain his respect. The respect of a demon can go a long way."

I let go of Robert and reached for the ball of light. When I touched it, it solidified into a solid ball of glass filled with swirling colors.

I looked up, and Altin was gone. "Robert?"

I blinked and found myself staring up at the ceiling of Penny's rundown house. Robert stood next to me, swaying side to side.

"Friend. Dream," he said, and pointed to my stomach.

I looked down to see the glass ball cradled on my belly. I sat up, wincing as my lower back screeched a protest. Rolling the ball in my hands, I stared at the lights within it, mesmerized by the flickering, swirling beauty. I could almost see images if I stared hard enough.

"What is that?" Suzy said, crawling over to me.

I showed her. "A gift."

"Yeah, but what is it?"

"I don't know—"

"An orb of power," Penny said from across the room. "Only one fae I know can make those, and he's supposed to be dead. So do tell me how you got one when you were sleeping?"

I stared at Penny. "I'm guessing this was from my grandfather then? Altin gave it to me."

Penny nodded. "He didn't go by that name when he was with Celia."

I smiled, thinking of my shady family history. "He went by Al, didn't he?" Al. Short for Altin.

"That he did."

I tucked it into my hip bag. "Alan, you stay here." I didn't see my gran which was good. She wasn't going to agree with what I was up to.

A quick look at the clock revealed it was only ten in the morning. We had twelve hours to deal with Joseph.

Twelve hours to find a way to stop the undead from popping up across Savannah like mushrooms after a rain. And I had a demon to talk to.

No problem, no problem at all. But before I did that . . . I had to look at the note Crash had left me.

I had to read his final words to me and put whatever 'us' could have been to rest.

22

I left the others in Penny's front room and let myself into a small room off the kitchen. It had the smell of stale garlic and old onions, so maybe it had been a pantry at one point.

The pull string for the light swung after I clicked on the single bulb. I pulled the yellow manila envelope out of my hip bag and looked it over.

The first thing I did was connect with that part of me that was witchy. The smell of herbs floated around me and I breathed it in, then let my hands run lightly over the envelope, looking for a spell. Or maybe feeling for a spell was a better way of describing it.

Nothing.

Then I pulled up that side of me that was connected to death and did the same thing. Clean there too.

Swallowing hard, I let out a slow breath and tried for the first time to truly connect with the part of me that was fae. A hot flash ran through my body, making me tingle in all sorts of inappropriate places. As if Crash was right there with me, touching me, drawing sensations through me.

But I got no bad vibes from the envelope, no burst of magic. Nothing.

Which meant he'd just left me a note.

I opened it up and a single sheet of paper slid out.

I recognized his writing.

Dear Bree,

I cannot tell you how much these last few weeks have meant to me. Even though I knew I'd have to let you go, I wanted to have as much of you as I could in the moments left to me. You make me unexpectedly happy, but I love you enough to know that you need and deserve your freedom from me and all that I carry.

Do not think for a moment that this goodbye has anything to do with you. My past has caught up to me, and there is no way for us to be together. I know you too well. You would never agree with the Dark Council and all they have planned for Savannah. I know that you will try to stop them.

This is not like the situation with the O'Seans. They fooled me into a pact that I did not see coming. A pact that you could—and did—break. The bonds between myself and the Dark Council run far deeper. They are woven into the fibers of my soul.

There is no saving me, Bree. You need to understand that. I can see you frowning now. You're trying to find a way around this. Your heart is too big, your hope too much for this world, and I do not want you to break on the rocks of despair.

I will never not love you.

But I need you to see me for what I am.

I am the bad guy*, Bree. I always have been, and from here on out, we will always be on opposite sides of the table.*

But for the short time we spent together I could just be me.

And I will be forever grateful that I had these weeks.

Crash

I couldn't see past the tears streaking down my face. How could he be so ducking perfect, and break my heart, and make me furious all in one page?

I folded it carefully and tucked it back into the envelope, folded that and put it in my bag. I wiped my face, took a deep, snot-filled breath and let myself out of the pantry.

Suzy and Kinkly were waiting for me there, on the other side of the door.

"Heard you crying," Kinkly said simply, and my lower lip trembled, and my vision fuzzed with tears. I hadn't cried like this over Alan. Of course, that relationship had been shit in the beginning, and it had suffered a long, slow death. This was the slicing of a limb, the cutting out of a part that I thought . . .

"Yup." I wiped my face again and the went to the kitchen sink and ran cold water. I splashed it over my eyes and neck, cooling myself. Suzy turned me around and hugged me tight. I closed my eyes, scrunching them up to stop the tears. "I got work to do, Suze. You coming?"

I stepped back, and she grinned. "You bet. Eric wants to help Penny with the spells she thinks she needs for tonight."

I would not think about Crash. I would not think about the fact that he'd written me that note. Nope, I would not think about trying to save him.

Sometimes you can't save the person you love. "He said he loves me," I whispered, and Suzy jerked.

"Bastard."

I gave a wobbly laugh. "Totally."

We left Eric and Eammon behind with Penny, and Gran stayed too in order to oversee the spelling. As for Alan, well, I wasn't interested in his particular brand of company seeing as he was a man—even if he was a dead one.

Suzy threw herself into the driver's side of her car and glanced over at me as I slid into the passenger side. "Advil is in the glove box."

I didn't argue, I knew I looked like a dumpster fire. I popped three of the little heavenly pills and dry swallowed them. Kinkly began to braid my hair back from my face.

"Warrior braids," she said when Suzy asked her what she was doing. "Meant to keep long hair from blinding you while you fight."

Good enough for me.

"Where are we going?" Suzy asked.

"To the council. I need to speak with Stark," I said.

"Who is that?"

"The guy nobody thinks speaks anymore, only he's spoken twice to me. I also need to warn the council that the Dark Council is here, and actively working against them." Because if any of them still wanted to keep their heads in the sand, I needed to open their eyes. And if by chance any didn't know . . . they needed to. We needed to work together.

If they wouldn't help, then I would go to Stavros, the demon the fae had told me about in my dream. While I was willing to work with a demon to save my city, it wouldn't be my first choice.

We parked outside of Death Row a few minutes later and let ourselves in through one of the secret doors.

"The council is here?" Suzy asked quietly.

"Hidden in plain sight," I said. "And also so they can spy on the comings and goings in Death Row."

We stepped out of the stairwell leading down into Death Row, and for a moment I just stared. The entire place was deserted. Completely empty of stalls, people, items.

"Oh, this cannot be good," Suzy said.

Kinkly fluttered ahead of us, then shot back. "Yeah, nothing at the end either."

Had they been evacuated?

I wasn't sure, and all it did was hurry my feet up—a possibility now that the Advil was kicking in.

I reached the far end of the hall and slid my hands over the doorway that I knew was there somewhere. I'd seen it from the other side when Roderick had taken me through the secret tunnel running behind Death Row.

My fingers brushed against an indentation, and I pushed my thumb into it. When the door slid slowly to the right, my friends and I stepped through the opening.

I knew the way—roughly—to the council chambers. But the sounds of shouting made it easier. Arguing. That's what was happening.

"Idiots," I said as I hurried toward the many, many flights of stairs leading down to the council chambers.

Suzy jogged along with me, and Kinkly kept just ahead of us. The sconces in the wall were lit with a guttering blue light that barely cast enough light for us to see by.

The double doors at the bottom of the stairs were open a crack, and Kinkly flew right in.

"Can she do that?" Suzy asked.

I shrugged. "I'm about to do the big version of zipping through." Reaching the doors, I grabbed them and flung them open. Epic, it felt epic until they bounced off the wall and back toward me. I scooted through, Suzy right on my ass.

"What is the meaning of this?"

I smiled up at Jacob, the necromancer whom I'd saved only a few days earlier. "Jacob Black, police officer and necromancer. Have you noticed the zombies in town?"

His jaw ticked. "Of course I have."

I didn't lose an inch of my smile. "And have you noticed they have nothing to do with Dr. Mori and his people and everything to do with the Dark Council ramping back up?" I didn't use Joseph's name. Not yet. Not unless I had to.

The men in the council went eerily silent. I had them by the short hairs now. Or so I thought.

I walked between the two desks that held magic that stripped you of any glamor, of any spells meant to do harm.

A tingle rolled over me, but that was it. "Do you understand that they are going to raise *all* of the undead of Savannah tonight?"

"You are telling us things we have known for weeks," barked a little man on the right. He wore glasses and could barely see over the railing around the room. I wasn't sure I'd noticed him the last time I was here.

I laughed. "You've known for weeks . . . and you've done nothing. Wonderful. Well, here's the deal. If we don't disrupt the undead spell before midnight, we're going to be hit with an entire army of goblins and the undead. We need to work together."

The thing was, I hadn't really counted on the sheer misogyny of the councilmen. I caught a glimpse of Roderick out of the corner of my eye, and he was shaking his head.

Jacob didn't laugh, but a few of the other men did. Okay, most of the other men did.

"You think we need your help? Please." The little spectacled man made a shooing motion. "This is not a place for a woman, certainly not a woman past her prime."

Suzy sucked in a sharp breath, and I could feel her vibrating next to me, her body humming with siren magic. I put a hand on her. "Not worth it, Suzy. Save it for later."

"Pricks," she muttered.

Kinkly zipped back to my shoulder, and I stared at each of the council members one at a time. There was no way I'd remember more than half of them. But I wanted them to see me.

"Then you could have very well doomed us all." I turned my back on them, but not before I'd locked eyes for a good moment with Stark. He gave me the slightest of nods and mouthed a word. I hoped I was right about it.

Dragging Suzy, who was literally spitting mad, I headed for the flight of stairs that one day would be the death of me, I was sure of it.

"How can they be so blind?" she screeched at the top of her lungs.

"Because they have been at the top for so long, they don't think they need to change. Or accept help. Or acknowledge that they might have been doing it wrong," I said between harsh breaths.

"How do we change it?" Kinkly asked.

I looked up at her. "Honestly, people like that don't change. All you can do is wait for them to die and make sure you teach the next generations to be better. To do better."

At the top of the stairs, I leaned against the wall. "Come on, we aren't done yet."

I led them out and around onto River Street to Vic's Restaurant, up yet another flight of stairs—I might have cried at that point—and into the men's washroom. I went straight for the last stall with the out of order sign on it, and opened the door, leading the three of us into the fae bar. "Ten minutes," I said as I walked through.

Without hesitation, I went straight to the booth I'd occupied with Stark.

"What are we doing here?" Kinkly whispered. "Karissa could be here. Crash could be here!"

"I know, but we aren't here for them," I said. Though Karissa . . . maybe she'd be willing to fight against Crash? I wasn't sure. I glanced at Kinkly. "You think she'd fight on our side?"

Kinkly shook her head. "No. She's no warrior queen. She'll wait to see who wins and then suck up to them."

I sighed. So much for that idea.

The blue-haired waitress came over. "What can I get you girls?"

"Nothing. We're waiting for a friend," I said.

Only a few minutes passed before Stark shuffled in from one of the doorways that ran along the far wall. He made his way over to our booth and squeezed in next to Suzy.

"They will not help," he said. "They still believe Mori and his people are to blame for the spell. They plan to raid the ghost ship tonight."

I winced. "Damn it. They will be as far from the fight then as they can be."

"Despite all the evidence to the contrary, they do not believe the Dark Council has been resurrected. Despite even what Marco said." He waved the waitress away. "The question is, what will you do, Sentinel?"

"Roll the dice," I said. "Where can I find Stavros?"

His bushy eyebrows shot up. "That is a gamble indeed."

I stared across the table at him. "Where is he, Stark?"

He sighed. "Not as far away as I'd like him to be. Go to 696 Fisher Street. He lives there, about as human as a demon can be. I do not know if he will help though."

"I have an offering of sorts." I didn't pull the globe out of my bag, though I wanted to. It had a strange draw that I wasn't immune to.

He reached across the table and put his hand on mine, his gnarled old fingers tightening. "I will be there tonight, young one. I may not look like much, but I still have it in me for one more battle, I think."

I put my hand over his. "Thank you."

"I should like to kick Joseph in the balls, at least once," he said.

I couldn't help the laughter—nervous laughter for sure, but still laughter. "In the balls?"

"Very hard, no less." He smiled through his bushy beard. "I will bring those who will stand with you. Jacob will come, I think. Roderick too. We will arrive just before the clock strikes midnight. In time for the ball drop, as it were."

"Roderick had better show up at the dance. Since he set me on this path," I muttered as I pushed to my feet. "Thank you, Stark."

He pressed his palms together and bowed his head over them. "May you protect us all, Sentinel."

I found myself making the same motion back to him, and as I walked away, I was sure I heard him whisper one more line.

"For if you do not, we are all doomed."

No pressure, no pressure at all.

23

I stood in front of a demon's house, wondering if I was at the right place. Because there was the definite sound of children playing and laughing inside. A woman's voice as she sung some sort of sweet lullaby.

An SUV in the driveway.

Kids' toys in the yard.

"What the hell kind of demon is he?" I whispered as I forced my feet up the steps. Suzy and Kinkly were waiting for me in the square across from the house. If I needed backup, they would come running-slash-flying. I blew out a slow breath as I lifted my hand to knock. "Gran is going to kill me."

I rapped my knuckles on the ornate wooden door, the sound reverberating not only through my ears but through my bones. Three times. Just like Stark had knocked on the table. Just like the Monica shapeshifter had knocked on the ground at Gran's house to awaken the demon at the Sorrel-Weed house.

The laughter and sounds of playing hushed, and I fidgeted. Seriously, what kind of demon—

The door opened to reveal a curvy woman with a child on her hip, flour on her face, and the biggest pair of brown eyes I'd ever seen on a person. The term doe eyes came to mind.

"I'm not buying whatever you're selling, girlfriend, sorry about that." She moved to close the door, and I did the thing I hated when it happened to me. I stuck my foot in the crack to keep it open.

"I need to speak to Stavros," I said, and then she took a good look at me. Leather shawl, pants, and gloves. Unkempt. Warrior braids, if Kinkly was being truthful.

She pursed her lips. "Honey, someone is here for you."

Honey.

Were these his . . . demon spawn? I looked at the baby in her arms for like a pair of horns or maybe a tail, but it looked like a normal baby.

The sound of footsteps from deep within the house grew closer and closer, until a rather slender man came into view. Average height, russet-toned hair, dark, dark brown eyes, and a scar that ran across his left cheek to his ear.

He wore a three-piece suit in navy blue with a crisp white shirt and bright red tie. "I'm on a Zoom meeting, Alexandra." His eyes shot to me, and I tried not to laugh. It sounded like a bad book title. *Zooming with the Demon.*

The laughter kept trying to burble up, so I bit the inside of my cheek. I really needed his help. The whole town did.

His eyes went to my foot in the door. "Whatever you're selling, we don't want it."

I didn't take my foot out of the door. "The Dark Council is raising every dead person in Savannah tonight, and I need help stopping them."

"What?" Alexandra asked. "What in the world is she—"

Stavros grabbed my arm and dragged me into the house. "Nothing, darling. This is my friend from college. I didn't recognize her in her *cosplay* outfit." He glared at me as I hurried my feet to keep up with him. "What a jokester!"

Through the beautiful, well-kept house he took me, to a door that led not down, as I'd have thought, but up.

At the top of the stairs, he flung open the door to an office and slammed me down into a chair.

He flopped into a chair across from me, behind a desk, and clicked to cut off the Zoom meeting. "Who are you?"

"Breena O'Rylee." I held out a hand and he stared at me like I'd gone mad.

"The one who killed the Sorrel-Weed demon? I went to school with him, you know." His eyes were hard. "I rather liked him."

I stared back, unfazed even though this was strange to say the least. "He tried to eat my soul, *you know*. So, I was well within my rights."

Stavros hummed a little. "Fair. What is this about the Dark Council?"

"Their spell to raise the undead of Savannah goes fully into effect tonight. They have a goblin army, too, and the council of Savannah has their heads so far up their asses they're going to need flashlights if they want to find their way out."

His lips twitched. "That is nothing new. What do you think I can do, and why would I bother to help you?"

"Because—"

"And don't say it's because it's the right thing to do. Despite what you might think, I *am* still a demon." He smiled, and the brown of his eyes deepened to a soul-crushing black.

"A trade. I have something you want." I dug into my bag and pulled out the orb. "Altin said you would want this. If he's wrong, then I guess—"

He reached for the orb, and I pulled back. "Yeah, no. Agree to help me first."

Stavros shook his head. "I won't help you, not for that."

Yup, my jaw hung open. "Why not?"

"While that orb does carry Altin's power, it is no longer needed. Karissa helped me." He smiled. "I think you should leave."

I stuck the orb back into my hip bag. I needed to offer him something else of value, so I picked up my knife. Might as well try.

"What about for this?"

I let him take the knife. He rolled it in his hands, walking it across his knuckles. "A knife that channels a death wielder's power. Nice work. The blacksmith made it, yes?"

"He did," I said and refused to get choked up. "Is it enough to secure your help?"

He handed it back to me. "It's useless to me. Only person it will work for is a death wielder." His eyes swept over me, and he slowly nodded. "Now it makes sense how you took Steve out."

"Steve?"

"The Sorrel-Weed house demon. That was his name."

The sound of his children floated up to me, and I knew that I had one last chance at convincing him. I stood up as if I were going to leave. "Thanks for your time. I hope you enjoy the day with your kids." I paused at the door and looked back at him. "I mean, just out of curiosity, what do you think will happen if the Dark Council achieves their goal? If everyone learns supernaturals are real, we'll be hunted, and even though there will be plenty of human casualties, too, the numbers are in their favor. Would be pretty terrible for a bunch of half demons, don't you think?"

His face paled, and I nodded. "Yeah, I wouldn't want my kids to be hunted either. But then again, I don't have kids."

"Death wielders can't," he said. "They can't hold life in their bodies."

My jaw tightened. "That explains things. Anyway"—damn it, I did not need to be catching more emotions—"have a good day with your kids. And your wife. Wonder what people would do to a woman that was banging a demon? You think it will be like the witch burning trials? Or more like the *Hunger Games*? If you do change your mind, you'd meet me at the old fort tonight. Around ten should do the trick."

I turned my back, went down the stairs, and let myself out the front door. The kids were screeching now, and I turned to see them waving from the window.

Bouncing light brown curls, round little faces, grins with gaps where teeth had fallen out. They were cute.

They were innocent even if their father was a demon.

I waved back, then crossed the square to where Suzy and Kinkly waited.

"What happened?" Suzy asked.

"Maybe," I said and didn't bother to look back over my shoulder at Stavros's house. "Maybe."

24

Suzy, Kinkly, and I drove back to Penny's house silently as the world ticked by like normal. People were out enjoying the weather, eating at restaurants, living life. A fire engine and emergency crew shot by us, sirens fading into the distance. Human life was going on. But if we didn't stop the rising of the undead, what then?

A police officer gave us a look as we slowed at a stop sign. "Full stop," I said to Suzy. "We do not need to be pulled over."

I stared straight ahead while Suzy executed a perfect stop, waited, and then took our turn.

No sirens behind us, thank gawd.

We arrived back at Penny's place after lunch, but I wasn't hungry. I found myself pacing, trying to come up with a way to face down Crash, Joseph, and the Dark Council.

"I have an idea," Kinkly said suddenly. "They think we're coming tonight, right? And all we really have to do is, you know, disrupt the spell, and then the rain will be just rain, correct? No more zombies?"

We all looked at Penny and I at Gran. Both witches nodded. "Correct. You need to disrupt it. Easiest way is with a handful of salt." Penny held up little pouches and tossed one to each of us. "This will be enough."

"The goblins sleep from noon until dinner usually. Like the rest of the fae, their sleep schedule is not on a human schedule," Kinkly said. "The fort is still having tourists in, so why don't we dress up and go in as a family? Eammon can be the bratty kid."

"Piss off, Kink," Eammon grumbled.

"Okay, bratty short teenager then." She snickered and flitted about his face while he swatted at her.

"I'll be coming too," Penny said. "I might be slower than you all, but I'll drink down the fairy honey to help me keep up some."

A witch, a leprechaun, a fairy, a siren, and a bigfoot go into battle with a whatever-the-hell I was. It sure as shit felt like the start of a bad joke. That or a really good story.

Let's go with the second one. I was tired of being the butt of jokes. I wanted to be a badass death wielder.

"Gran, can you come and help keep an eye on things? You too, Alan."

Everyone startled, Alan included. "You'd bring him?" Penny asked.

"You want to spy for Marge, you're about to get an eyeful." I shrugged. "I mean, it isn't going to be a secret after tonight."

He shrugged back.

"Monica will be there," I said. "All in red leather, no less."

Alan frowned. "I don't like her anymore. She's also a man sometimes."

I looked at my friends and blew out a tired breath. "Okay. Kinkly, I think it's a good idea. We try to disrupt the spell now, while the goblins are asleep and the undead are mostly tucked away from the humans."

"About the humans, how are you going to keep them safe, exactly?" Eric asked. "Because I know that is important to you, to all of us."

I nodded. "It is, but I don't want to make the call until we are going in. I don't want to tip our hand." Officer Burke very well could be working for Joseph, but she also had a responsibility to the town. I was banking on her wanting to keep her job.

And just like that, we were as ready as we were going to get to save the day, rescue Sarge and Corb, and maybe, just maybe, stop the zombie apocalypse.

I could not wait for this week to be over.

The drive out to the fort wasn't quiet. You'd think going into a fight where we were outnumbered, out-magicked, and outgunned, we'd be depressed and silent.

Nope, we were drinking every last drop of fairy honey we had left and enjoying those last moments together.

Eammon was singing some version of ninety-nine bottles of beer on the wall involving fairy honey and an orgy. Eric and Suzy joined in, and Kinkly snapped her wings to the beat. Penny thumped her cane on the floor of the car for the bass, and I just hummed along, harmonizing. Laughing at the chorus lines.

Distantly wondering if our plan, such as it was, would work.

The initial goal was to get to the supernatural prisoners and set them free. Hopefully that would mean we'd have more firepower.

Each of us carried not only a pouch of salt but a small flask of fairy honey to help us move any injured and exhausted prisoners to safety. It would also give a boost to anyone who chose to help us fight Joseph.

"Roderick had better pay up after this," Suzy said as we drove up to the fort's gravel parking lot, a cloud of dust billowing around us as we stopped.

I blinked over at her. I'd almost forgotten there was a pot of gold at the end of this dark rainbow. "Yeah, he'd better."

It would be the only good thing to come out of this job.

Alan and Gran went first, heading past the entrance and straight for the tunnel system. Their job was to scout out exactly where the spell was being kept, and then one of them would come back for us. We weren't going to venture into the belowground tunnels until they were done snooping.

Eric and Suzy linked arms and sauntered off to the left, as if they were a young couple touristing it up. Eammon stayed close to Penny, and they headed to the right. Kinkly and I stayed on the central path and walked across the ring fort, straight to the opposite side.

"Thanks for the braids," I said.

"You really got stop thanking people," she said. "Do you know how much you owe me?"

I smiled. "Everything."

She laughed and sat on my shoulder. "What about Feish?"

Her question caught my heart off guard. "What about her? She's tied to Crash, and he's bonded to the Dark Council."

A couple pushing a stroller gave me a funny look. I shrugged. Whatever. I looked for where the sun sat in the sky. The afternoon heat was high, and we still had a couple hours before the goblins were up and at 'em.

"But maybe her bonds to him can be severed. You know, like you did before, except permanent?" Kinkly said. "I miss her."

I sighed. "I miss her too." I missed her blunt words. Her loyalty, inasmuch as she was allowed to give it. And her unintentional humor.

"You should not miss friends who are bad friends."

I froze on the spot and turned to see Feish standing up against one of the support columns, partially hidden in the shadows. I hurried over to her. "Feish."

Shit. She was on the wrong side.

Her eyes filled with tears. "I left eviction notice for you. I knew Boss would hurt you. I hoped . . . you'd take me with you. But it didn't work."

I closed my eyes, and my head hung forward. "Oh, Feish, I wish you'd told me."

Kinkly fluttered around our friend's head. "We still love you, Feish. We know it isn't your fault."

Feish let out a burbling cry and covered her face with her hands. I caught her up in my arms and hugged her while she sobbed. "It will be okay, my friend," I whispered against the side of her head. "I know right now it feels like the world is crumbling, like there is no way out, but I promise you it will be okay."

She sniffed and looked up at me. "How? How can you say that? This is the worst! Worst ever!"

Boy, didn't I know it. The ten of swords was all but burning a hole through my bag as if begging me to pull it out.

"Because the story isn't over yet," I said. "Because we are still here, and that means there's still hope."

Feish shook her head. "Boss is a mess."

"Good." I smiled. "Feish, what can you tell me about the bond between you and Crash?"

She looked from me to Kinkly. "You think you can break it? But you aren't a witch. Not really. Like a baby witch at best. Weak magic, you know."

I shrugged. "Maybe what you need isn't a witch, but a fae with some power."

My jaw dropped as the possibility of what I'd just said hit me. I had an orb of power in my damn handbag. I reached in but didn't pull it out. Of course, I couldn't just throw it at her. A memory surfaced of a spell I'd seen in the book of curses. Breaking bonds. "Was it fae magic that bonded you to him?"

"Of course." Feish looked offended by the suggestion that it might have been anything else. "Boss did it himself. Big, strong, blacksmith-made bond to keep me close to him. To keep me safe. But I want to stay with you, Bree. I want to be a good Feish."

She clasped her hands together and lifted them to her big lips. And I knew then that what I was going to ask her to do was dangerous. Because if anyone ever found out . . .

"What if we released you from the bonds, Feish, but you stayed with him?" I asked quietly. "For a little while?"

She blinked those big bulbous eyes up at me. "You mean like . . . spy on him?"

I nodded. "See what you can find out?"

She shrugged. "I guess. But I already know everything about him. As soon as I am free of the bonds, then I could tell you all his secrets."

Well, shit. "Okay, then let's do it."

We didn't have long. There were humans everywhere, and we were in a public place. But this was the only chance we were likely to get, and I was going to take it. I pulled out the book of curses and flipped it open to the spell about breaking connections.

"We're going to mix it up," I said softly. "Fae magic and witch words."

Why not, am I right?

I gave the spell book to Kinkly to hold up, and I read through it a couple times before putting my hand on Feish's shoulder.

I could do this.

I wrapped my fingers around the orb in my handbag and started to recite the words from the book of curses.

Now, let me just say, I should have thought this through. Like, I really should have thought it through. But the idea of freeing Feish was too compelling. If I couldn't free Crash, then at least I could make sure she didn't go down with him.

"The bonds of time release, the bonds of power release, the bonds of frailty release. Thrice bound, thrice called, thrice burned, thrice felled, thrice hidden, thrice revealed."

The liquid spilled out of the orb and into my palm, liquid that was both clear and a rainbow of colors ran up my arm and straight to Feish. She gasped as it curled around her, like glittering water, and then sunk under her skin.

"It's working!" she whispered. "The bonds are falling away!"

Kinkly snapped her wings. "Yes!"

Feish's expression shifted into a frown. "Oh no."

"Oh . . . no?" I took my hand from her and tucked the spell book back in my bag. "What do you mean, oh no?"

She grimaced. "Should have thought about this. I felt the bonds go."

"Right." I tipped my head and then closed my eyes, understanding what she was getting at. "Let me guess, Crash felt them break too."

Feish burbled, "He did."

Time to rumble.

Whether we were ready or not.

25

I grabbed Feish by the webbed hand and dragged her with me, heading for the underground bunker out back. "We have to hurry then. If he knows, he'll tip them off."

"I'm sorry!" Feish wailed, and I squeezed her hand.

"No, this is not your fault. Not your fault, Feish!" I looked around for Kinkly. "Kink, go get the others. Tell them we're going in."

She was gone in a flash of glitter. I fumbled with my flask of fairy honey and gave a sip to Feish. Her eyes widened.

"Holy hot sea water, that's good stuff!"

We slid to a stop at the entrance to the underground bunker, and the others met us there seconds later. Penny wasn't even breathing hard, and her eyes glittered.

"Let's kick some ass!"

"What about Celia and Alan?" Eric said. "Shouldn't we wait for . . . oh, hi Feish."

Feish flopped a hand. "Bree broke the bonds between me and boss, and now he knows you are all here."

All eyes landed on me. I cringed. "Sorry!"

"Well, into the lion's den then," Penny said, leading the way down into the hole.

I motioned at Eric. "Phone."

He pulled it from his pocket—mine had totally died after its dunk in the river—and I dialed the hospital first.

"Message for Dr. Mori please," I said, and the operator patched me through to his voicemail. "Mori, I'm at the fort and the disease we discussed is rampant here. Some backup would be great."

I hung up and dialed one other number.

"9-1-1, what's your emergency?"

"You might want to evacuate the old fort. Heard a bomb's been planted. Jacob Black knows about it, so confirm with him, but move fast."

"Wait, what—"

I hung up before she could ask questions.

I flipped the phone into the air to Eric, then followed the others down into the depths of the earth. Yup, it sounded creepy, but in daytime it wasn't so bad.

I slid to the front of our group and the dead end I knew was an opening. I bent and called up my connection to death—hah, dead end, death, good one—and the hidden door slid open.

Eric went first and then helped Penny, Suzy, and Eammon.

Eammon grumbled and swatted at the bigfoot. "I've got it, I'm not an invalid. Just short!"

I was the last one down and closed the circular door so no unsuspecting human would fall through.

I knew the tunnel went to the central chamber, and it was there that we would split up. We had to find the cauldron with the spell and rescue the other supernaturals. Hopefully Gran and Alan would find us soon with info on the cauldron.

Assuming that Joseph and Crash weren't hanging out there.

We moved quickly but quietly, and soon enough we'd arrived where I'd last seen Crash.

The space was empty.

"Feish, where is the spell?" I asked.

"Well not here, that would just be dumb."

Not here.

Ah, duck me sideways. We all turned to look at her. "Not here?"

She shook her head. "No, Missy is doing the spell. It's at her place."

Missy.

Penny let out a low hiss like a pissed-off cat. "Imma wring her neck like a damn chicken! She told me the back bedroom was packed full of boxes! That's where it is, I'd bet my last dollar on it!"

"We still have to get all of the prisoners out," I whispered. "Penny, you, Eammon, Suzy, and Eric go to Missy's. Stop that spell!"

I sent them away, and they hurried back out through the tunnel. I turned and grabbed Feish's hand. This was not how I imagined things going down, but here we were.

"You and I are going to get Sarge and the others out."

"Good plan, they are this way!" Feish tugged me along, and I let her lead. Kinkly fluttered down and landed on my shoulder.

"We're sure that the bonds are broken?"

"Yes," I said firmly even though the second she asked the question, doubt filtered in. Could I have really severed bonds that Crash, who had hundreds or even thousands of years of experience, had wrought?

Then again, I didn't have a lot of time to question things. Two zombies lurched out of the shadows.

One rode Feish to the ground while she squawked. The other came for me.

I pulled my dagger from my hip sheath and grabbed the outstretched hand closest to me, yanking the zombie close and driving my blade up and into its heart. It grunted and then slumped to the ground. Leaping past that one, I grabbed the zombie on top of Feish and pulled it up enough that I could safely dispatch it too.

"You okay, Feish?'

"Yeah, yeah, just a little bite," she grumbled as she held up her forearm. Bite marks firmly set in her flesh.

Kinkly gasped, but I shook my head. "Not now, Kink. Later."

Because I knew there was nothing we could do about it in that moment. We had to get everyone out, save as many lives as we could. Even if it meant acting like I didn't care that Feish had probably just been handed a death sentence.

"They never bother me before," she whispered. "Why now?"

We stepped into a second circular room, across from a wall of cells with all sorts of critters in it.

Sarge saw me first. "Bree! Get out of here!"

But my gaze was stuck on Crash, sitting slumped in a chair next to a table. Several empty whiskey bottles were laid out on the table in front of him. He lifted alcohol-laden eyes to me.

"Feish. You broke the bond?"

"I asked her to," Feish said, clutching at her bitten arm.

He groaned and lurched to his feet. "You can't have any of them." He waved a hand at the cages. "You have to go through me first."

"Done," I said. "Kinkly, help Feish get the doors open while I deal with the blacksmith."

He winced. *Yeah, that's right, I'm not even going to use your name, big boy.*

I wasn't going to think about kissing him or anything else either.

I pulled Robert's finger bone from my hip bag and held it out. Between one blink and the next, he swayed at my side. He, at least, couldn't be hurt like my other friends. At least that's what I believed.

Crash lunged for Feish, and I leapt forward, tackling him at the waist and tangling up his legs. The move wasn't pretty, but it was effective.

I was on his back, and he was face down, but that didn't last. He flipped me over in a flash, and I found myself on my back with him on top of me. I scrambled to get a knee between us. My breath came in pants as I fought to get out from under him.

"Hurry!" I yelled at Feish and Kinkly.

They didn't answer.

"Robert!" I screamed, but I didn't even get a 'friend' in answer.

"He can't save you now," Crash said, his mouth against my ear. "No one can. You should have left town."

I let out a scream as he got both my wrists tangled up with one hand and pinned me to the ground. Time seemed to pause in the way it does when adrenaline is pounding, and I found myself staring up into his face, our bodies flush against each other as our breathing came in gasps. It was not lost on me that this was as close as we would ever get again to being together.

I wrapped my legs around his waist, and his eyes widened until I started to clench them tight. I probably couldn't break a rib. But maybe I could cut his air off.

With a grunt he went to his knees, taking me with him. I was pretty much sitting in his lap, legs wrapped tightly around him, hands still captured in his clasp.

One leg at a time, he pushed until he was upright, if a bit wobbly. I let my legs drop and kicked him in the thigh. He spun me around and clasped my chin with his free hand so that I had no choice but to stare at the scene in front of me.

Joseph and Monica had Feish and Kinkly. Monica held Kinkly by the wings. "Flying rats, if you ask me."

And she tore the left wing right down the middle as Kinkly screamed.

I screamed with her. "Monica, I'm gonna mess up your already ugly face when we get out of here!"

She sniffed and threw Kinkly into a tiny metal box. An iron box. Kinkly huddled in the middle, avoiding the iron bars.

Feish was shoved into the cell next to Sarge. He draped an arm over her, and she leaned into him.

"They caught us, Bree."

Yeah, they had caught us. But we weren't done yet. Eric, Eammon, Penny, and Suzy still had a chance to stop the spell. They had to.

"You can't have her," Joseph said, motioning to me.

Crash grunted. "I'll do as I please."

Nope, I should not have felt an excited shiver at those particular words.

Liability. That's what Crash had called me. I was his weakness. Could I use it against him after all?

As soon as the thought crossed my mind, I threw it out. Not that I wouldn't do anything to save my friends, but I wasn't that good of an actress. Plus, he knew me too well to believe I'd abandon my principles so easily.

"Throw her in the cell with the others," Joseph barked. "We have things to do. And I *will* deal with her later."

Crash's hands tightened on me, but he walked toward the cell.

He put me in it and walked away.

26

Fifteen minutes before the blood storm came and all the dead in Savannah rose up and tried to eat the living. Fifteen tiny little minutes. I sat with Sarge and Feish, as close to Kinkly's little cell as we could get.

Neither Gran nor Alan had shown back up. Did that mean they were caught too? Or hiding?

Corb was apparently in another cell block, which . . . was good. I wasn't sure I was up to seeing him right then.

"You're sure you can't call on Robert?" Kinkly whimpered the words out.

"No. I've tried," I said. And I had, multiple times in the last ten minutes. Sarge and Feish had seen

Joseph reduce him down to a bone with a single flick—a bone he had pocketed before walking away.

I put my hand to my hip bag. Crash hadn't taken it. I still had my knife. I still had the orb, though it was not as bright.

No Gran.

No Alan.

"If Penny can stop Missy, we have a chance," I said.

That's what I told myself, but as I pulled out the tarot card that I'd been given just a few days before, I felt the message all the way to my toes.

This really was as bad as it got.

And I had to pee.

There was a bucket at the back of the cell that I used—and I was not the first, so let's just say it wasn't my favorite part of what was turning out to be a pretty bad day.

"Footsteps," Sarge whispered.

I stood at the front of the cage, the other inhabitants not even looking up.

When the visitor stepped into view, I felt a moment of pure happiness, something I'd never thought I'd experience upon seeing a demon. "Stavros."

"You started without us?" He snapped his fingers, and four other demons stepped out from behind him, all wearing business suits. All looking very much human.

"We took a chance to sneak in while everyone was sleeping."

"That's always good with a vampire," Stavros said, "but it doesn't work if they know you're coming."

I had to do like the double blink to make sure he was really there, and this wasn't a dream. "Come again?"

"Vampire. That's what you're stuck on, isn't it? You thought Joseph was just a really snazzy necromancer, didn't you?" He barked a laugh, came to the door and unlocked it simply by running his finger over the keyhole. "Everyone is above ground now, and the sky is filling with clouds. Where is this spell we need to stop?"

I stepped through the open door and grabbed his arm. "What time is it?" Hoping maybe I was wrong. Maybe we had more time.

"Quarter to midnight," one of his friends said.

"We have fifteen minutes to stop it, and it's in the Victorian district with Missy," I said. I scooped up Kinkly's cage and held it up to him. He opened the door with the touch of his finger. Demon powers had their perks apparently.

"Can you get there in time?" I asked, and he shook his head.

"No."

I put my hands to my head. How were we going to stop Joseph? Especially if he was a vampire? The spell, it was still all about the spell. If we stopped that, then . . . then we had a chance.

An idea came to me in a flash. I wasn't sure it would work, but we had nothing to lose. "I need a cell phone."

The same demon who'd given me the time offered me his phone. "Might be dodgy this far underground."

"I'll take that chance."

I dialed.

"Hello, this is 9-1-1, what is your emergency?"

"I need you to patch me through to Officer Burke in the Savannah PD," I said. "I'm her undercover partner!"

There was dead silence for a moment—not just from the operator, but the people around me. One of the demons snickered.

"I can patch you through to the police station. But, for future reference, we're not a dispatch."

"I wouldn't have asked if it wasn't an emergency," I said, but she was already gone, and the phone was ringing once more.

"Officer Wrightone," Kevin's voice drawled. "How can I direct you?"

"Officer Burke," I snapped. Trying to sound official.

"Sure thing."

A beep.

"Officer Burke," Abigail said.

"Abigail, listen to me."

"Oh my God. Is this O'Rylee again?"

"Don't hang up! The undead are going to get worse in about—" I looked at Stavros, and he showed me his watch, "—thirteen minutes if you don't go to the Victorian district, to Missy Haverstock's home. She's at 543 Blackstar Ave. Take salt and throw it any bubbling pot you find."

"Are you serious?" she breathed out. "Are you freaking serious?"

"Twelve minutes," I said.

"And why aren't you doing it?" she yelled.

"Because I'm dealing with a damn vampire!" I yelled right back at her, and then I hung up. Handed the phone back to the demon on the left.

"Thanks."

"Shouldn't thank a demon," he said.

"Might be the end of the freaking world as we know it," I said. "But I can still have manners."

The ground rumbled, dust fell from the ceiling, and the lights flickered. I nodded. "I think that means it's time to go kick some zombie ass."

Stavros laughed. "I don't want to like you, demon hunter."

"There's a club," Sarge said. "I started it on Facebook. All the people who didn't want to like Bree but now do."

I laughed and turned to Feish. "Lead the way. You know how to get up top quick?"

Holding her arm, she bobbed her head. "Let's do it."

There was no resistance below from Joseph, Crash, or anyone who worked for the Dark Council.

"Nine minutes," Stavros said. "I hope you were right to trust that human you called."

"She's all we've got." Because if Penny and the others had failed . . . I didn't know who else to turn to.

Feish led us up a set of narrow stairs, and we popped out underneath one of the openings in the ring fort set up for cannons. I peeked into the courtyard to see Joseph standing in the middle of the open space.

Damn, he *did* look like a vampire now that I knew the truth about him. Actually, who was I kidding, I had no idea what a vampire looked like, or why one would look different from any other critter.

Crash stood to his right. Missy stood on his left. A bubbling cauldron sat between her and Joseph. Shit.

I jerked around to look at Feish, and she shrugged. "Maybe they brought it here?"

We still had time. I had to believe we still had time then. Though part of me was terrified at what might have happened to Penny, Eammon, Eric, and Suzy. What would Officer Burke find at Blackstar Ave.?

"What do you want us to do?" Stavros asked quietly.

"Spread chaos," I whispered back. "See those goblins over there?" I gestured to a group of them waiting at the front of the gates facing outward. Maybe thinking the council would come in that way, guns blazing? They clearly expected someone to try to come through that way. Seems they didn't think much of me and my friends and so hadn't guarded their backsides.

Booyah bitches, I'm about to bite you in the ass.

"If you can tackle them," I continued, "we'll take on the undead as they come through."

He grinned. "Scaring goblins, that was our pastimes as teens."

He and his four friends were gone in a blink, using the cover of the ring fort to make their way closer to the goblins.

"Sarge, you shift, go for Missy," I whispered. Kinkly clung to my ear for balance.

"I can't fly," she said in a quavering voice.

"We'll fix you and Feish up as soon as we deal with those dinguses out there." I lifted a finger to her. "Just hang onto me."

She patted her hand against my finger, and then I looked at Feish. "I'm going to give you the salt to put into the spell."

I handed her the bag of salt, and she clung to it with her webbed fingers. "I'm going to keep the two of them distracted." I couldn't bring myself to say Crash's name.

I needed an explosion of some sort was what I was thinking. And I had a not-quite-empty orb of power still in my hip bag. If it broke, I was hoping for a great big bang. I scooped it out and lobbed it overhead, aiming for Joseph's feet. It caught the light, and the first drop of blood that fell from the sky landed on it, splattering its pristine surface.

"Tonight, we take Savannah back!" Joseph yelled. "Tonight, the shadow world finally comes into its own!"

The goblins cheered.

Crash held his fist to the sky.

Missy cackled, a perfect witch laugh if ever I'd heard one.

The globe fell right into the boiling cauldron.

Did I get an explosion? You bet I did.

27

When the orb landed in the still-boiling spell, it shattered with a boom that threw everyone backward.

I felt the concussion of it my chest, felt my heart think about stopping. Saw my friends tumble through the air. Even had time to consider that maybe that hadn't been the best idea.

I slammed into one of the pillars and slid down it as the dirt and wind from the explosion blew past me. I forced myself to my feet. "Feish?"

"On it!" she burbled as she crawled toward what remained of the magic spell.

Missy screeched in unreal octaves as Feish managed to pour salt on the puddles. I wasn't sure it needed any further nullifying after the explosion, but I wasn't taking any chances.

My friends were all getting up, but so were the goblins. "Now, Stavros!" I yelled.

When the five demons emerged from the shadows, they looked nothing like uptight businessmen. They each stood well over ten feet, and their bodies had morphed into the monsters I knew demons to be. And boy, were the goblins not happy to see them.

They scattered, screaming like pigs to the slaughter, as the five demons laid into them.

Kinkly clutched my ear. "We did it."

"I hope so." I looked for Sarge and found him shaking his fur free of the dust and dirt, one big paw on the back of Missy's neck as he held her face down. "But there is someone I want back."

Joseph had Robert. The idea of facing a vampire was terrifying, but right then he was flat on the ground. He'd taken the brunt of the blow. Crash was twenty feet off to the right, also face down.

My instinct was to check on him, but I turned to Joseph. Still feeling plenty of kick from the fairy honey, I ran to his side, quickly searching his pockets until I found the finger bone that I knew was Robert.

"Seriously," I said. "You have to stop getting stolen."

I took a step back, Robert clutched tightly in my hand.

A very strange sensation came over me, and it took me too long to realize what was happening.

I was yanked to the ground so fast that I didn't even have a chance to blink. I was just suddenly flat on my back with Joseph on top of me. All I had was Robert. I couldn't reach my knife.

"Robert!" I screamed his name, and he was there, every bony bit of him between me and Joseph's fangs.

Joseph snarled. "You think you've stopped me, but you haven't!"

"Not friend," Robert snapped and spun, clamping his teeth onto Joseph's wrist. Like a dog with a bone, he pulled Joseph off me, and I rolled onto my hands and knees.

"He's dead, you know that." Joseph smiled and pointed his free hand at Robert, who suddenly seized up, powerless to move. "He's dead, and now I'm going to make sure you don't have him anymore."

"No!" I reached for him even as Robert arched his back, his actual body coming into view for a split second.

Blue eyes met mine. "I'm sorry, Bree. I couldn't keep you safe."

Joseph snapped his finger and the body shriveled into nothing. A burst of sparkles, and Robert was gone. There was no finger bone. Just dust.

I dropped my hip bag and pulled my knife free.

Joseph laughed. "You can't be serious?"

"Do I look like I'm laughing?" A commotion at the gate rolled through the air, and I smiled. "The calvary has arrived."

His face twisted up. "That council is useless."

The gates swung inward, and there were only two from the council. Stark and Roderick. But they weren't alone. Penny, Eammon, Eric and Suzy were there too.

Roderick strode forward first. "I believe, brother, that you are done."

A strange look glimmered in Joseph's eyes, but I didn't need an interpreter to tell me what it meant. He knew he was done, but he wasn't going down alone. Before I could even think of moving, he was on me in a blink, his hands so tight on my wrists that I had no choice but to drop the knife.

"No, I am just beginning," he growled, and his fangs descended.

Joseph was going to bite me.

I wondered if I'd taste out-of-date, like milk past its expiration. That was the thought I had as his fangs drove deep into my neck.

Let me be clear, it did not feel good. Paranormal romance has it all wrong. There is nothing sexy about the sensation of dagger *teeth* going into your flesh. The pain was immediate, and I screamed as he gnawed on me, not unlike how Robert had gnawed on Joseph's wrist.

Kinkly punched at his face, scratching and clawing for all she was worth, but she was too small to do any damage.

Shouting filled the air, and then suddenly I saw Gran to my left. I couldn't hear her either, until I could. Suddenly, she was so loud she might as well have had a megaphone.

"You can stop him, Bree. Your father could do it and so can you! You have the strength!"

I dragged on the connection I had to the dead and pulled it around me as tightly as I could. I didn't know what the duck I was supposed to do with it, but I hung onto it for dear life and kept drawing on the power until I was full up.

Full up, and then I let that power go—all into Joseph.

He froze and pulled away from my neck. Whimpered, "No. No, you can't—"

Maybe I could have found out more about what I'd done, what I could do, if I'd had more time. There seemed to be a lot of maybes in my life lately.

The thing was, the tip of a sword sliced through his neck, spraying me with his blood as his head rolled from his shoulders.

"Yes!" Kinkly yelled. "He deserved that and more!"

I fell backward, and a well-muscled arm caught me. I blinked up as the world faded to nothing but his eyes. Blue and gold. "Let me go," I whispered. "You have to stop saving me and let me go."

"I'm trying," he whispered back. "I'm trying."

I was handed off to someone else—and then I found myself looking up into the face of one of Stavros's friends.

"Damian, you are the best with wounds," Stavros said. "Can you patch her up?"

Damian, back in a three-piece suit, bent over me. He had dark hair and strange indigo eyes that would never pass for human. Gorgeous. His mouth twisted up, and he showed off some rather sharp teeth. "She'll heal, but she'll have some scars. He chewed on her pretty good. He didn't hit an artery, though, and I think that's what he was going for."

Tears tracked down my cheeks as I was triaged right there in the middle of the fort, my wounds cleaned and stitched up. My neck wrapped in soft cotton.

The chaos of the aftermath was something else. Crash gathered up his goblins and left without a word before Stark or Roderick could confront him. In a blink, he was gone.

Missy screeched to the high heavens she'd been framed, and I watched with glee as Penny knocked her out with a single punch to the head. She was put into a waiting van after that, right along with Joseph's body. That couldn't be comfortable.

"Can you check my friend?" I held my hand out for Kinkly, who looked shyly at Damian as he did his thing.

"Her wings can be patched, that's not a problem. It'll take some time to heal is all."

"And Feish?" I groaned as I spoke.

Damian turned to the river nymph. "Same. The zombie bite won't affect her like it would a human. She'll be off for a week or so. But that's about it."

Relief flowed through me. My friends would be oaky, and with the relief a weight slid off me.

I sat up, wobbled a little, and then made it up to my feet courtesy of a few helping hands.

"Stavros, I'm sorry I broke the orb."

"I didn't want it anyway," he said. "And you were right. This town . . . I want it for my children." He drew himself up a little. "I'll help you when I can, Sentinel. Because I doubt this is the last we will see of the Dark Council."

I could have cried right there. The fairy honey was finally wearing off.

I was hurt in both body and heart.

"Thank you." I didn't hold out my hand. I hugged him. I hugged a demon, and he hugged me back.

Gran tsked, but I ignored her.

"Wait, where is Alan? And what happened to you, Gran?" I asked as I stepped back from Stavros.

"Gone," Gran grumbled. "I chased him for a bit, but he took off for his master I'd guess. And that Joseph, he had a ghost trap and I got stuck in it! Phaw, I should have seen that coming!"

Alan must have seen enough then to give info to Marge. Good riddance.

Sarge, still in wolf form, stepped up next to me. I put a hand on his back and limped toward the front gate. "Roderick, there are others in the tunnels. You should get them out. Me and my friends, we're going home."

Roderick gave me a stiff bow, his eyes drifting to the body of his brother. "Of course. Stark and I will make sure the cleanup is complete, that the humans will know of no issue here this night. Well done, Sentinel. Well done."

Stark bowed over his hands to me which made me think of Dr. Mori. He hadn't come when I'd asked for help. When I was sure he could have helped.

I almost didn't care. I wanted to leave, to go to Gran's house. My bed, a shower, food, and a whole lot of whiskey, not necessarily in that order.

But life, karma, fate, whatever you want to call it, was not going to be so kind.

28

I stood in front of the raging inferno that had been my gran's house only hours before. The fire department was there, doing what they could to save it, but they obviously thought it was a lost cause. By the time we got there, they were more concerned about saving the houses on either side.

Gran cried out and went to her knees. "No, No!"

I stared at the house I'd come to Savannah to save from being sold. The one I'd tried to buy from first Alan and then Crash. The one I'd spent the rest of my life in, making new memories.

And now it was gone.

Ann, her mom and their house goblin, Bridgette, met us there. Bridgette tugged on her big ears. "We called it in, as soon as we saw the flames. But it was too late. I'm so sorry."

Ann—little witch in training with Penny—gave me a hug. "I'm sorry your house burned down, Bree. You can stay with us if you want."

I forced a smile and hugged her back. "Thanks, my young friend. I'll keep that in mind."

They all stayed awhile with me as Gran and I watched the last of the timbers fall and the firemen doing their best to keep the flames from leaping to the neighboring houses.

Penny took the others back to her place after the first hour. I slumped across the street with Gran and watched my future—or what I had thought was my future—go up in flames and smoke and ash.

The tears finally came, close to dawn. The birds were singing as the firetrucks pulled away. As the last of the water was spread across the ashes of my past. I pushed to my feet and walked to the gate, letting myself into the garden. The plants were scorched. The earth still warm.

The oak tree was gone.

I slowly turned.

The oak tree hadn't been burned to the ground.

It had been dug out.

"No."

I hurried to the base of the tree and dug with my fingers, not caring that the soil and rocks tore at my flesh. I needed to know, and soon the answer became obvious. Maybe it should have been from the moment I saw the flames.

The box holding the fairy cross was gone.

"Gran," I breathed out, my voice scratchy. I stared at the tree, then turned and looked to the house. "This was no accident."

"What do you mean?"

I thought about Crash buying the house, and about Monica helping him.

I bit my bottom lip. "Someone waited until we were preoccupied with the fight, then they came and . . . they were looking for the fairy cross. And when they couldn't find it in the house . . ."

"They burned the place down?" Gran shook her head in disbelief, then she reeled. "This was never about zombies, was it?"

I shook my head. That didn't feel quite right. "It was about showing the world that the supernatural is real. It was about showing off their strength and putting fear into our hearts." What had Dr. Mori said? "Joseph was a harbinger of what is to come. And the bonus? It kept us all busy and out of the house. Busy enough that they could hunt for the items they knew they needed."

All to get their hands on another ingredient for a spell that was so deadly it had only been used once before. About the spell I'd stolen from Joseph. I thought about the perfectly cleaned forge. Which meant that they had at least two ingredients.

I put my hands to my face, then just lay on the soil next to the dead tree. The tree Robert had called home. And there I let myself cry for all I'd lost, for the future that looked so very dark, and for my friend. My friend who had never wavered in his loyalty to me.

Time passed, and I woke up and headed back to the safe house, where I told my friends about the fairy cross. About Robert. About the zombie spell being a distraction to keep us busy and away from the house long enough for others to go in and get what they wanted. But also that it was just the start of things.

I was pretty sure I knew who'd roasted the house.

Monica hadn't been at the fight. At the time I hadn't even spared a thought for her.

And now I knew what she'd been up to.

Kinkly fluttered loudly from the other room. "Roderick wants to speak with you. He'll be here tonight."

I shrugged, despair wracking me in a way I wasn't sure I'd felt before, except for maybe once before after my last miscarriage. I showered, ate some food that Eric put in front of me, and went and lay down on one of the sleeping mats.

I dreamed of the river and the steamboat. It sat at the dock, and a plank had been laid out for me. I walked up it to the deck to find Dr. Mori waiting for me, a faint smile on his stern lips.

"You can come back to shore now," I said.

He smiled at me, truly smiled. "You are a very good sentinel, Breena. Well done. I look forward to training you."

How did I tell him that right then it didn't feel like much of a win? I didn't. "I lost a friend. Actually, I kind of lost two." I mean, Crash and Robert were both gone.

"Robert is not truly gone. He's dead." Dr. Mori smiled wider. "But not *dead*-dead as you so eloquently put it."

My heart thumped a little harder with a glimmer of hope that scared me for how much I wanted it. "You mean . . ."

"He will regenerate," Dr. Mori said. "It will just take time. If you gather the dust from his bones and place it in his grave, he will come back to you. He will always come back to you."

Well, that was easier said than done. The dust had been gathered; Penny had done that so we could give him a proper burial. But finding his grave? That was maybe a bit more difficult. I didn't know his last name, or even the date he'd died.

Mori motioned me toward the table of light and shadows. "I think you should look more closely at this side." He gestured to the light side of the table. "It is important for you, I think, to see the truth."

Movement across the board drew my eyes. Penny's house. All my friends were there. Penny, Eammon, Eric, Suzy, Sarge, Kinkly, and Feish. I smiled and brushed a finger across Feish. "I never doubted," I paused. "Okay, I doubted a little."

Mori just let me look, and as I took in Savannah, I found my eyes drifting to Factors Row. I knew Jinx wouldn't be there—she'd disappeared as surely as Corb had.

No, Jinx wasn't there.

Someone else was. I sucked in a sharp breath and couldn't help but reach out and brush my hand across Crash's back.

"His intentions . . ."

"They are good, even if he is fighting for the Dark Council," Mori said. "That is perhaps the best and worst of this table. Just because he is here," he flipped the table over, "doesn't mean he can't be here too."

And there he was, in the shadows. "How long did it take you before you realized people could be on both sides?"

"Longer than I wish it had." Sorrow laced his words, and I wondered how many people he'd lost because of a judgment made at this table.

"Why are you showing me this now?" I asked.

"Because you are my student now, and I wish to guide you. When you wake, you will be presented with an offer that will be very hard to refuse. You have all these parts inside of you, and they call to different supernaturals. There is nothing wrong with owning them all. And there is nothing wrong with choosing a single one."

I looked hard at the calm man in front of me. "You're saying I should refuse whatever is offered?"

"I did not say that. But the choice will be hard. And you need to know that the blacksmith . . . well, he is a complicated man. More than most."

He tipped his head at me, and the dream scattered.

I dug deeper into my blankets, refusing to get up. Nope, that wasn't going to happen. I had to pee. Badly.

Duck walking to the bathroom, I barely made it. I tried not to think about what Mori had said, or about Crash and how he made me feel. How much I still cared what happened to him.

I waited quietly for the hours to pass, for the sky to grow dark, and was not surprised when a knock came at the door shortly after true sunset.

My friends, who'd stuck close but had kindly let me stew in my own funk, watched me as I got up and opened it. Roderick stood with his hands tucked behind his back.

"Perhaps you and I could take a stroll?"

Yeah, there was no way I was inviting him into any house from here on out. Assuming what the humans said about vampires had any basis in truth. "You going to bite me?"

He blanched. "No."

"Are you sure that's a good idea?" Gran asked, her ghostly touch feathering the back of my arm.

"I'll be okay, Gran. You wait here."

I closed the door, not caring that I was wearing slumpy pants and a tank top with a sports bra under it. I slipped on my one pair of footwear—my boots—and followed Roderick down to the green square two blocks over from the safe house.

I didn't wait for him to talk. "You could have told me he was a vampire."

"Actually I couldn't. It is in the creed. We do not speak of each other." He walked slowly, allowing me to easily keep pace even though I limped a little.

"Did you know that Crash was on the Dark Council?"

He shot me a look. "I did not believe that the Dark Council was back in play. Jacob left shortly after your visit to the chamber. He was an original member of the Dark Council. Apparently you tipped him off."

I groaned and put a hand to my head. "Damn it, I totally figured it was Clovis! Is that how they knew we were coming? Me barging into the chamber?"

"Most likely."

Double damn it. I needed to learn to keep my mouth shut. "You were trying to bend me to your will the other day, weren't you?"

He sighed. "I had to be sure that if Joe got a hold of you, he couldn't break your mind. Which, by the way, is like a steel trap. Whatever you've done to fortify yourself against manipulation, it holds well."

"A narcissistic, gaslighting ex-husband and some good counseling." I managed a smile. "Who knew that could be a weapon against a vampire?"

He chuckled. "Yes, well. You did as I asked, and I have your payment." Roderick handed me an envelope. "And because of everything, I doubled it."

A million dollars.

I should have been jumping for joy. I should have been damn well jubilant. I took the envelope quietly. "Thanks."

His eyebrows shot up. "Thanks?"

"They used the zombie apocalypse as a distraction to burn down my gran's house and take the fairy cross. I'm pretty sure Crash took the remnants of the angel wings too. They have most of the building blocks of what is, by all accounts, a very, very bad spell. I don't know the name of it, but," I turned as his jaw flapped open, and I caught a glimpse of the fangs he so carefully kept covered.

Spluttering, he grabbed the bench closest to us and sat down. I sat next to him and stared at the large building to our left.

"Maybe you can see why I'm struggling a bit. That and Joseph sort of killed Robert."

I rubbed a hand over my face. Touched a finger to my bandages. The bite wounds ached.

"That is not particularly good news. Are you sure about that?"

"I know. It's terrible. Robert has stood by me when a lot of other people haven't."

Roderick turned to me. "I meant about the fairy cross and the wings."

"Right." I sighed. "Right." But honestly, I just couldn't find a way to be more upset. I was too tired.

He stood. "I must take this news to the council—"

"Why?" I almost shouted the word. "So they can sit on their thumbs while they twiddle them? Jaysus, Roderick. They're useless."

He rubbed a hand over his face. "What would you have me do? We can't do nothing. That spell . . ."

I stared at him, taking in the way he was falling to pieces in front of me. "You know what the spell does, don't you?"

"I do," he whispered, "and it's worse than any zombie infestation, Breena O'Rylee. It is a spell that will usher in the downfall of Savannah and the humans here and much, much more. If put into play . . ."

And then he told me what it would be. He told me exactly how bad it was, what we were facing.

The darkness that we faced was deeper than that of any night that had ever fallen.

He spoke slowly, "*Draculean famisheen*. The spell will . . . it will create a vampire army. The entire town of Savannah would be turned in a matter of weeks. It was covered up once before. The humans believe it was the yellow fever. The reason why there were bodies being buried alive is because . . . they were coming back to life."

My gorge rose as I clung to the bench. "And here I thought things couldn't be worse than zombies."

Roderick stared hard at me. "They won't make the same mistakes again, Breena. The Dark Council is mostly made up of vampires. They will be very, very careful not to be stopped. That you even know this much, it is deadly for you."

I nodded and turned around, numbed by what he was saying. A vampire army. The entire town.

I couldn't see straight by the time he was done. My heart was racing, and my vision had blurred from the shock of it. I knew only a few things. I had to tell my friends. I had to tell Gran and Penny and hope that we could come up with a solution. Because I couldn't let this happen. Not here.

Not again.

When I managed to stumble back to the safe house, Roderick's million-dollar check in hand, I barely got through the door before I heard a voice that made me want to run back into the night and sleep out in a park somewhere.

"Is she here or not?" Karissa asked. "I wish to speak with her. I have an offer I don't think she will want to refuse."

Steeling myself but feeling like I didn't have it in me to be diplomatic, I made my way to the kitchen on the left.

"What the duck do you want, Karissa?" I snapped the question out, and everyone jumped, Karissa included. Yes, that was as diplomatic as I could be after the last twenty-four hours.

She turned and stood, all dressed up as if she were going to a ball. "I want to make you an offer."

"So I heard. Spit it out." I folded my arms and stared her down.

She smiled. "I can give you your Robert."

"I already know how to bring him back. That's not an offer—"

She held out a vial that she spun in her palm in a lazy circle, the liquid in it a deep red. "But can you bring him back to life for good? Once he is here, can you lay flesh on his bones and make him a man again? I had to borrow him to make this little beauty." She winked. As if stealing Robert was a big joke now.

I stared at that vial. My heart ached. I still remembered kissing Robert in that dream. We'd never talked about it. I couldn't talk about it because . . . because it rivaled anything else I'd ever experienced, and in my mind it was fruitless. I had bad enough taste in men, I didn't need to go chasing after a dead one.

I looked at Penny and then Kinkly. "Is she full of shit?"

Penny answered, somber, "It is a true gift, one that the fae rarely are willing to part with."

I stared hard at Karissa, knowing that there would be a high cost for this. Dr. Mori hadn't needed to give me a heads up for me to figure that part out. "And what, exactly, do you want from me?"

Her smile was wicked, that was the only word for it. "I want you to give up every part of you that is fae. No more of our magic. No more being able to enter fae bars or the land of Faerie on your own." She leaned in closer. "No more zing when you are near Crash."

I took a step back.

This was more than just giving up Crash. She was asking me to give up a part of myself that I'd only just started to understand. The part that Altin had been able to reach me through. The part that connected me to the land in a way that even being a witch didn't.

But . . . but if I did it, I'd get Robert.

I'd get him for real.

And I'd have to give up Crash forever.

Could I do it?

I stared at the red vial. "When do you need my answer?"

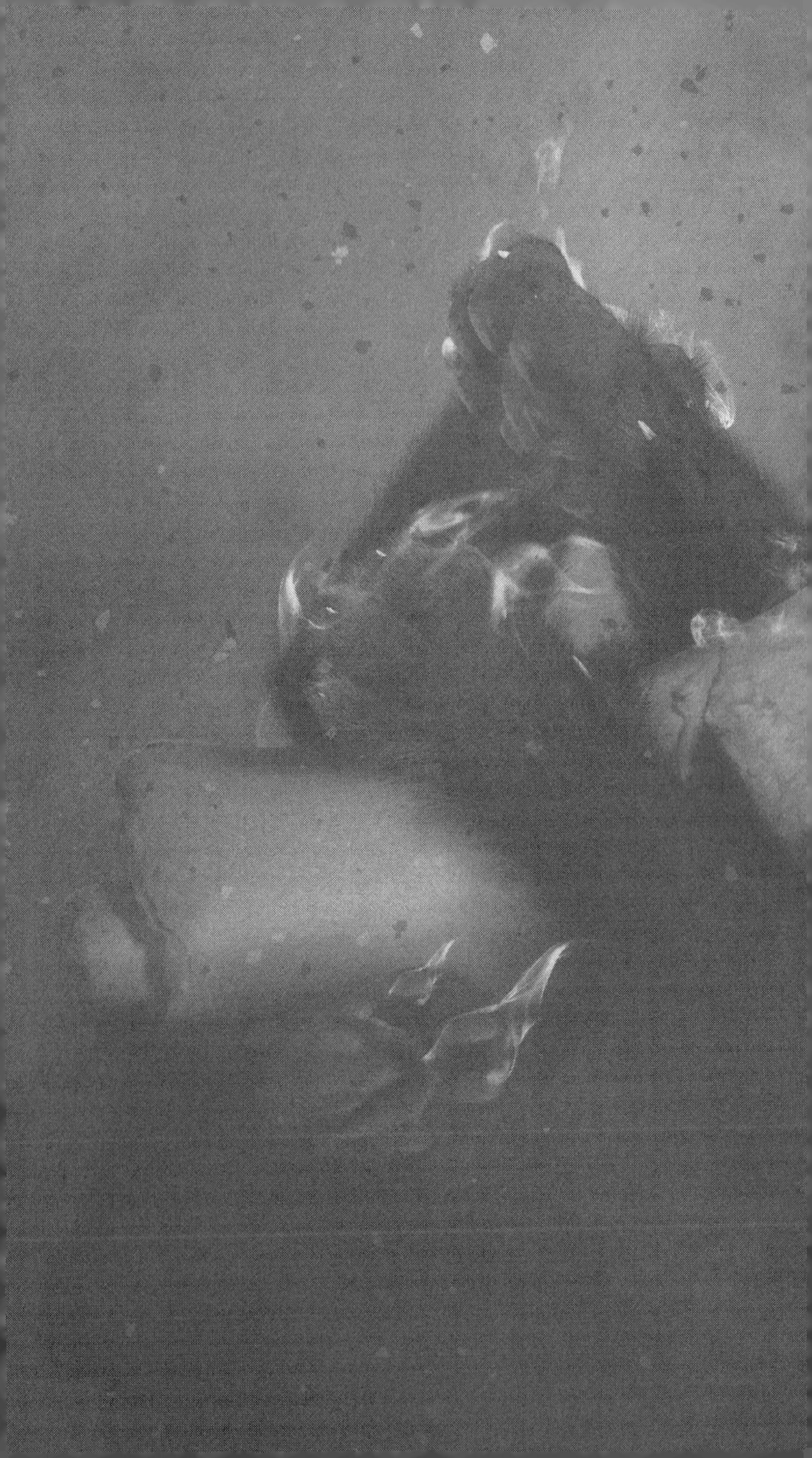

About the Author

Did you know that I write something different at the back of every book in the about the author section? I could copy and paste, but where's the fun in that?

I love horses, and I have a small herd of my own (yes, I count 3 as a herd). They keep me busy outside of my writing, and they help keep my sanity. You'll see me put in horses into a number of my books (including the Forty Proof series) and I love hearing from readers who understand and appreciate the small, accurate details I'll use :) It's makes my day.

Also, I may like whiskey. Maybe Bree is me. (Then again, I haven't seen any walking skeletons lately, if that happens I'm throwing all in for my bounty hunter license!)

Follow me these places, my website if you want a real surprise! www.shannonmayer.com

TEN OF SWORDS

I hope you enjoyed this installment of the Forty Proof Series! Be sure to keep an eye out for the next book, **Midlife Zombie Hunter**, which will be available 2021.

Need more than that to tide you over? You can check out more of the amazing authors in paranormal women's fiction genre at:

www.paranormalwomensfiction.net

OR you can check out my big list of books at:
www.shannonmayer.com

Made in the USA
Columbia, SC
06 January 2025